# An Eye For An Eye

**Inspector Stone Mysteries, Volume 2**

Alex R Carver

Published by ARC Books, 2017.

AN EYE FOR AN EYE

**First edition. May 30, 2017.**

Copyright © 2017 Alex R Carver.

ISBN: 978-1386411062

Written by Alex R Carver.

# 1

"Blam! Blam!"

The sawn-off shotgun in the hands of the masked man boomed twice in quick succession, filling the shop with the smell of cordite and doing fatal damage to the two women in front of him. The younger of the two, who appeared to be about a decade older than his forty years, flinched when she saw his finger tighten on the trigger; by contrast the older woman, who could have been the younger woman's mother, didn't react, she simply stared at him, accepting her fate almost stoically.

They were brave, he couldn't deny that - much as he disliked the thought, he had to admit the two Indian women were braver than any of the British women he had known, none of them would have been so calm in the face of death - but he had seen the fear they tried to hide, fear which remained even as he stared into their eyes and watched the life fade from them. He took pleasure in their fear, and more in the thought of the pain what he had done would cause to those who cared for them.

At a distance of no more than three feet the shots were powerful enough to lift both women, neither of whom were all that big, off their feet and throw them into the shelves by the counter, from there they slid to the floor. Blood stained the front of their saris, while alcohol from the bottles smashed by their bodies mixed to make a puddle of liquor beneath them, the fumes from which were so strong

1

they overpowered the acrid smell from the shotgun and left him a little light-headed.

With a smile on his lips, Kurt Walker dumped out the spent shells and reloaded with brisk efficiency, his eyes on the women as he watched them for any sign of life. He didn't see how they could be alive, but he wasn't about to take any chances. When neither woman had moved after almost a minute he bent to pick up his rucksack, into which he shoved his shotgun, the money the younger of the two women had handed over in the hopes of making him leave, several bottles of whiskey - his preferred drink - and all the cigarettes he could fit.

Once the bag was full he shouldered it and turned away from the two bodies on the floor. Without so much as a backward glance, he left the shop. In a couple of strides, he was at his car, where he slid behind the wheel after tossing the rucksack into the foot-well in front of the passenger seat.

The engine started on the first turn of the key, and Kurt quickly pulled away from the kerb, tugging his balaclava off as he headed down the road. He had never enjoyed wearing balaclavas, he found them uncomfortable - his discomfort was made worse by the heat of the day, it was over twenty degrees, far too warm for the garment - and he exhaled in relief when he felt fresh air stroke his face.

## 2

Detective Inspector Nathan Stone got out of his car and looked around, his hazel eyes taking in everything. A small crowd, almost certainly made up of the residents of Mead Street, had gathered and he noted the anger etched into the faces of several of them, Asians all, anger that was brought into sharp relief by the blue light that continued to flash from the top of the police patrol car parked outside Bhaskar's Convenience Store on the corner of Mead Street and Victoria Road.

Nathan hoped the attack he was there to investigate wasn't racially motivated. If it was, he didn't doubt there would be a lot of trouble, especially if he couldn't solve it quickly.

The non-Asians in the small group didn't appear angry, but there was shock, sadness, and a mix of other emotions on their faces. They stood in small knots, their conversations hushed as if they were afraid to either draw attention to themselves or disturb the scene.

In addition to the patrol car outside of Bhaskar's, the occupants of which were nowhere to be seen, a second patrol car was down the road, filling the gap between a green Kia Picanto and a red Ford Ka; the officers from that patrol car were keeping the crowd back from the shop, an easy task since none of those gathered showed any inclination to push forward. There was a restlessness to the crowd, but none of them seemed willing to do more than stand and watch events, despite there not being much to see.

An ambulance occupied the middle of the road, preventing cars passing, its siren silent, though the blue lights atop it flashed every few seconds, illuminating the little that evaded the light from the patrol car. The paramedics were leaning against their vehicle, leading Nathan to conclude there was nothing that could be done for the victims in the shop; that was not good news since it meant he was almost certainly there to investigate a murder rather than an assault.

"Jones is here."

The comment drew Nathan's attention away from his surroundings and across the car to his partner, Detective Sergeant Stephen Burke, whose emerald eyes were looking past him to the other side of the road. Following Stephen's gaze, Nathan spotted the silver Mercedes that belonged to Doctor Daffyd Jones - it was easily recognised by the personalised number plate 'DRDJ94' - the senior medical examiner for Branton Police, and the man who attended virtually every murder scene, thankfully a small number, in the town.

"Let's hope he's been here long enough to have the preliminaries out of the way." While he had great respect for the doctor, Nathan had little patience for the almost compulsive rituals he went through before getting down to work.

Nathan got the first surprise of his new case when he stepped through the door and saw who had responded to the initial nine-nine-nine call.

"What are you doing here, Frank?" His voice revealed how unexpected it was to find his long-time friend, Sergeant Frank Wells, there. "I didn't think you were allowed out of the station anymore, something to do with too many crashes while on patrol, wasn't it," he said, a smile playing about his lips.

Wells shot his friend a less than amused look and pushed away from the shelf he was leaning against. The limp he had been left with by his last crash obvious the moment he took his first step towards Stone. "I'm here because Vaughn thought the situation might need someone with tact to handle the uniform side of things; since I was already on patrol, shepherding WPC Beck," he indicated the very nervous female constable who, to Nathan's mind, seemed far too young to be in uniform, "on her first time out, he figured I was the best person for the job."

"Judging by the looks on the faces of the people out there, tact is definitely going to be needed; fortunately, I have Stephen for that."

Wells gave that comment the smile it deserved; he knew Stone was perfectly capable of being tactful, polite, and considerate, when the occasion called for it.

After trading a few more comments with his friend, while his partner looked on without joining in, Nathan made his way to the back of the shop, where he could see Dr Jones. As he got closer he saw the two women on the floor of the shop, their limbs entangled and their chests sporting matching red stains.

In appearance, both women were similar, to the extent that Nathan wondered if they were sisters, or otherwise related - both were short, barely over five feet, though it was hard to be sure of their heights given their position on the floor, clearly of Indian descent, and wearing long saris. The only immediately obvious differences between the two women were that one of them looked older than the other and had a peaceful, almost serene, look on her face, as if she had accepted her fate.

"It's definitely murder then," Nathan said, taking in the scene at the doctor's feet. In addition to the two murdered women, there was a mess of chocolate bars swimming in a pool of alcohol from the broken bottles knocked off the shelves.

"That's what I like about you, Nathan, you're not afraid to state the obvious," Daffyd Jones remarked, looking up over his shoulder at Stone. "I hope you're paying attention, Stephen; if you ever want to make it to inspector, you need to be able to look at a crime scene like this and know instantly what it is you're dealing with."

Though there was no hint of it in the doctor's appearance, both detectives knew him well enough to know when he was being sarcastic - it wasn't difficult, when he wasn't talking about purely medical matters, Daffyd Jones was nearly always being sarcastic.

"Working with Nathan is a constant learning experience," Burke said with a perfectly straight face.

A trace of a smile played about Daffyd's lips as he straightened, not that that made much of a difference since he still needed to look up to match eyes with the two detectives. At five-foot-five he was short, though the lack of inches in his height was made up for by those around his waist.

"I take it we're looking at a shotgun, Daff," Nathan said, deciding that it was time to become serious and begin his investigation.

Daffyd nodded. "I'd guess it was a sawn-off, fired at a distance of about three feet, to judge by the spread of the pellets. They were thrown backwards into the shelves, no surprise there, being shot at such close range, and I'm sure I'll find bruising as a result of that, but they won't have felt anything. Both women died instantaneously. It's not much, but it might be a comfort to their family," he said in a compassionate voice. "I'll be able to tell you more after the P.M., but right now everything looks pretty straightforward from my side of things." He looked sadly at the women at his feet. "Who'd want to do a thing like this?" he asked, more of himself than of either Stone or Burke.

"Have you got anything else to do here?" Nathan asked of Daffyd, aware that there was little he could do until the doctor was finished.

"No, I've done all I can," Daffyd said, knowing that he had done nothing except confirm that the two women were dead. "Are forensics on their way?"

That was a question to which Nathan didn't know the answer, and he turned to Sergeant Wells in the hope that he did.

"They're about ten minutes out. Apparently a bus broke down on Castle Bridge, they've had to divert. I imagine it's chaos around there."

"I imagine you're right," Nathan agreed. "Let's hope they don't run into any more delays. Do we know who the ladies are?"

"Not for certain," Wells answered. "We believe they are the wife and mother of the owner, a Mr Vikram Bhaskar, but that hasn't been confirmed yet." Anticipating the next question, he said, "We don't know where Mr Bhaskar is; according to his neighbour," he gestured in the direction of Victoria Road to make it clear which neighbour he was referring to, "he left in the shop's van a little over an hour ago."

"Who reported this?" Nathan asked.

"A Mrs Dormer, she was walking past the shop on the way home when she heard the gunshots. She's outside in the crowd now, at least she was."

"Did she see anything?"

Wells shrugged. "She didn't mention anything, but I only spoke to her briefly."

Nathan regarded him steadily for a moment before saying anything more. "Would you start the house-to-house enquiries? I've a feeling we won't learn much, even if there are a few nosey neighbours out there, but anything is better than nothing."

"Sure thing," Wells said agreeably, he knew as well as Stone did how important the most minor of details could be. "Come on, Elsa." He gestured with a jerk of his head for the young female constable to follow him. "Anything else you want me to do?"

Nathan shook his head. "I trust you to get on and do anything that needs doing," he said, "without me needing to tell you." Though the sergeant had never passed the detective's exam, he had more than enough experience to know what might need to be done to help an investigation.

NATHAN AND BURKE WERE standing to one side, keeping out of the way of the white-suited forensics specialists, who were working the crime scene with their usual silent efficiency, when Vikram Bhaskar arrived. The bell over the door jangled noisily, announcing his arrival and giving the two detectives enough warning to intercept him before he could interfere with the work the forensics team was doing.

"Mr Bhaskar?" Nathan queried, moving to place himself between the older man, whose Indian heritage was obvious in both his features and his clothing, and the specialists who were photographing, dusting, and otherwise sampling the area around the two murdered women, whose extremities had been covered with plastic bags to protect any forensic evidence there might be on them.

There was no reply from the man being blocked, his attention was all on the activity at the rear of the shop. Though he had stopped when his way was barred, it wasn't until the question was asked a second time that he showed any sign of being aware the two detectives were there.

"Yes, I'm Vikram Bhaskar," he said, nodding slowly without taking his eyes from the two bodies that were partially visible between the forensics officers.

"I realise this isn't a good time, Mr Bhaskar," Nathan said in a compassionate voice, "but can we talk?"

"W-what h-happened?" Vikram Bhaskar asked, his face pale and grief-stricken.

"That's what we're trying to find out," Nathan told him. "At present it looks as though your wife and mother - we'll need to formally identify them later, once they've been taken to the mortuary - were killed during a robbery. Do you have any idea who might be responsible?" He knew the odds of Bhaskar being able to name a suspect were slim, but he had to ask.

Vikram Bhaskar shook his head. "No. Neither my wife nor my mother has ever done anything to anyone, and I've always told them not to be brave if anyone robs the shop, especially if they have a weapon. We're insured against that kind of thing, so there's no reason to be brave."

"Have you had a problem with robberies?" Burke asked. He wondered if Vikram Bhaskar's instructions to his wife and mother stemmed from trouble the family had been experiencing. "Or any other kind of problem?" He hesitated to raise the subject of racism, he didn't want to put the thought into the older man's head, but it was a possibility they had to consider.

Again, Vikram Bhaskar shook his head. "N-not for a long time. We've been here for thirty-five years, and we get on well with everyone in the local area. We-we had some trouble in the beginning, people weren't happy that we bought the shop from the previous owner when he retired, but there's been none of that for years. I know some of my fellow shopkeepers have had trouble over the last few years, mostly from people who think all Asians are Muslims, and all Muslims are terrorists." His grief slipped for a moment, replaced by disbelief that anyone could be so ignorant, an opinion that was shared by both detectives.

"So you have no enemies, no-one who would want to hurt you or your family?" Nathan queried, wanting that confirmed. "Either in the local community or elsewhere?"

"No, no enemies at all."

It would have been easier, Nathan thought, if there were enemies, at least that would give him a starting place for his investigation. In the absence of known enemies, they had to work on the notion that the motive for the murders was robbery. That didn't sit well with him, though; there was something about the situation that suggested a motive other than robbery to him - he knew of plenty of incidents where people had been hurt, and even killed, for much less than what the man who had robbed the Bhaskar's must have gotten away with, but none of those had involved a shotgun.

"I notice you have CCTV cameras around the shop," Nathan said, his eyes moving from one camera to the next; he counted five, one in each corner, and one angled to cover the till. "Would you mind showing us the footage?"

Vikram Bhaskar opened his mouth to respond to the question but no words came out.

Disturbed by the look of horror on the shopkeeper's face, and the way his eyes went wide, like those of a cartoon character, Nathan glanced over his shoulder to see what had caused the change in expression. The forensics officers had moved apart so they could continue their work, with the result that Vikram Bhaskar was, unfortunately, afforded an unimpeded view of what had happened to his wife and mother. Nathan quickly shifted sideways to block the distressing sight.

"Mr Bhaskar. Mr Bhaskar," he repeated. "Can you show us the footage from your CCTV cameras?"

"Yes, yes, of course," Vikram Bhaskar agreed, once he realised what had been said. He led the two detectives through the shop, skirting the forensics team, and into the back; it was as he was leading them from the store room to the room that had been converted into an office that it occurred to him he didn't know the names of the two men with him. "Who are you?" he asked.

Nathan's eyes widened as he was reminded of his omission, it wasn't like him to forget the courtesies. "I'm very sorry, Mr Bhaskar," he apologised, "we should have introduced ourselves straight away. I'm Detective Inspector Stone, I'm in charge of this investigation, and this is my partner, Detective Sergeant Burke." He held out his hand, which was shaken briefly and perfunctorily.

The setup that allowed Mr Bhaskar to record and watch the footage from the cameras in the shop was old, Nathan saw that the moment he entered the office - if it was old to someone as technologically inexperienced as him, he could only wonder how bad it must look to his partner, who was up on the latest in computer technology. A quick glance at Burke revealed the horror the elderly, if not to say antique, equipment inspired in his partner; his expression was bland, but it was there in his eyes.

Nathan and Burke both waited patiently while Vikram Bhaskar stopped his recording, so he could search the footage for the first appearance of the person who had robbed him of his family; it wasn't easy for the monitor was small, and the image split into six - five of the little squares showed the shop as seen by each of the cameras while the sixth was dark.

When the darkly dressed and balaclava wearing figure appeared, Nathan leant forward so he could watch events more closely. The robbery didn't last long, only two or three minutes, and then the three of them watched as the two Mrs Bhaskars were shot for a second time; Nathan said nothing, he didn't want to add to the distress Vikram Bhaskar was already suffering, but as he watched the murders he couldn't help thinking there was something wrong with the scene.

It wasn't until he had watched it for a third time that he realised what was wrong; there was no need for the two women to be killed, no need at all. Though there was no audio to go along with the video, and the image was small, Nathan could see that both Vikram Bhaskar's wife and mother were cooperating with the armed robber and offering no resistance - he didn't need to kill them.

Why the robber had killed Mr Bhaskar's wife and mother, Nathan couldn't fathom. Robbery, even armed robbery, carried a much lighter sentence than murder, and a double murder, such as the one he had just watched, was likely to receive a life sentence, with a minimum of twenty years.

"Can you give us any idea of how much money he might have gotten away with?" Nathan asked; he doubted it was enough to justify one murder, let alone two.

Vikram Bhaskar was silent for a few moments as he thought about the question; he finally answered the inspector in a voice which reflected his own uncertainty in what he was saying, "It depends on whether he just got the money in the till, or what was in the safe as well. We had a good day yesterday, and there was a little over three hundred pounds in the safe, waiting to be deposited tomorrow, and there should have been somewhere in the region of a hundred pounds in the till this morning." It struck him then just how cheaply the robber had valued the lives of his wife and mother. "I-I won't be able to give you an exact f-figure until I-I cash up the till."

"That's alright, Mr Bhaskar," Nathan said reassuringly. "Will it be alright if we take the disk and have the footage analysed by our experts? They might be able to spot something that will enable us to identify the killer."

"Of-of course." Vikram Bhaskar nodded as he ejected the DVD and then looked around for a case to put it in, so it wouldn't be damaged.

3

Kurt Walker looked around as he walked up to the gates to remove the padlock; there was no-one to be seen, not that he expected to see anyone on a Sunday afternoon, and he quickly pulled the chain free, so he could push the gates open. He returned to his car then and drove through, stopping again once he was on the other side, so he could secure the gates.

He worried that the new padlock he had put on when he decided to use the place as a hideout would be spotted by someone who would raise an alarm, but so far there had been no problems. He supposed that was because most people passed the old industrial estate in cars, and didn't have the time to see something as small as a new padlock.

He parked his battered old Honda Civic down the side of the building he had picked at the rear of the estate, where it was out of sight of anyone passing along the road. He wasn't concerned that anyone might connect it with the robbery at the Bhaskars, but the presence of a vehicle on the estate, even one as beat-up as the car he was driving, might get people talking, and he wanted to avoid that.

With the bag containing his spoils from the shop in one hand, and his takeaway in the other, he left the car and nudged open the back door of the building with a foot. The interior was gloomy, despite it being early afternoon, for the sunlight had a hard time penetrating the thick layer of dirt and grime that coated every pane of the numerous windows that had once made the building a light and airy place to work.

What little light did penetrate the windows was barely sufficient to help Kurt avoid tripping over the debris that remained from when the building had housed a thriving business. The air was thick with dust and the musty smell of decay; compared to the smells he had become accustomed to, however, firstly while working as a garbage man, his first job after leaving school, and later while in prison, it was nothing to trouble him.

The gloom deepened as Kurt crossed the landing at the head of the stairs and entered the office where he had made his home. A crude curtain hung over the window, preventing the small amount of sunlight that penetrated the grime-coated glass brightening the room. He didn't enjoy being surrounded by such darkness, it was too great a reminder of the cell he had occupied until recently, and he quickly groped for the electric lamp he had positioned just inside the door.

The lamp blazed on, filling the office with light and chasing away the darkness. In one corner of the room, where he had shoved it after deciding the office would make a good hiding place, was the furniture that had belonged to the company's last manager - all of it was dusty, stained, and showing signs of age, which was why he had elected not to use any of it. In place of the old furniture he had a folding, camp chair, a thin sleeping bag, and a blanket he had folded up as a pillow; it wasn't much, but it was enough for now.

Kurt tossed aside the bag containing his ill-gotten gains and sank into the camp chair. A low rumble from his stomach reminded him how hungry he was, and he quickly took his takeaway from the bag and unwrapped it; it being Sunday he would have preferred a roast dinner: beef, pork, lamb, chicken, he didn't really care which, any would be better than the cheeseburger and chips he had, but under the circumstances he was happy enough just to have a decent meal.

He couldn't help but smile as he lifted the cheeseburger to his lips; six weeks ago, he had dreamed about having a proper cheeseburger, one with all the trimmings, and decent chips, now he had one and he wanted something else.

As he chewed on his first mouthful he reached over to the camping stove; a warm glow settled over him the moment he turned it on, dispelling the chill that had long since permeated the antique brickwork of the building, which the outside temperature didn't seem to affect. He then grabbed a bottle of cider from the box next to his chair, chilled to a nice temperature by the room's atmosphere, and drained half the contents in a single swallow before stretching out a hand to flick on his radio.

Content, he settled back to enjoy his food and drink while wondering if there would be anything about what he had done on the news yet. If there was, it might give him some idea of whether the police had any clue who was responsible for murdering the Bhaskars - he doubted it, he was confident he had left no clues to either his identity or his motive at the scene.

# 4

Unhappy with the task he had been given, Chris Grey knocked on the door in front of him. This was the fifth of the houses across from Bhaskar's Convenience Store he had visited, and with each one his resentment grew - this was a job for uniformed officers, not a detective, it simply wasn't fair that he was being treated this way; his mistake had, after all, been genuinely that, and the sort of thing that could have happened to anyone.

What justice was there in the world when he was punished for another's lack of attention? How was it his fault that the superintendent and DCI had had coffee spilled on them when they had been the ones distracted; if they had been paying attention they wouldn't have walked straight into him as he carried a tray bearing three mugs of coffee to the CID offices.

It wasn't his fault, everyone knew that, but there was no justice to be had for a junior officer like him. The incident had happened almost a fortnight ago, and ever since he had been stuck with every demeaning and dirty job that came along. How long the situation was going to persist he didn't have a clue, he suspected it was going to be some time however for Superintendent Vaz was a woman, and had suffered more than DCI Collins as a result of having her chest assaulted by scalding coffee.

Grey was ready to give up and move on to the next house, after knocking twice and waiting for more than a minute, when the door swung open. The passage beyond the door was empty, leaving him to wonder if his knock had drawn the attention of a spectre, until a sound from around his knees made him look down. A young boy of about four was holding onto the door, a pride-filled expression on his face, as if opening the door was an achievement only recently learned.

"Hello," Grey said in a bright voice, pushing aside the irritation he was feeling as he summoned a friendly smile. "Is mummy or daddy home?"

For answer the little boy swung the door shut, slamming it with all the strength his four-year-old arms possessed.

Grey stared at the door, uncertain what to do. He was tempted to knock again, after all, someone had to be home with the child, but after a moment he decided against it - he had already given the boy's parents plenty of time to respond to his knock. Instead he walked along to the next house, so he could try there.

"Did you knock?"

The question made Grey freeze, his hand raised in prepared to knock on the door in front of him. Slowly, he lowered his hand and turned to look back up the street, where he saw a young woman leaning out the front door of the house he had just knocked on.

"I did," he said with a nod as he returned to the house. "I'm Detective Constable Grey, do you mind if I speak to you?" He noted the wetness of the young woman's hair, and the robe she was wearing, and concluded that she had been in either the shower or the bath when he knocked, which explained why she hadn't answered before.

"What about?" the young woman asked, suspicion and concern warring on her face as she clutched her robe tight to keep it closed.

"There was an incident a while ago, across the road at Bhaskar's," Grey told her. "We're speaking to all your neighbours in the hope that someone saw or heard something that will help us find the person responsible."

The young woman looked past Grey and across the road to the shop, where the van belonging to the forensics team was parked. "Sure, come in."

The flash of leg that was revealed as the young woman showed him into the living room and then turned away to head upstairs made Grey change his mind - it was possible that door-to-door enquiries wasn't such a bad job. When she returned, barely a minute and a half after leaving, dressed in a pair of skimpy shorts and a halter top, Grey was glad about the previously unwanted chore.

"Run upstairs and play in your room, Thomas, mummy needs to talk to the policeman," she said, guiding her son out of the room and giving him a gentle push towards the stairs.

"Do you mind if I ask your name?" Grey asked once the young woman had joined him on the sofa.

"Ally, Alison Murray. What happened at Bhaskar's?" she asked.

Grey didn't answer straight away, he needed a few seconds to consider what or how much he should reveal. "There was a robbery that went wrong," he told her. "Mr Bhaskar's wife and mother were killed." The news drew a gasp. "Can you tell me where you were an hour ago?"

"I was just coming home from mum's with Thomas."

"So you weren't at home at the time of the robbery?"

Alison Murray shook her head. "No, sorry."

"That's alright," Grey dismissed the apology. "Have you see anything or anyone unusual in the area recently?"

A puzzled look crossed Alison's face as she pushed herself up from the sofa and walked over to the window, so she could look out on the street. "What do you mean, unusual?" she asked over her shoulder, her attention on the shop across from her house; she stared at it as if she could see inside to what was going on there.

"This is a fairly out of the way neighbourhood," Grey said. "It's not really on the way from any place to any place, so the chances are that anyone on the street, whether on foot or in a car, is going to be someone you know, if not well then at least by sight. If there's been any strangers around, you've most likely taken note of them, even if you haven't realised you're doing so."

It was like a light-bulb went off behind Alison's eyes. "There was something. It was as I was coming home, I was just turning the corner down the road when I passed a car I don't remember seeing before. It was gone in just a few moments, but I remember thinking that it must have been someone visiting because it was new to me."

"Can you describe the car?" Grey reached into his jacket pocket for his notepad and pen. It was a slim hope, he knew, but he couldn't help thinking that if he could provide valuable information that led to the arrest of the murderer, he might be restored to the good graces of Detective Chief Inspector Collins and Superintendent Vaz and given duties more befitting his rank and abilities.

"It was blue," Alison said confidently, though the confidence vanished from her voice almost immediately. "That's all I can tell you, I'm afraid."

Grey frowned in dismay. "Are you sure?"

Alison screwed up her face in concentration. "It was definitely blue, dark blue, and it looked old - not ancient, but it definitely wasn't new."

"How about make or model? Did you see anything that would make the car easy to identify?"

A shake of her head answered the question. "No, sorry. I'm not very good with cars. About all I can tell you is that it was blue, and it wasn't a mini or a Beetle; it wasn't anything expensive either, it was just an average car."

Grey made a note of that, though he realised it wasn't much help. "Did you see anything of the driver?" he asked, mentally crossing his fingers.

"I got a glimpse of straggly black hair and stubble," Alison said, "but that's all."

The genuine look of apology on her face surprised Grey, after all it was hardly her fault she hadn't paid more attention to the car and its driver, she hadn't even known that a crime had been committed. "That's okay," he reassured her. "What you've told me isn't much, but it's more than we had before."

## 5

"Nathan."

"Sir?" Nathan quickly hid his surprise at seeing his superior in the office on a Sunday.

With a sharp jerk of his head, Detective Chief Inspector Collins indicated that Nathan was to follow him, he then turned and strode away through the CID department.

Nathan glanced curiously at his partner as he got to his feet. Burke had no more idea of why the DCI was in the office than he did, however, and merely shrugged. Since his partner couldn't enlighten him, he left his office and hurried after his superior, catching up to him when he reached the DCI's office.

"We don't often see you here on a Sunday," Nathan said once he was seated. "Is everything alright?" He assumed not since Collins was still dressed in his golfing clothes, which meant he had come to the station straight from the course; the expression on Collins' face suggested he hadn't even had the time to finish his round with the chief superintendent.

"No, everything is not alright, everything is very far from alright," Collins said in an abrupt voice.

"What's up?" Nathan suspected he knew the answer, but he didn't want to mention it until Collins did in case he was wrong.

"Why don't you tell me; tell me about the Bhaskars."

Nathan ran a hand through his sandy hair while fighting the urge to grimace; he had hoped Collins wouldn't hear about the Bhaskar situation, at least not until he had something to report other than the nothing he currently had. "We don't know much," he admitted reluctantly, "but at the moment it looks like it's a robbery gone wrong." It wasn't what he believed, but he had no evidence to support his feeling that the situation was something more.

"A robbery gone wrong, is that all?" Collins was dubious. "The Herald thinks differently. Roger Kelly called me at the golf course to ask if I was concerned about racial tensions; he hinted that the paper will be running a story about the murders being racially motivated."

"Kelly wants the murders to be racially motivated," Nathan said cynically, well aware of how the new editor for the Branton Herald thought. "If the murders have a racial motivation, and tensions in the town increase - which they will if he has his way - then the paper will sell more copies, he'd love that. If that were the case, though, Louisa would have been in touch, she's their lead reporter, she'd be the one writing the story, and I haven't heard from her.

"I'll speak to her, see if I can find out what's going on, but if Kelly's calling you, not Louisa, the chances are the story's at least seventy-five percent rubbish, and he's stretching whatever he's got, if not making it up entirely, which is something Louisa would never do. If it comes to it, we'll know how true the story is when we see what name is on the by-line; if it's Louisa's then there's a good chance the story is true, she's not likely to write a story about racial tensions if she can't back it up, and if it's got Kelly's name on it, then we can be reasonably sure it's rubbish."

"That won't help us any, though," Collins remarked. "Once the story hits the stands the tensions will exist, whether they did before or not." He was silent for a few moments as he contemplated the problems he was facing. "The best way for us to head this off is to get something solid to counter it with, so tell me what you know."

"As I said, we don't know much at present. We have a DVD containing CCTV footage from Bhaskar's convenience store, which is now in the hands of the computer experts; I'm hoping they'll will be able to enhance the footage and discover something we can use." As far as Nathan was concerned, the tech experts performed miracles with their computers; his abilities when it came to them were limited to typing up his reports.

"Is that all you've got?" Collins wanted to know, disappointed.

"No." Nathan shook his head. "Christian called in a short while ago, he's with the officers conducting the door-to-door enquiries; it seems that a dark blue car, possibly a Honda, not known to the local residents, was seen leaving the area around the time of the robbery. The driver had dark hair and stubble. Unfortunately, that's all we know about him at the moment, and none of the residents were able to provide the license number of the vehicle." It would have been too great a stroke of fortune, he thought, to get such a useful piece of information so early in the investigation.

Collins was silent for a moment and then he said, "What are you doing to find the car?"

Nathan was tempted to comment that without a license number, the odds of them finding the car were somewhere between slim and non-existent; added to which he hadn't had an opportunity to set anything in motion because he had been summoned by the man across from him. He held his tongue, however, and instead said, "I've got DC Hill going through footage from CCTV and traffic cameras in the area." He decided not to say that Hill was actually waiting for the footage to arrive, so she could begin checking it.

"I want to be kept up to date with this case." Collins ignored the look of annoyance that flashed across his subordinate's face. "If this was a racial crime, I want to know about it, so we can head off tensions in the community. And if it wasn't, I want to be able to get that out to the press as soon as possible."

# 6

"    *...* To *recap today's lead story, residents in the quiet area of Mead Street were left in shock following a robbery that went horribly wrong. According to reports, a masked figure entered Bhaskar's Convenience Store on Mead Street armed with a sawn-off shotgun and, after taking the money from the till, shot Mrs Amala Bhaskar and her mother-in-law, Manjula Bhaskar, killing them both in what is suspected to be a racially motivated attack.*

*"The police have spent the afternoon questioning the residents of the streets surrounding Mead Street in the hope of discovering a lead to the killer, and are appealing for anyone with information to come forward. They are especially interested in speaking to anyone who might have seen a dark blue Honda in the area around midday."*

Kurt Walker smiled as he listened to the news report on the radio. If the police knew no more than the newsreader, and he was sure they didn't, then he had nothing to worry about. The partial description of his car was nothing to worry about, he had already taken steps to ensure it wouldn't be recognised the next time he went out before he knew anyone had seen him leaving the area of Bhaskar's.

After finishing his takeaway, and while working his way through a couple of bottles of cider, he had changed the car from dark blue to green. His paint job wasn't perfect, but he didn't care about perfect; once he finished what he was in town to do he would be getting rid of the car. In addition to changing the colour, he had changed the license plates, front and back, just in case someone had spotted the license number and given it to the police; fortunately, he had a plentiful supply of replacement plates, as well as paint, so he could change both as many times as he felt it necessary.

When the news report finished, Kurt reached over to turn off the radio before settling down in his sleeping bag. It was still early, and he wasn't all that tired, but he had little to do to keep himself occupied, other than play the silly games he had downloaded onto the tablet he had bought so he could access the internet. Normally he would have gone to a pub or a snooker hall and passed a few hours there; he wanted to keep a low profile for the time being, though, and thought it best to avoid doing anything that involved other people, just in case he was somehow recognised.

He wished, briefly, for a warmer place to hide, and then turned his thoughts to his plan for tomorrow - his plan was as simple as the one he had followed that lunch time, as all his plans were, but he still felt the need to go through it in his mind to make sure he wasn't missing anything.

# 7

Nathan and Burke both stood a respectful distance to one side while Vikram Bhaskar examined the faces of the two women, their bodies discreetly covered by sheets. Nathan could see that Bhaskar's face was twisted with grief and wished he had thought to check whether there was anyone who could come along to provide support to the newly made widower.

It was a couple of minutes before the distraught shopkeeper turned away from the bodies, and when he did there were tears in his eyes, though he refused to let them fall.

"Can you confirm that this is your wife, and your mother?" Nathan asked in his most gentle voice.

Vikram Bhaskar nodded his head slowly, his eyes glistening. After a moment he found his voice. "Yes, that's my Ama, my Amala, and my mother, Manjula."

"Thank you, Mr Bhaskar, I know this can't have been easy for you." Nathan's voice remained gentle as he reached out to take the shopkeeper by the arm. "Let's go and have a cup of tea."

"I REALISE THIS IS A difficult time for you, Mr Bhaskar," Nathan said once they had settled in a cafe down the road from the morgue, and the waitress had supplied them with a pot of tea. "And I hope you won't take this the wrong way, but can you tell us where you were yesterday lunchtime, at the time of the robbery?"

If he thought the question was being asked because the detective thought he was involved in the murder of his wife and mother, Vikram Bhaskar didn't let it bother him. In a voice that was flat, as if he was afraid to let go the control he had over his emotions, he said, "I was at the cash-and-carry, and then I was at temple; I can provide you with the receipt, and Ibn Hanifa, he's the Brahmin, can confirm I was at temple."

"That won't be necessary," Nathan assured him quickly. "We just need the information for the case file. We have no reason for thinking that you were involved in what happened." As he said that he found himself struck by a feeling of recognition, just as he had been when he first met Vikram Bhaskar at the shop; he had no idea how or where, but he was sure he knew Vikram Bhaskar from somewhere.

Burke washed down the slice of toast he had been snacking on and then entered the conversation. "Were you able to contact your son and daughter, and your brother?" he asked, remembering what Vikram Bhaskar had said the previous day about getting in touch with his family.

"Yes. Ravi had to go to work this morning, but he promised to be here this afternoon. And Lali and Kunwar should be home either today or tomorrow, depending on when they can get away from college and university." The pride he felt in his children was obvious to the two detectives, as was the distress he felt at the loss of his wife and mother, though his voice remained calm as he spoke. "Have you made any progress in identifying the man who murdered my Ama and my mother?"

"Our inquiries are ongoing," Nathan said, as unhappy with his inability to provide any solid information as he was sure Vikram Bhaskar was. "We have leads we are following up on, and we hope to have something soon. We'll keep you informed as the investigation progresses; if I can't speak to you myself, DC Laughton, the liaison officer we gave you, will pass on whatever information we develop. Right now we're looking into the blue Honda that was seen in the area around the time of the robbery."

DETECTIVE SERGEANT Mason rapped sharply on the door and then stepped back to watch the front of the house. He was sure it was a waste of his time - he didn't think the man he was there to speak to was who they were looking for - but he had been ordered to question the owner of the Honda Civic identified from CCTV footage and believed to have been used in the robbery and murders at Bhaskar's Convenience Store, and that was what he was there to do.

"Sergeant," DC Hill said warningly as the figure appeared from around the side of the house. Despite the assurances from her superior, who was positive there was nothing to worry about because they weren't at the home of a double-murderer, she couldn't help the feeling of trepidation that overcame her at being there without backup - given the choice she would have had every armed officer in the area with them.

"Good morning, sir. We're looking for a Mr Harold Willis, is that you?" Mason asked, alert for any sign of danger that might indicate he was wrong about the situation.

"Who wants to know?"

"Police." Mason responded to the question, which was asked in a tone that betrayed nothing more than a normal measure of caution and curiosity, by whipping out his warrant card and holding it up in an almost aggressive manner. "DS Mason, we'd like to talk to you about your whereabouts yesterday, and about your car."

"My car?" Harold Willis looked bewildered. "Why do you want to talk to me about my car?"

"We have reason to believe it was used in the commission of a crime, a very serious crime." Mason looked past Willis to the elderly, and not in very good condition, Honda Civic that sat in the drive. "Perhaps we could go inside," he suggested. "I'm sure this isn't a conversation you want us to have out here, where your neighbours can see."

For a moment Harold Willis looked as though he was going to say he didn't give a damn what his neighbours saw or heard, he didn't, though. "You'd better come round the back, I was in the garden when you knocked." With that he turned and disappeared back round the side of the house.

"So, how can I help you?" Willis asked of the two detectives once they reached the garden and he had settled himself on the bench in the sun.

Without preamble, Mason got down to business. "Where were you yesterday lunchtime, around midday, Mr Willis?" Now he had met the owner of the Honda Civic, he was certain he was not the man responsible for the murders at Bhaskar's; that didn't keep him from fixing the elderly man with a look of suspicion, however.

"I was here," Willis said, "enjoying the roast dinner my wife cooked. She dished it up at about midday, as always, and we stayed at the table until about one."

"Is there anyone, other than your wife, who can vouch for you being at home?"

"My neighbour, Anthony Healey." Willis indicated the property next door. "I was helping him fix his fence when Jean, my wife, called me in for dinner, that was about a quarter to twelve."

"Did you lend your car to anyone yesterday? I assume it wasn't stolen since it's still outside in your drive."

NATHAN GLANCED BRIEFLY at the screen of his mobile before answering the incoming call. "Justin, how'd it go with Mr Willis?"

"It's a dead end," Mason said.

"A dead end?" Nathan hadn't expected much after discovering who the suspect vehicle was registered to, but he had hoped there would be some information to be gained from his subordinate talking to Harold Willis.

"Yeah. Willis was at home yesterday lunchtime with his wife, his neighbour, and his neighbour's wife to confirm it. His car wasn't stolen, and he didn't lend it to anyone; in fact, the car hasn't been used in the last two months," Mason said. "It needs work, apparently there's something wrong with the engine and it needs a new part, which he can't afford right now because he's retired."

"Are you sure about that?" Nathan asked. He might know only a little more about cars than he did about computers, but he knew enough to be aware of how easy it was to make it appear as if a car was out of action.

Mason bit back the comment that rose to his lips; it would do him no good, he knew, to respond to the suggestion that he hadn't done a proper job. "Of course I'm sure; I checked Willis' story and the car won't start, it won't even turn over, and it's been listed as off the road with the DVLA for the past six weeks. There's no way the car's been moved in the past couple of months. I even checked with the neighbours and they confirmed, a couple of them at least, that the car was in the Willis' drive all day yesterday."

"Good job, especially in such a short time." Nathan was amazed that Mason had managed to get an answer from the DVLA so quickly, it normally took several days to get a response to an enquiry that couldn't be answered by a search via the police database. "Any idea how we've got an apparently duplicated car on our hands, or how we're going to find it?"

Mason didn't answer straight away, he was too taken aback by being asked for his opinion. "Not a bloody clue," he said finally, wishing he did have one; he would have liked nothing better than to have a clue, or an idea that would lead to the killer of the two Mrs Bhaskars, not that he would have told Stone - he wanted the credit for bringing in the killer, if it was possible to arrange it.

"Is there any connection between Mr Willis and the Bhaskars that might explain why the killer chose to use a duplicate of Willis' car? Or is it just a coincidence?"

"I didn't think to ask," Mason admitted reluctantly.

Nathan gave a little shake of his head. "You'd better go back and ask then," he told Mason, knowing his subordinate wouldn't be happy with his instructions.

# 8

His eyes darting around, checking for potential witnesses, Kurt strode up the road. He was once again dressed darkly in jeans and a black pullover - he had little in the way of spare clothing - which would have made him difficult to see in the dusk were it not for the street-lights illuminating the deepening darkness. He would have liked to avoid the pools of light that lit him up at intervals but that was impossible, all he could do was move through them as quickly as possible.

When he reached his destination, without seeing anyone or anything to give him pause or make him postpone or abandon his plan, he stepped off the pavement and into the shadows of the drive.

Kurt pulled down his balaclava as he walked up the drive, past the BMW that was parked there. It startled him when a security light blazed on, chasing away the concealing shadows; he had done a recce of the house, so he should have known about it, but, somehow, he had missed the light. His footsteps faltered momentarily, but he quickly regained his stride and approached the front door, taking out the knife he had brought - the weapon was a lethal-looking thing, a hunting knife with an eight-inch blade that was guaranteed to inspire fear in all but the most hardened of people - from the bag on his shoulder as he did so.

With the knife held at his side, where it wouldn't immediately be visible, he reached out to ring the doorbell. He heard it echo in the passage beyond the door, and a few moments later he heard footsteps as someone responded to it. Behind his balaclava he smiled in anticipation of what was to come.

The moment the door swung open, and before the man who stood framed in the doorway could react, Kurt lunged. He thrust the knife he had brought into the stomach of Terry Fielding, who collapsed over the blade with an explosive gasp of pain.

Kurt took Fielding by the shoulder and shoved him off the blade before entering the house and slamming the door behind him. He could see Fielding trying to draw breath, to either scream or yell for help, and he quickly dropped on top of him, his hand going to his mouth to cut off his efforts; at the same time, he buried the knife in Fielding's stomach for a second time.

Again and again he stabbed Fielding, half a dozen times in total. He didn't stop until his victim lay still beneath him.

Kurt pushed himself to his feet when he was done and bent to wipe the blade of his knife clean on Terry Fielding's shirt. He then left the body, and the slowly growing bloodstain on the carpet beneath it, to check the house, though he was sure there was no-one else home.

Once he had assured himself that he was the only one there he stole some of Terry Fielding's clothes - it was petty, but the man was almost the same size as him and he needed something to wear other than the bloodstained clothes he was in then - and began filling his bag with the Fieldings' valuables, starting with the jewellery he found in a polished wooden box on the dresser in the master bedroom. Robbery was not why he was there, but he could think of two very good reasons for taking whatever he could find: the first, and most important, was that it would throw the police off the trail when they investigated Terry Fielding's murder, and the other was because he could always do with the money he would get from selling the jewellery.

ADAM FIELDING SWUNG his keys idly as he strode up to the front door of his family's home. He was late, he should have been home twenty minutes ago, and was worried he would be punished, but the absence of his mother's car suggested he might be lucky and get away with it - his father was nowhere near as strict as his mother, and could probably be talked out of punishing him.

All thoughts of being punished, and how he could avoid it, were driven from his mind when he opened the door and saw his father on the floor of the passage, his chest a bloody mess. His mouth fell open as a scream boiled up out of him, destroying the night's peace.

NATHAN WAS NOT HAPPY, and he was sure it showed on his face as he got out of his car. He had been enjoying a peaceful evening at home with his family, an event that was all the more pleasurable for the infrequency of it, and he wasn't pleased that it had been disturbed, especially for something as unpleasant as murder.

He wasn't the only unhappy person, his wife was tolerant and understanding, but couldn't completely conceal how she felt about his being called away, while his son had been vocal about having playtime with daddy cut short. Even his partner was showing his displeasure, Nathan saw as he joined Burke at the start of the drive.

"Evening, Stephen," Nathan greeted his partner.

"I'm glad you didn't say good," Burke said. "I was ten minutes away from finishing Le Mans." His frustration was evident in the lines around his eyes, though he was more in control of himself than his superior.

"You were what?" Nathan asked, bewildered. He guessed Burke was talking about a computer game of some sort, but he had no interest in games, and virtually no time for them, so he had no idea what game it could be.

"Ten minutes away from finishing the Le Mans 24-hour race," Burke said. "It's a race on Gran Turismo for the Playstation, one of the older versions anyway. You have to race for a full day. It's hell on your thumbs, and you have to keep stopping for a rest. I've been working on it for weeks now, and I was looking forward to finishing it tonight." He sighed. "Oh well, it'll be waiting for me when I get home." He pushed his frustration aside and became his usual, professional self. "What do you know about the situation here?"

Nathan smiled grimly. "I was about to ask you the same question. All I was told is there's been a murder, and I was to get here as soon as I could." He saw Constable Ramirez then, comforting a teenage boy, and he diverted away from the front door.

"Hi, are you the one who called the police?" he asked in a gentle voice.

"Y-yes," Adam Fielding answered with a stammer.

"Can you tell me about it?" Nathan asked, his eyes moving from the teen to Ramirez, who had an arm around his shoulder. "Excuse me, let me back up; what's your name?"

"A-Adam, Adam M-Fielding."

"Okay, Adam, you reported that someone has been killed, can you tell me who?"

Tears fell from Adam's eyes and his chest heaved as he was wracked by sobs. "My-my dad, he was...he was..." His voice failed him, and he sat there sobbing on the grass in front of his family's home, his cheeks wet with tears.

It was almost five minutes before Adam, with the help of Constable Ramirez, got himself under control. "I'm sorry," he apologised once he managed to stop his sobs - tears continued to run down his cheeks and drip onto his t-shirt but he had his voice back. "I'm sorry," he repeated.

"There's nothing for you to be sorry for," Nathan reassured the teen. "Do you feel up to telling me what happened?" he asked.

"I-I don't know," Adam said, though he quickly dispelled the uncertainty his words suggested by continuing. "I-I was late home. I-I w-was supposed to get home before ten but it was about tw-twenty past when I made it home. I thought I was going to be in trouble. When I opened the door and saw d-d-dad lying there, covered in blood, I froze; I think I screamed."

"That's perfectly understandable," Nathan told him comfortingly, recognising the look of embarrassment that swept across the youth's face. "It's nothing to be ashamed of. It's completely normal to react like that when you discover something has happened to someone you love, regardless of the circumstances." He looked away, giving the teen a few moments' privacy in which to compose himself. "What did you do after that?" he asked, wanting to get all he could from Adam Fielding before he viewed the victim for the first time; he knew he would almost certainly have to question Adam again later to get his statement, but it was possible the teen would say something while he wasn't thinking that would prove to be the key to the case.

"I-I." Adam sniffed back a few more tears that threatened to fall and started again. "Once I could move I called the police. I-I told them where I was and what had happened. I'd just hung up when my neighbour, Mr Peterson arrived." He waved a hand at a figure Nathan hadn't previously noticed in the shadows of the garden.

"Mr Peterson." Nathan turned his attention to the neighbour, who moved forward upon being called until he was clearly visible in the light that shone through the living room window and lit up most of the garden. "Can you tell me what happened after you arrived?"

Mr Peterson nodded, his face was as pale and shocked as that of the teen now next to him, but he was more in control of himself. "I came running around here when I heard Adam scream. I didn't realise it was him until I got here and found him in the doorway, on his knees. I didn't see Terry straight away; when I did I froze for a few seconds. Once I recovered I led Adam away, out of sight, and went back to check Terry." He paused so he could swallow against the dryness in his throat. "There was so much blood. I've never seen so much. I was almost afraid to touch him, but I had to check, had to be sure if he was..."

Nathan gave a brief, understanding, nod. "Was he...?"

"He was dead," Mr Peterson said with a cautious glance at Adam, concerned by how he might react to his words.

"You didn't hear or see anything until you heard Adam's scream?" Nathan asked. He realised suddenly that Burke was no longer with him and looked around for his partner, he found him in the doorway of the house, his voice just barely audible as he spoke to someone in the house.

"No, nothing," Mr Peterson said with a shake of his head. "I've wondered about that since I saw Terry, but there was nothing."

Nathan studied the man before him briefly, looking for any sign he might be lying or concealing something. "Thank you, Mr Peterson, Adam; if you don't mind, I'll need to speak to you both again, so I can get full statements from you. If you'll excuse me now." Without waiting for any kind of acknowledgement, he turned away and made for the front door and his partner. When he got there, he saw that it was Dr Daffyd Jones that Burke was talking to. "Evening, Daff; it's good to see Stephen and I aren't the only ones who've had our evenings disturbed." Though his tone was light, his expression was serious.

Daffyd looked up from the body he was squatting over. "Evening, Nathan," he returned Stone's greeting dolefully. "Three murders in two days," he shook his head sadly, "what is this town coming to?"

"Nothing good," Nathan remarked as he studied the body of Terry Fielding from the doorway, he didn't want to get any closer in case he disturbed evidence. "How many times was he stabbed?"

Jones carefully moved aside the shirt he had undone, he had to peel it away from Terry Fielding's chest, to reveal the injuries. "Six times. Three times in the stomach, twice in the left lung, and this one," he indicated a barely visible stab wound just to the left of the centre of Fielding's chest, "may have nicked his heart."

"Which one killed him?" Nathan asked.

Jones gave himself a short while to consider the question before he answered. "He could probably have survived any one of the three to the stomach, maybe even all three if he got to the hospital quickly enough. The two to the lungs would most likely have been fatal, either one of them, as would the one to the chest, especially if it did nick the heart, which I won't know for sure until the P.M.."

"Any sign he tried to defend himself?" Nathan couldn't believe that Fielding had made no effort to protect himself, unless the first wound was fatal, yet from the position and posture of the body that was how it appeared.

Jones shook his head. "None that I've seen so far. Hard to believe, isn't it," he remarked. "He's not a small man, you'd think he'd have been able to put up some kind of fight, even if he was taken by surprise. Maybe he knew his killer."

That possibility had occurred to Nathan. "How long has he been dead?"

"No more than a couple of hours," Jones said. "Possibly less. I should be able to be more accurate after the P.M.."

"Adam. Oh my God! What's happened?"

Nathan turned away from the doorway at the panicked, and obviously female, voice. His eyes zeroed in on the elegantly-dressed woman striding across the small lawn towards the teen, who was still being comforted by Constable Ramirez. He guessed the woman was Adam Fielding's mother, and the wife of the murdered Terry Fielding, and he quickly made his way towards her; it wasn't until he was at her side that he saw past the stricken look on her face and recognised her.

"Paulina!"

"Nathan." Paulina Fielding's voice was as filled with surprise as Nathan's.

# 9

Nathan was relieved to be able to put down the drinks when he reached the table, the disposable cups were poorly insulated, and he was sure if he had had to carry them much further he would have dropped them, simply to avoid doing permanent damage to his fingers.

"Here you go." He gave Paulina Fielding the white coffee she had requested, took the black coffee with three sugars for himself, and handed the hot chocolate to Burke - his partner was a coffee snob who had refused to put up with a distasteful and inferior coffee from a hospital vending machine, a description that Nathan found surprisingly restrained.

"Do you feel up to talking now?" Nathan asked of Paulina Fielding once he had taken a couple of sips of coffee and felt the caffeine and sugar begin to take effect.

At the house Paulina had been too consumed by grief and shock over what had happened to her husband, and concern for her son, who had sunk further into his own shock after relating the details of what he had discovered upon his return home, to talk. When they made it to the hospital she had been busy with her son's doctor, and making sure her son was going to be alright - the doctor assured her he was, though it was likely to take time, and Adam was almost certainly going to need therapy.

Wearily, Paulina nodded. "I guess I can't put it off any longer." Lifting her eyes, she met Nathan's. "Ask your questions, Nathan."

"Thank you." Nathan hesitated before he started; this was different to a normal case, this was someone he knew, someone he had known for a long time, though he hadn't known her husband. Finally he decided how best to proceed. "Where were you tonight?" It wasn't a very original opening question, but it was one that had to be asked.

Paulina's eyes hardened as she looked at Nathan, and her hands tightened on the cheap plastic cup that held her coffee. The cup squashed slightly, making the murky brown liquid threaten to spill over. "You think I might have done it?" The question was asked in a barely audible whisper.

"Of course not," Nathan assured her quickly. "You were a prosecutor for a long time, though, you know I have to ask these questions. So, where were you tonight?" he asked when Paulina nodded. Her obvious reluctance to answer the question worried him, it suggested she had something to hide, and he found himself wondering if it was to do with her husband's murder; it was not something he wanted to think of someone he had worked with, but he was professional enough not to let friendship get in the way of his job, and to know that when it came to murder, the spouse was more often than not the person responsible.

"I was out with a friend from work," Paulina said finally.

"What friend, and where were you?"

Paulina's eyes moved away from Nathan to dart all around the cafeteria before settling, briefly, on her coffee, and then darting around the cafeteria again.

Nathan was disturbed by his friend's evasiveness. "What friend, Paulina, and where were you? You know you can't avoid telling me; the longer you try and keep the information from me, the more like a suspect you look.

"I was at a restaurant, having dinner, there's plenty of witnesses who can confirm it." After hesitating for a while longer, and enduring a hard look from Nathan, Paulina added, "It was one of the partners, I was having dinner with one of the partners from work."

From the look on Paulina's face, Nathan realised what it was she wasn't saying. "Did your husband know about you and the partner from work?" The discovery that his friend was having an affair didn't sit well with him, not least because it gave her a motive for murdering her husband.

Paulina nodded, though the look on her face was a little uncertain. "Yes, well, not about him specifically. Terry knows, knew," she corrected herself, "that I've been seeing someone, but he never showed any interest in knowing who it was. Our marriage has been over for a while now, a couple of years to be honest - we tried counselling, but it didn't work - but we've held off on getting divorced; we discussed it and decided to wait until Adam has finished school, we don't want to put him through a divorce with his exams coming up."

Nathan accepted that, it made it a little less likely that Paulina was involved in or had instigated her husband's murder, but it was still a possibility that had to be looked into. He didn't know how much Paulina earned, just that she had been on a very good salary while with the Crown Prosecution Service, was earning a lot more in the private sector, and that there had been talk of an inheritance from a childless great-uncle; all in all, he suspected there was a fair amount of money that would have to be divided up, which was likely to be a strong motive for trying to circumvent the divorce process.

"What's the name of the partner you've been seeing, and where did you have dinner?"

Paulina hesitated once again, the unhappiness visible on her face deepening, but then she surrendered to the necessity of answering the question. "His name is Kevin Michaels, and we had dinner at The

Golden Dragon. You will be discreet when you speak to him, won't you?"

"Of course," Nathan reassured her.

"Thank you." Paulina gave a brief smile of gratitude. "We can't afford to have too many people find out about us yet; Kevin's in the middle of getting a divorce, if his wife were to find out, well, it could make things difficult. Not only that, the other partners would not appreciate the bad publicity this situation would generate."

"Okay, so you have an alibi, and people who can confirm it." Nathan gave his partner a few moments to scribble down what Paulina had said before he continued. He realised that an alibi didn't mean Paulina could not be behind her husband's murder, she had met plenty of people during her career who would probably not be averse to committing murder for the right amount of money, but there were other questions he needed to ask before he looked into that. "You said your husband knew about your affair, though he didn't know who it was with; did he have a problem with you seeing someone else?"

Paulina shook her head. "No. As I said, our marriage was over. We'd discussed the situation, and we both knew where we stood; we've just been waiting for Adam to finish his exams before we did anything formal."

"So he wasn't doing anything to stop you being with this Kevin Michaels?"

Again, Paulina shook her head. "No. It's all been very civil."

"Okay. Can you think of anyone who might have wanted to hurt your husband?"

"No. I can think of plenty who would want to hurt me, almost everybody I put behind bars, but no-one who would want to hurt Terry, he is, was, one of the nicest guys you could meet. Never a bad word for anyone, got on with everyone."

Nathan didn't think he had ever met anyone who was that nice, and he always doubted how people were described in the aftermath of their death, but he accepted that for the time being while he thought of any other questions he needed to ask.

# 10

Vikram Bhaskar's sleep was troubled, not that he really thought of it as sleep; his eyes were closed but he didn't think he actually drifted off at any point. Nonetheless, he was startled into full wakefulness when he heard noises; he wasn't sure what the source of the noises was, but they set his heart to racing, and his first instinct was to call the police.

He quickly squashed that thought, realising that it was just panic resulting from what had happened to his wife and mother. There was no point in calling the police until he was sure of what was going on.

He threw back the blanket he was using to keep himself warm and got up from the sofa - he hadn't been able to face the bed without his wife next to him. When he reached the window, he pulled back the curtains so he could look out on the street below. It wasn't until he opened the window that he realised the noises that had disturbed him were voices, and they were coming from right below him, from the front of his shop.

The slurring of the voices he could hear suggested the people they belonged to were drunk, and that worried him. A glance at his watch revealed it was after two a.m., which was far too late on a Monday night for anyone to be out with anything but mischief on their mind.

He collected his mobile phone from the coffee table and made his way, barefoot, across the living room to the passage. He was tempted to go and wake his brother, who was asleep in their mother's room, but Ravi had had a long journey and he didn't want to disturb his rest.

Alone, he descended the stairs, a sense of trepidation building within him the closer he got to the front door. It threatened to overwhelm him as he slowly, and as quietly as he could, pulled open the door; the moment he did the volume of the voices doubled, making it easier for him to hear what was being said.

"...you'll wake someone up!"

"Who cares. If the old bastard comes out, I'll make him regret ever coming here. He should have stayed home with the rest of his Islamic State buddies..."

Bhaskar froze at the words, which sent an icy shiver up and down his spine, as though he had just plunged into a freezing winter lake. He pushed the door to; he didn't shut it since he wanted to hear what else was said, but he did want to reduce the chances of any of the men out in the street noticing that the door was open. Why people thought he was a Muslim, he didn't know, but that was pushed from his mind by fear when he heard the next comment.

"We should just kick the door in and treat him like his kind treat the people they kidnap. Let's see how he likes being beheaded."

Bhaskar had to fight the urge to slam the door and run back upstairs when he heard that. Instead he closed the door as quietly as he could and walked up the stairs, dialling the emergency operator as he went.

"Police, please," he said in a whisper.

# 11

Nathan yawned mightily and took a sip of his caffeine-rich double espresso while he waited for Kevin Michaels to arrive. Next to him, Burke struggled to contain his delight at their meeting someone in a place that served decent coffee, he wasn't doing very well at it, but Nathan ignored him and focused on his espresso.

"Inspector Stone?"

Nathan looked up at the inquiry and nodded. "Yes, that's me," he told the tall, rake-thin, smartly-dressed figure who had appeared at the table he was sharing with Burke. "Kevin Michaels, I take it."

"That's correct," the middle-aged barrister answered with a controlled smile. "If you will excuse me for a moment, I'll just get a drink." Without waiting for a response, he strode away to the counter.

While Nathan watched Michaels, Burke filled in another answer in the crossword he had been doing to pass time and then folded the newspaper and pushed it aside. Together they waited for the barrister to return with his drink; fortunately, there wasn't much of a queue, so they didn't have to wait long.

Kevin Michaels got straight down to business once he was seated across from the two detectives. "You said on the phone that you wish to talk to me about my relationship with Paulina Fielding."

"That's correct," Nathan said with a nod. "I understand from Paulina that you have been involved with her for some time now, and that her husband, Terry, was aware of the relationship, but that your wife is not. She also told us that the two of you were having dinner last night when her husband was murdered, is that correct?"

"That's right, we were at The Golden Dragon," Michaels said. He showed none of the concern that Nathan and Burke had expected given Paulina Fielding's statement that he wished to be discreet because of his divorce. "I couldn't believe it when Paulina told me what had happened, it was such a shock. I've met Terry a few times over the years, at work functions, he was a nice guy, friendly to everyone."

"So we've been told," Nathan said.

"Yet you had no problem sleeping with his wife," Burke remarked.

Nathan watched Michaels to see if he was going to react to the hint of reproof in his partner's voice.

"Their marriage was already over, as was mine, before we became involved, and Terry was aware that Paulina was seeing someone, though I don't believe she told him it was me."

"He wasn't resentful of the situation?" Nathan couldn't help wondering how he would feel if he were in that situation; he suspected that even if his marriage was over he would have a hard time dealing with his wife being involved with someone else. That didn't help him to come up with either a motive or a suspect for Terry Fielding's murder, however.

Michaels shook his head. "Not as far as I'm aware," he said. "From what Paulina told me, he accepted it without a problem. Their marriage had been on the rocks for a while before they decided to end it. She thought he was interested in someone, and had plans he couldn't follow through on if they stayed together. All he insisted on, apparently, was that Paulina was discreet and agreed to wait until after Adam's exams are over before they divorced."

"So he wasn't putting any barriers in the way of Paulina divorcing him and the two of you being together?"

"No. They even had a tentative agreement regarding the division of assets - it was only agreed verbally, but they were both happy with it; Paulina was going to keep the house and assume full responsibility for the mortgage repayments, and she was going to compensate Terry for his share of it."

"Could she afford to do that?" Nathan didn't know the value of the Fieldings' house, but a conservative guess put it at twice what his own was worth, which meant Paulina needed at least two hundred thousand pounds to pay off her husband for his share of the property.

Michaels shrugged. "I couldn't say. I have no idea what sort of state Paulina's finances are in, nor am I interested, I care about her, not her money. Besides, as a partner, I earn considerably more than she does," he said that with a smile that contained more than a trace of smugness. "I can only assume, since she made the offer, and Terry accepted it, that she either has the money or a way of getting it. Maybe she intends re-mortgaging the house."

"What about her son?" Burke asked. "Do you know what's supposed to happen to him?"

Again, Michaels shrugged. "If they discussed what they were going to do about Adam, Paulina never told me."

"Okay, let's get a few details," Nathan said, deciding that they had gone far enough along that line. "You had dinner at The Golden Dragon last night; can you tell us where and when you met Paulina? Did you pick her up from home, did she meet you at your place, or did you both meet somewhere else?" They already had Paulina's version of what had happened, now they needed Kevin Michaels' to see if both versions matched.

"NATHAN."

Burke hid a smile while Nathan schooled his features and did a quick one-eighty.

"Hello, Louisa," he said in as neutral a voice as he could manage. "How did you find me?" He was not happy to see her, even though he knew she wasn't responsible for the stories in The Herald over the last couple of days that suggested his failure to catch the Bhaskars' murderer was the result of racism and incompetence.

"Oh, you know me, Nathan, I can find anyone," Louisa said with a quick laugh. "Actually, it was a bit of luck, one of the juniors was on a coffee run and saw you and Stephen, and knowing I've been after a chat with you he called to let me know where I could find you. Fortunately, I was able to get here before you disappeared, though only just, it seems."

Nathan glanced over his shoulder to where his car was parked, less than two dozen feet away; another minute, perhaps less, and he would have reached it and been on his way, without being troubled by one of the last people he wanted to see just then.

"So, who was it you were talking to in The Roasted Bean?" Louisa asked, her nose twitched as if she could smell a scoop and was determined to ferret it out. "A witness to the murders of the two Mrs Bhaskars, or is he connected to last night's murder? From the description I was given, I'd say he's something to do with the Fielding murder, a solicitor or a barrister?" she probed, watching Nathan's face for a reaction that would tell her if she was on the right line.

Nathan wondered how Louisa could look so awake and energetic when he was sure she had spent just as much of the night awake, investigating the murder of Terry Fielding, as he had. "You know I can't tell you that."

"I'll find out sooner or later, from somewhere."

Nathan didn't doubt that for a moment, he could even guess how she would find out; he was well aware that there were officers working at Branton Police Station who would be only too happy to give Louisa whatever information she needed for a story. Just because she could get the information from somewhere else, that didn't mean he had to make things easy for her by giving her what she wanted.

"Is there any truth to the rumour that Paulina Fielding was having an affair?" Louisa asked, hoping to catch Nathan off-guard. The abrupt widening of his eyes, which he controlled quickly, but not quickly enough, suggested she had hit the nail on the head. "Was it her lover you were talking to a short while ago?" Another direct hit. She was pleased, she had gotten confirmation, if not proof-positive, of her suspicions much quicker than expected. "Is he a suspect in Terry Fielding's murder?"

"Why do you insist on asking questions you know I either can't or won't answer?" Nathan asked a question of his own, exasperation and tiredness adding more bite to his voice than he intended displaying. "Sorry," he apologised. "I haven't had enough sleep."

Louisa dismissed the apology with an airy wave of one hand. She had been on the receiving end of far worse questions and comments, and even one or two punches, during her time as a journalist. As far as she was concerned, if she couldn't handle that kind of thing she was in the wrong profession. "Because I know how much it annoys you, and I'm always hopeful you'll get caught by surprise and let something slip you don't mean to.

"What steps are you taking to handle the rising tensions in the Muslim and Hindu communities?" she threw out in the hope that he was tired enough to be incautious.

"You mean the tensions your boss has created?"

"Yes, those." She might not be responsible for the stories, or the racial tensions they had stirred up in Branton, but that didn't mean she was going to ignore the situation now it existed. She would, however, ensure that whatever she reported on the tensions was accurate.

"You'll have to speak to my superiors about that," Nathan told her. "My priority is solving these murders."

"What progress have you made? Three murders in two days, that's serious, and very worrying for everyone, no matter where in town they live; what do you say to the rumours the murders are connected?"

"That's the first I've heard of such rumours." Nathan glanced at Burke to see his reaction, and was answered by a brief shake of his partner's head. "I'd be careful about reporting such rumours if I were you," he advised.

"You know me," Louisa said. "I never report something without the proof to back it up."

"It's a shame your new editor doesn't seem to feel the same way."

Louisa could only nod her agreement of that sentiment. "I told him those stories wouldn't go down well, but he's not concerned with facts and responsible reporting; as far as he's concerned, if it sells, he'll print it."

# 12

The custody suite was a hive of activity when Nathan and Burke returned to the station. They were held up for nearly five minutes before they were able to make it through and head up to the CID offices.

"Briefing room," Nathan called out the moment he reached the offices.

While the officers and detectives under him filed into the small briefing room and took seats, Nathan picked up a thick black marker and drew a line down the middle of the white space on the board that dominated the main wall of the room.

"Okay everyone, settle down," Nathan said once everyone but Burke was in the briefing room and had seats. The murmuring that had filled the room quickly died away, and everyone's attention moved to the front, centring on him, something which had unnerved him the first time he led a briefing. "I'm sure you're all aware by now that we've had another murder." There was synchronised nodding from almost everyone in the room. "I'll come to Terry Fielding's murder in a bit, first, though, I want to deal with the Bhaskar case.

"We have no suspects as yet, but we do have some information: the experts are still analysing the CCTV footage from the shop, but they have been able to give us a few things, such as that the killer is approximately six feet tall and stocky, probably well-muscled, with size ten feet - we know that from several boot prints that were left by him after he stepped in the alcohol." He pointed to the photographs taped to the board behind him, the one on the left was an un-manipulated image which made it hard to see the boot print on the floor of the shot, while the image on the right had been played with to make the print more visible. "They aren't likely to be much help in finding us a suspect, but if we can come up with one they might help us to link him to the murders."

"You really think so?" Mason asked pessimistically. "From what I can see, they're not going to help us at all. Even if we find a suspect, which isn't too likely, there isn't a single distinctive thing about that print, it could belong to a million boots."

The negative attitude didn't surprise Nathan, he was used to his subordinate's efforts to undermine him and no longer paid attention to them. It was easy to ignore Mason on that occasion, because Burke chose that moment to enter the briefing room with two mugs of strong Costa Rican coffee.

"House-to-house enquiries were conducted on Sunday afternoon," Nathan continued the briefing after enjoying a long swallow of his coffee, "with the result that we were given a description of a vehicle possibly used in the Bhaskar's robbery and murder," he said for the benefit of those officers who hadn't been at the previous day's briefing. "Unfortunately, the blue Honda Civic, which we believe was used, presents us with something of a problem. Justin?"

Mason was caught by surprise when Nathan surrendered the floor to him, but he recovered quickly. "After examining footage from the CCTV and traffic cameras in the area around Mead Street, we were able to put a license number to the vehicle we were looking for. The car is licensed to a Mr Harold Willis. DC Hill and I spoke to Mr Willis yesterday afternoon, that's when we discovered our problem - the car in question has been off the road for the last couple of months, and is not only registered as off the road but is non-operational." He paused for a moment to make sure everyone was paying attention to him. "Questioning of Mr Willis' neighbours has established that the car hasn't moved from the drive where it's been parked in weeks. Someone has made a duplicate of Mr Willis' car, either to throw suspicion onto him, or simply to divert suspicion away from himself; it could even be that the killer simply got a car from a chop shop with no idea it was a duplicate."

"Have you had any luck in locating the car that was seen leaving Mead Street?" Nathan asked. "The real Honda?"

Mason shook his head. "Not yet." His disappointment at the failure showed on his face. "But a re-examination of the footage we have has revealed that the car in question is a newer model of Civic to that owned by Mr Willis. We have the description of the vehicle out on the news, but as yet the only responses we've had point us in the direction of Mr Willis, meaning they're useless." Mason saw Nathan open his mouth to ask another question and hurried on. "I've requested footage from all other CCTV and traffic cameras in the area to see if we can spot the car, and follow it to wherever it's been hidden."

"Is there a connection between Mr Willis and the Bhaskars?"

"Not that we're aware of," Nathan answered the question from Sergeant Wells while ignoring DCI Collins, who had slipped into the briefing room and assumed a position near the door. "When questioned by DS Mason, Mr Willis claimed only to have heard of the Bhaskars from the news following Sunday's incident. Nonetheless, we're looking into the possibility. DC Hill has been given the task of looking into the backgrounds of the Bhaskars and Mr Willis, both for a connection between them and for a motive for the murders. Lisa," he invited the young officer to reveal what she had discovered.

Hill wiped her hands on her trousers nervously as she stood and made her way to the front of the room. "Starting with Mr Willis," she said. "I've been unable to find anything that connects him to the Bhaskars; he says he is currently out of work, but the truth is he retired about six months ago - his last job was as a carpenter with a local construction firm, prior to that he was in the army. He has a few traffic offences on his record, but nothing beyond that. I've been trying to find out about his military record, but no luck so far, and I can't see there's going to be anything in there that will either connect him to the murders or make him a suspect. Sergeant Mason has already established that he has an alibi and his car was not the one used in the murders."

"You might find out who tried to frame him, if that is the reason a duplicate of his car was used," Nathan told the young detective. "I'll make a few calls and see if I can get you access to the records." He didn't say so, but he suspected it would take a call from someone senior to him to get the records.

Hill nodded. "Yes, sir." It was a moment before she realised she was supposed to continue with her report. "The Bhaskars don't have so much as a parking ticket between them, and, as far as I can tell, they've never been in any trouble, at least not where they were the instigator. Mrs Bhaskar, the elder, came over here in the seventies with her husband and their eldest son, Vikram. I wasn't able to find out much about their first few years here, other than that they had a second son, and then a daughter who died as a baby. They bought the shop in nineteen-eighty-one, and have been running it ever since.

"They've had some trouble over the years: robberies, vandalism, and some racist incidents, but nothing that might be a motive for murder. I'll keep looking, see if there's anything I missed."

# 13

" ... *Speaking at a press conference this lunchtime assured the public that there is no cause for alarm, and no reason for believing that the murder of Terry Fielding is connected to the murders of Mrs Amala and Mrs Manjula Bhaskar. According to DCI Collins, Terry Fielding's murder is almost certainly connected to his wife's work - Paulina Fielding is a prominent local barrister who formerly worked for the Crown Prosecution Service - while a racial motive has not yet been ruled out in the case of the Bhaskar murders."*

Kurt was both pleased and annoyed as he listened to the news report on his radio. It was good news that the police hadn't linked the murders, and were in fact looking in opposite directions - it amused him that they believed the Bhaskars to be a racist attack - but not so good that they were on the right track when it came to looking for Terry Fielding's killer.

He quickly reminded himself that he didn't have too much cause for concern; even if the police figured out who they were looking for, and he was sure there had to be a lot of potential suspects amongst those Paulina Fielding had prosecuted, they had to find him. That wasn't likely to be easy since he looked considerably different from any of the pictures either the police or probation might have of him. Not only that but he was living under the radar; no-one knew where he was, or even what he currently looked like. He figured the odds of him being found were somewhere between slim and none, assuming he wasn't about to be inflicted with a case of bad luck, which he didn't consider likely.

"*Following an incident at Bhaskar's Convenience Store last night,*" the news reporter continued, "*tensions within the Asian community have risen sharply, tensions which DCI Collins sought to play down. Though it is believed to be unconnected to the double-murder that took place there on Sunday, a gang believed to consist of three or four men painted racist slogans on the shop's shutters in support of the murders, calling them a suitable response to the actions of Islamic extremists around the world, even though the Bhaskar family are Hindu, and not followers of Islam.*

"*DCI Collins has called for calm, and promised that anyone guilty of racist behaviour will be prosecuted to the full extent of the law. The response to last night's incident was described by Ravi Bhaskar, Manjula Bhaskar's second son, who spoke to the Herald this morning, as inadequate, and a far cry from the response they would have got if they were white and the vandals Asian.*"

Kurt reached out to turn the radio off, he had heard enough, he wasn't on the police's radar, so he could relax for the time being. Since he didn't have to worry about the police, he turned his attention to the next target on his list; everything he knew was on the pad he pulled from his bag, and in his mind, nonetheless he went over it all again to be sure he hadn't forgotten or missed anything. He had waited a long time for his revenge and didn't want some silly mistake to be the reason he failed.

# 14

After sending Mason and Grey round to the rear of the house, Nathan strode up the path to the front door, Burke at his shoulder. He rang the bell, or tried to, he heard nothing, so he rapped sharply on the door. He knocked for a second time after about half a minute, impatient for a response - with so much going on, he was keen to get at least one of the cases keeping CID busy cleared up before anything new could crop up.

Nathan had just raised his fist to knock for a third time when the door swung open to reveal a woman in her early to mid-forties.

"Good afternoon, Detective Inspector Stone." He held out his warrant card. "Is Lester Crowther home?"

The question was answered not by the woman in the doorway, who held the door open just far enough for her to see who was on the doorstep, but by a series of heavy thuds. Nathan interpreted the noises as someone jumping down the stairs and then running down the passage towards the rear of the house and reacted quickly. Springing forwards he put his shoulder to the door and knocked it from the woman's grasp, sending it into the wall of the passage with a crash.

Aware that he had Lester Crowther's - he assumed that was who was making for the kitchen - escape blocked, but not willing to stand back and wait to see if Mason and Grey succeeded in stopping him, Nathan hurried after the fleeing figure. He reached the kitchen,

Burke on his heels, in time to see Crowther being wrestled to the ground just outside the back door.

"Lester Crowther?" Nathan asked when he reached the now handcuffed figure, who spat grass and dirt as he was hauled to his feet. "We have a few questions we'd like to ask you, down at the station," he told the man whose fingerprints had been positively identified from those found on the can of spray-paint left at Bhaskar's Convenience Store.

SILENCE FILLED THE interview room for several long moments, which stretched on for more than a minute, after the recording equipment was set up. Finally, when he saw Lester Crowther shift nervously in his seat, Nathan decided it was time to start the interview.

"As previously stated, Mr Crowther, you have been arrested on suspicion of vandalism, conspiracy to incite racism, conspiracy to commit acts of racially motivated violence, and suspicion of murder." That last one made Crowther's eyes widen, which didn't surprise Nathan since he had only added it to provoke a response. "Do you have anything you'd like to say at this time?"

"Yes I bloody well do," Crowther said sharply over the protests of the duty solicitor in the chair next to him. "I never killed nobody. If you think I did, you're dead wrong, I'm no killer."

"You are a racist, though, aren't you, Mr Crowther," Burke said from his position next to Nathan. "And you did, along with two friends, paint racist slogans, including incitements to violence against the owner and his family, as well as against followers of Islam, on the shutters of Bhaskar's Convenience Store on Mead Street last night."

Crowther was about to respond to that allegation, as forcefully as he had to the suggestion that he was a murderer, when his solicitor laid a restraining hand on his arm.

"What evidence do you have to support this allegation?" Frank Rawlings asked on behalf of his client.

For answer Nathan reached down to the floor and lifted a clear plastic bag to the table. "This can of spray-paint was found at the scene by the officers who responded to the emergency call, it was on the pavement outside Bhaskar's Convenience Store. Forensic analysis of the can discovered fingerprints, which were identified as belonging to your client from his police record." He saw that that news came as an unwelcome surprise to the solicitor. "This can places your client at the scene, and links him to the graffiti painted on the shop's shutters. Not only that, but Mr Crowther was overheard discussing breaking into the shop to kill Mr Bhaskar and his family." After allowing that to sink in he leant across the table to fix Crowther with a hard, penetrating stare. "I'm not particularly keen on racists, Mr Crowther, they taint everyone, but since I have three murders to solve, a case of vandalism, even one that's racially motivated, is not high on my list of priorities.

"Since that's the case, I'm going to offer you a deal. If you tell me who was with you last night, and where I can find them, as well as whatever you know about the murders of Mrs Amala and Mrs Manjula Bhaskar, I'll recommend leniency - a suspended sentence, or perhaps even a caution."

It was clear from the looks on the faces of both Crowther and his solicitor that they had not expected to be offered such a deal, especially so soon into the interview. Several long seconds passed before either of them responded.

"I'd like to speak to my client privately," Rawlings said.

"Of course, not a problem." Nathan had anticipated that response. "Would either of you like a drink?" he asked as Burke stopped the recorder and got to his feet. A double nod answered the question. "I'll have someone take care of that straightaway."

"Get the good stuff," Nathan told Burke once they were out of the interview room, having been in there for barely five minutes.

"For them?" Burke asked, surprised. He was reluctant to surrender any of the high-quality coffee he bought with his own money to anyone other than his partner, and a select few lucky individuals.

Nathan shook his head. "Of course not, for us; they can have the regular stuff."

WHILE HE WAITED FOR Rawlings to finish discussing the situation with his client, and for Burke to return with the coffee he desperately needed, Nathan called forensics to see if they had made any progress with the mountain of evidence they had to sift through from the two murder scenes. He was disappointed to learn there was nothing new on the Bhaskar case, but there was some good news on the Fielding case, so he didn't feel too disheartened.

"Do you think it belongs to his killer?" Burke asked when he returned to the custody suite with the two mugs of coffee and heard what the forensics department had discovered. Like his superior, he found the news potentially case-breaking, though he kept his excitement in check, knowing that it might turn out to be nothing.

"They wouldn't commit themselves," Nathan said after sipping at his coffee and expelling a sigh of satisfaction. "You know what they're like, unless they're a hundred percent certain about something, they won't commit. They said the blood could belong to Terry Fielding's killer, or it could belong to another victim, someone we don't know about. It might not even have anything to do with the murder; Terry Fielding could have got the blood on his shirt in any of a number of ways, and the killer just happened to wipe his knife on that spot."

"You think that's likely?" Burke was doubtful.

"No." Nathan shook his head. "That stretches the bounds of coincidence too far. Whether the second blood sample belongs to another victim or our killer, I don't know - the killer, I hope - but we might have some idea by the end of the week, when the DNA results come back, and they've been run through the system."

"ARE YOU READY TO TALK now, Mr Crowther?" Nathan asked when he and Burke returned to the interview room.

It was Rawlings who answered. "My client wishes to make it clear that he is prepared to co-operate, but that he has no knowledge regarding the murders that took place at Bhaskar's on Sunday. My client also denies being the one to suggest breaking into the shop to kill Mr Bhaskar and his family."

Nathan looked dubious at that, but didn't comment on the statements, instead he asked, "What is your client prepared to say?" He could tell from the look in Crowther's eyes that he wanted to accept the deal he had been offered, it only remained to see if he was going to say anything that would actually be worth it.

Rawlings said nothing until he received a nod from his client. "Mr Crowther is prepared to give you the names of the two gentlemen who were with him last night, as well as where they can be found. In addition, if you guarantee that he will not be charged with anything, he is prepared to give you the names of those you have been looking for in connection with the Jennings' robbery."

Nathan kept his face expressionless, but he couldn't keep his heart from giving an involuntary lurch; he was sure that next to him, Burke's was doing the same. The Jennings' robbery was a case they, and the rest of the department, had been trying to solve for almost four months: a gang - they didn't even know how many people were in it - had raided Jennings' Electricals' warehouse, making off with a van-load of assorted electronic goods, from microwaves to TVs to Playstations and X-boxes. The cost of the robbery had been calculated at around forty thousand pounds, and that was only the value of the stolen items, it didn't include the damage to property made when the gang broke in.

"We would certainly be interested in those names," Nathan said, being careful not to show just how interested he was. "But we need more than just names to guarantee no charges. Names alone won't be enough to get convictions."

Crowther looked appalled. "Giving you the names is dangerous enough," he said in a panic. "If I give you anything more than that, they'll know for sure you got it from me, especially if I get off scot-free."

"That's a chance you'll have to take, Mr Crowther," Nathan told him unsympathetically. "I'm sure you're aware that the courts, given the current national climate, are not looking kindly on those who commit racially motivated crimes, regardless of the nature of the crime. With tensions the way they are locally, I don't think it would be too hard to push for a quick trial, in the interests of public safety, and your own of course - I wouldn't like to be in your shoes if it were to get out that you decorated a murder scene with racist slogans."

"That's blackmail," Rawlings said quickly in a tone of deepest disapproval. "I would have thought, inspector, given your reputation, that you would act more professionally than that. I could report you."

Instead of being offended by the accusation, Nathan was amused by it. "That wasn't blackmail, Mr Rawlings, it wasn't even a threat. It was an observation. The situation is not looking good for your client; I'm sure you're both aware of the interest the Herald has in this story, an interest which is bound to result in them discovering your client's name; when that happens, life is likely to become unpleasant for him. That can all be avoided, if he gives us the names, and enough information to help us prove the case against the gang who robbed Jennings'.

"If he does that, we'll make sure no charges are laid against him, and that his name is kept out of the Herald." He knew he shouldn't be making such an offer without first discussing it with his superior, but he was confident Collins would go along with it when he heard.

"And how do you expect to accomplish that last part?" Rawlings wanted to know. "You've just said the press is very interested and they'll learn my client's name, now you're saying you can keep it from them - which is it?"

"YOU THINK THE DEAL is a good one?" Collins asked, stalling for time while he ran the pros and cons through his mind; he was already pretty sure Nathan thought it a good deal, otherwise he wouldn't have brought it to him.

"Yes," Nathan said. "The Jennings' case is much bigger than vandalism, even if it is racially motivated, and we've been trying to crack it for a long time now. Besides, if we agree to the deal, we'll close the vandalism case as well as the Jennings' case, that'll look good in the monthly crime figures," he knew how much they mattered to Collins, "and in the papers."

"You're certain this Mr Crowther had nothing to do with the murders?"

"Positive," Nathan said. "I never thought he was involved, I only brought it up in the interview to try and rattle him, which it seems to have done."

Collins had suspected as much, he had used similar tactics himself. "And keeping his name out of the papers, how do you plan on achieving that?" He didn't think it was possible, given how aggressively the Herald's reporters had been chasing down every story they stumbled on since the new editor took over.

"Louisa's a professional, if I agree to give her an in on the Jennings' case, I'm sure she'll cooperate. Nothing before the arrests, of course," he said quickly when he saw that Collins was about to protest. "I'll just make sure she has the information first, ahead of any of her rivals."

"She might go for that, but will her new editor?"

"I'm sure she can get him on side, one way or another." Nathan was sure that the moment she had learned who her new boss was going to be, Louisa had discovered everything there was to know about him, including the things he hoped to keep private.

"Okay, now, what do we know of the gang behind the Jennings' job?"

"Nothing so far, beyond that there are four people in it. Crowther refuses to say anything substantial until he's been assured that he won't face any charges." Nathan could understand that, like the majority of criminals, Crowther didn't trust the police. "He's given us the names of the two who were with him at Bhaskar's, though, and he's hinted that the Jennings' gang are planning another job for this weekend."

"Is he telling the truth, or just trying to make sure he gets the deal and avoids jail?"

"I'd say he's telling the truth, but I'm not sure it's a chance we can afford to take even if you think he's not. We need to wrap up the Jennings' case, and if it turns out the gang is planning another job and we had a chance to stop it but didn't, we'll end up looking incompetent."

That was the last thing Collins wanted. "Okay, tell Mr Crowther he gets his deal, as long as what he gives us is good enough to get convictions."

# 15

Louisa's face had a knowing look when Nathan joined her in the booth she had taken in the corner of The Stag's Head pub.

"I'm guessing you didn't ask me here for purely social reasons," she said, her eyes on Burke, who was at the bar.

"No, I didn't," Nathan admitted as he slipped into the booth and set his glass of coke on the table.

Louisa hid her curiosity as best she could and sipped at her Malibu and coke. It had been a while since Nathan expressed an interest in talking to her officially, though, and she couldn't conceal her interest completely. "Alright, what is it you want?" she asked finally.

"I've got some information for you," Nathan told her. "But I want an agreement before I give you it."

"What sort of an agreement?" Louisa knew from dealing with Nathan in the past that whatever information he had for her would be good, but it remained to be seen whether it was good enough for whatever he wanted in return.

"We're on the verge of making arrests in the Jennings' case." Nathan was pleased by the reaction that news garnered. "And I'm prepared to give you the names of ours suspects, on a couple of conditions."

"What conditions?" Louisa watched Nathan's face for some clue while she sipped at her drink.

"Firstly, you don't print the names, or anything about the case, until after the arrests have been made." Nathan doubted Louisa would have a problem with that, it was a pretty standard condition for being given exclusive information. "And secondly, you keep the name Lester Crowther out of the paper when you do any future stories on the vandalism at Bhaskar's."

Louisa was an experienced reporter, and it only took her a few moments to realise what the situation was. "Crowther's given you the Jennings' gang in exchange for not getting charged over the vandalism?" The slight inclination of Nathan's head was all the answer she needed. "I'm sure Roger will love hearing that no-one's being charged over racist vandalism. I can already see him planning headlines about insensitive and racist police disregarding community feelings, he'll have a field day." She waved a hand dismissively to show what she thought of her editor and what he would make of the information she had been given. "The readers won't be too happy either."

Nathan gave a grim sort of smile. "Don't worry, your readers will be satisfied, even if Kelly isn't," he assured her. "Crowther won't be charged, if his information proves accurate, but his two companions will be; you'll get those names ahead of anyone else as well."

The two of them haggled back and forth for a while over how much information Nathan would give Louisa, when he would give her it, and when she would be able to make use of it, before finally reaching an agreement they were both happy with.

# 16

Jamie landed lightly on the other side of the fence and turned to see if his friends were following: Aaron was halfway to the top of the fence, but Matt remained on the ground, his eyes darting all around as though he expected to see a security guard or police officer appear at any moment.

"What'sa matter, Matt, scared?" Jamie taunted his friend. "You afraid of getting arrested? Or is it ghosts you're afraid of?"

"There ain't no ghosts," Matt declared, though his voice reflected his uncertainty.

Jamie laughed mockingly. "You sure about that?" he asked as his eyes left his friend to dart around the abandoned and rundown industrial estate they were planning to explore. "Don't worry, if there are ghosts about, one look at you and they'll be the ones running scared." He laughed again, this time teasingly rather than mockingly. "Come on, get your butt over the fence, we ain't got all night."

Matt looked up at the sky, which was darkening rapidly as dusk drew in, and then at Aaron. He was reluctant to climb the fence and enter the estate, not because he feared ghosts, he knew Jamie had just said that to scare him, not even because he feared being arrested - it wasn't something he particularly wanted to happen since it would look bad when it came to applying for colleges, and he didn't like to think how his parents would react if he was arrested - but because he was concerned about who they might encounter in the abandoned buildings, or rather what might have found them a perfect place to make a home.

While his friends looked on, amused by his efforts, Matt heaved and scrabbled until he found his footing and was able to pull himself up to the top of the fence and then drop down the other side.

"Dammit! Mum's gonna go mad when she sees this," he swore, poking a finger through the hole torn in his t-shirt by the fence.

Jamie muttered something that sounded suspiciously like 'mummy's boy', but he looked all innocence when Matt focused his attention on him.

Sensing an argument brewing between his friends, Aaron stepped in to defuse things. "Come on, if we're gonna explore, let's explore, before it gets too dark to see anything." He accepted Matt's stiff, abrupt nod as agreement while Jamie, ever the leader of the trio, was more vocal.

"Sure, let's go." Jamie set off towards the nearest building, without looking back to see if his friends were following.

"How do we get in?" Aaron asked as he and Matt joined Jamie in peering through the broken and dirty panes of glass at the interior of the building. He didn't want to appear scared or cowardly, as Matt did, but he was relieved when Jamie dismissed the window as a means of entry, even if his manner was insulting, since he was sure that climbing through it would result in one of them, if not all of them, cutting themselves.

"The door, you idiot," Jamie told him, leaving the window and walking along the wall to the sturdy-looking door that was set in it. He took the handle, turned it, and pulled, only to discover that the door was locked and wouldn't budge.

"Now what?"

Jamie scowled at Aaron before answering the question by kicking the door, dislodging splinters of wood and paint.

"You can't do that," Matt said.

"Why the hell not?" Jamie asked as he kicked the door for a second time, causing it to crack. "You think anyone's gonna care if I kick the door in? Hell, they're not even gonna know." His third kick split the door in two, leaving one half hanging from the hinges, while the other half fell away. "Come on, let's see what we can find."

KURT WAS WATCHING A film when he heard the dull thud. It was barely audible, and he wasn't initially sure he had actually heard anything. The second thud was louder, and he paused the film, so he could try to identify the noise and work out if it signalled a threat to him. The third thud had him on his feet and searching in his bag.

His hand closed momentarily on his shotgun, he had it half out of the bag before he changed his mind and let go of it. The shotgun would enable him to deal with whatever trouble he might encounter, but the noise it would make might draw more attention and cause him more trouble than it saved him. Thinking that, he let the gun fall back and took out the knife he had used to kill Terry Fielding.

A few spots of blood marred the gleaming brightness of the long blade, but he didn't care about that. If anything, the blood was likely to make the weapon more frightening to anyone who saw it.

With the knife at his side, ready to be used but out of sight until it was needed, Kurt left the office. The dust that coated the floor served to help quieten his footsteps as he made his way along to the staircase and descended to the ground floor. The noises he had heard came from somewhere off to his left, from outside the building in which he had made his den, so he made his way over to the windows on that side. He could see nothing, thanks to the grime that coated the windows and the deepening dusk outside. Even rubbing clean a small portion of one pane did nothing to improve his ability to see what was going on outside.

Reluctant to expose himself, but knowing he had to locate the source of the noises, he left the windows and headed for the door he had prised open with a crowbar. Cautiously, all his senses alert for trouble and his knife at the ready, he pulled the door open and exited the building.

AARON KICKED AT A STACK of something that sat on the floor next to a desk, it was paperwork of some kind, but the light was too dim for him to see what, and he didn't care anyway. He had no interest in paperwork, least of all paperwork from a business that had been closed for years.

"I thought you said we'd find some good shit lying around," he said accusingly to Jamie as the stack of paperwork, dry and brittle from its long years of abandonment, exploded into fragments that rose up to fill the dusty air of the office he was exploring with his friends. "There's nothing here but rubbish, old rubbish."

"I think it's pretty interesting," Matt said as he continued to search through the drawers of the desks in the office, piling up an assortment of knick-knacks left by the people who used to work there that he liked the look of: key-rings, pens, coins, and all manner of other trinkets, many of them, he guessed, had been left behind unintentionally, forgotten in the process of shutting down the business.

"You would," Aaron said in disgust. "You're the only person I know who finds crap interesting."

"You can learn a lot from what other people consider crap." Matt pulled open another drawer and reached in to search it. "Damn!" he swore sharply. Yanking his hand from the drawer he lifted it to his mouth to suck at the blood that glistened as it ran down his finger.

Aaron gave a short, sharp laugh, amused by the reward his friend's curiosity had received, but it was quickly cut off by a scurrying sound. His hand dived into his pocket as the three of them turned towards the noise, and pulling his phone out he unlocked it, so he could turn on the torch function. He played the light around the office as he searched for the source of the scurrying; it wasn't long before it was revealed to be a rat, large and black, with a long tail and eyes that shone redly.

"I think we should get out of here," Matt said when he saw the rat; he wasn't great with animals at the best of times, and a rat in a dark, abandoned building was one of his worst fears.

"There must be a nest somewhere nearby," Jamie said, turning in time to catch sight of the rat's pink, worm-like tail as it disappeared through the door they had left open.

"Let's find it," Aaron suggested, sure his friend was thinking the same as him.

KURT WAS TEMPTED TO head back inside when he saw nothing and no-one as he searched around the building that housed his hideout. He wanted to return to his film, it was one he hadn't seen before, but thought it best to continue looking around. If there was trouble nearby, he wanted to find it and deal with it before it threatened his den and left him in danger of going back to prison. There was no way he was going back inside if he could avoid it, he had vowed as much when he got out; no matter what he had to do, he would not be locked away again.

He had checked half the exterior of the building that occupied the other corner at the rear of the industrial estate when he found the broken door. The damage was fresh, he could see that despite the encroaching gloom, and he realised what he had heard was someone breaking in the door. He didn't think it was the police, or anyone looking for him - he had no reason for thinking that anyone had the slightest clue he was there - but he knew that ignoring what he had found was a risk he couldn't afford to take.

Once through the remnants of the door, Kurt paused to give his eyes a chance to adjust to the darkness, not that it was all that much darker than outside. When he could make out the outlines of the machines that had once filled the building with noise and thickened the air with dust - a different kind of dust to that which now coated everything - and the smells of oil, heat, and other such things he moved forwards.

He placed each footstep as carefully as a poacher stalking a rabbit, determined to avoid noise wherever he could on his way to the far corner of the building; he saw no sign of anyone down any of the aisles formed by the parallel rows of machinery, but he didn't allow himself to relax.

In his father's day, he remembered, the factory had fabricated all manner of machine parts. How long it had been since the machines were last turned on, he didn't know, just as he didn't know why the industrial estate had remained abandoned for so long; it didn't make sense to him, but then, it didn't matter either, and he quickly forced aside the reminiscences of his childhood, so he could focus on the present.

He found no sign of whoever had broken in the door as he searched the ground floor, not until he reached the stairs leading to the first floor. That was when he heard the voices, and a few moments later he saw the vague outlines of three people at the head of the stairs. From the voices and what he could see of their owners he figured they were young, just teenagers, and no threat to him - he guessed they were looking for fun, not for trouble or him - so he melted back into the darkness to listen and observe and make sure he was right.

"DO YOU THINK THIS PLACE has a cellar?" Aaron asked as he followed Jamie down the stairs, the light from his phone piercing the darkness in search of the rat that had startled them in the office, or any rat that might happen to cross their path.

"How the hell would I know?" Jamie asked, throwing a look over his shoulder that would, if it had been seen, have made it clear he thought his friend was an idiot. "Why?"

"The nest'll probably be down there, if there is one."

"What's that?" Matt asked suddenly from behind the other two, a note of alarm in his voice.

"What's what?" Jamie wanted to know irritably, sure Matt had been spooked by another rat; how his friend could be scared of something as pathetic as a rat, he didn't know, but he did know it was ridiculous. He followed Matt's pointing finger with his eyes and saw 'what', it was a boot, black, and just barely visible at the edge of the light from Aaron's phone. "Who's there?" he called out.

KURT CURSED UNDER HIS breath as he wondered how he had been spotted, he was sure he was out of sight. Tightening his grip on the knife, he moved further back into the darkness of the factory, hoping the teens wouldn't come looking for him, and that they would assume they were mistaken and hadn't really seen someone. He quickly realised he was not to be so lucky as the sound of footsteps approached, they were muffled by the dust that lay thick on the floor but still echoed off the walls and the machinery, making it seem as though they were closing in on him from all directions.

He continued to back up and hope the teens would forget about him; he didn't want to hurt them, they were just looking for fun, but when they appeared in front of him, and the light shone brightly in his face, he reacted automatically. He lunged with the knife, the bloodstained, eight-inch blade reaching for the figure holding the source of the light.

Aaron twisted away but wasn't quick enough to evade the knife. He felt a sharp pain in his arm as the blade sliced into him, drawing blood and making him drop his phone. The light blinked out when the phone hit the floor and smashed, and he panicked, more than he had when he saw the knife coming towards him.

With his left hand clutched to his arm in a futile effort to stem the flow of blood, Aaron made to flee from the danger he could see and ran straight into Jamie, who was right behind him. They fell in a heap, taking Matt with them. Aaron's howl of pain mingled with the cries of alarm and fright from his friends until they became one sound, whose source couldn't easily be determined.

Aaron untangled himself from his friends, scrambling over them as he got to his feet, and hurried back the way they had come, searching the darkness for the closest and quickest way out of the abandoned factory. He could hear rapid footsteps coming from behind him and, not knowing who they belonged to, sped up, biting his tongue to hold back the cries of pain that threatened to betray his location when he bumped into the silent and rusty machinery, prompting a fresh stream of blood to flow from between his fingers and run down his arm.

A barely perceptible lightening of the darkness led him to the door Jamie had kicked in, and he burst out of the building into the fresh air at a run. The fence was only a dozen or so yards away, but some instinct made him turn away from it and race along the side of the building, so he could disappear around the corner. He hoped his friends had been able to get away and find the exit, but he was too afraid of the wild-looking man with the knife to stop and find out; all he could think about was escaping, and once he was out of sight of the door he made for the fence.

Climbing the fence to get into the industrial estate had not been all that difficult, but climbing it to get out was. It was too dark for him to tell how bad the cut on his arm was, but he didn't need to see it to know it was bad. If it hadn't been for the adrenaline the fear sent racing through his system, he didn't think he would have made it over, he did, though, and the moment his feet touched the ground on the other side he raced away into the darkness.

He didn't stop until he was on the other side of the patch of wasteland that stood at the back of the industrial estate, and had reached the narrow alley that led between houses to the street. Only then did he look for some sign of his friends, or the man with the knife.

To his enormous relief, he saw his friends appear out of the darkness at the far end of the alley after a minute or so; he had never been so glad to see them. While he waited for them to reach him he looked beyond them, trying to see if they were being followed. He saw no sign of the man with the knife, and finally allowed himself to relax, a little, at which point he became aware of the pain in his arm that twisted his face into a grimace.

"You alright?" Matt asked, his face pale and his voice shaky. His chest heaved as he tried to regain his breath after his panicked flight; how he had got over the fence, he didn't know, he had no recollection of reaching it let alone climbing it.

Aaron didn't trust himself to speak; now the danger was past he felt sick - he liked to think he was tough, but he had never been attacked by someone with a knife, and he could feel his whole body shaking; he was sure if he opened his mouth to speak he would puke. That thought, and the desire not to look weak in front of his friends, made him clamp his mouth shut and swallow against the nausea that made him want to spill his guts.

"What do we do now?" Matt asked when it became clear Aaron wasn't going to answer his previous question.

As always it was Jamie who took charge. "We go to your place and call the cops," he said setting off down the street.

"Why my place?" Matt looked nervously over his shoulder while he followed his friends, as if he expected the knife-wielding lunatic to appear at any moment and attack them again. "Jamie, why my place? Mum'll be home, and she'll do her nut when she hears where we've been." He followed along for a little longer and then said, "Come on guys; can't we go to one of your places?"

"Shut up, Matt!" Jamie snapped. "Stop bitching like a little girl. We're going to your place because it's closest. We've got to call the cops about that nut-case before he attacks anyone else, and Aaron needs his arm looked at."

KURT STOOD AT THE FENCE and cursed fluently as he watched the darkness swallow the teens. He could have climbed the fence and continued the chase, he might even have caught them, though he doubted he could have done so before they reached the houses that were separated from the industrial estate by the fifty or so yards of wasteland, but he had enough sense to realise that doing so would only make his situation worse.

Instead of pursuing the teens, he swore until he had exhausted his extensive repertoire of profanity, which took him a short while. Only when he was done did he leave the fence.

Since he couldn't stop the boys, and he was sure they would call the police at their first opportunity, he realised he had to get away and find himself a new hiding place. As much as he wanted to, he couldn't leave it to chance that the police would ignore the report of the attack when they got it; he was sure they would search the industrial estate and all of its buildings thoroughly for him.

He didn't know where he could go; the industrial estate was the perfect hiding place - at least it had been - and he couldn't think of anywhere that came close to being a match for it. As he thought about it, though, Kurt realised he didn't need to know where he was going, at least not right then; the important thing was for him to get away before the police arrived. He could find himself a new hiding place later, once he was safely away from the estate.

With quick strides, he made for the building that housed his lair, darting up the stairs when he reached them. He packed up his things as rapidly as he could, shoving them untidily into the two bags he had, taking little care whether he damaged them in his haste; he could replace anything he broke, but not if he delayed too long and was caught.

He took a final look around to be sure he had everything, and spied the bottle of whiskey he had allowed himself as a reward for dealing with the Bhaskars and Terry Fielding. Snatching it up he spun off the top and lifted it to his lips so he could drain it; the moment the last drops of the fiery liquid burned their way down his throat he tossed the bottle aside to smash against the wall. He watched the fragments of glass cascade to the floor in the light from his portable lamp, then spun on his heel and departed.

It took him just a couple of minutes to reach the gates, where he stopped his car and hurriedly got out, so he could unlock them. He abandoned his usual caution in his haste to get away before the police arrived, and he left the gates standing wide once he had driven through.

# 17

"Nathan."

He stirred as his name was called, but it wasn't until it came again that he woke. Sleepily, he forced his eyes open, so he could look around for the person who had disturbed him - it was his wife.

"Sorry to wake you," she apologised. "It's Stephen."

"Thanks." Nathan was annoyed by the interruption to his sleep, but knew there was no point in taking it out on either his wife or Stephen, who wouldn't be calling without a good reason. He fought off a yawn as he took the phone his wife held out, putting it to his ear he dropped his head back to the pillow. "What's going on, Stephen?" he asked.

"Sorry to disturb you," Burke apologised. "But we've got a possible lead on the Bhaskars' killer."

That brought Nathan fully awake; he sat up quickly, throwing back the quilt so he could swing his legs round and get to his feet. "What sort of lead?"

"A phone tip," Burke told him. "I'll explain when I get there, I'll pick you up on the way."

Nathan grumbled but accepted that. He tossed the phone onto the bed once his partner had hung up, and quickly pulled out fresh clothes so he could get dressed. A check of his watch revealed that it was about half-six, which meant he had only had a couple of hours sleep, but that was about as much of a nap as he had expected so he didn't feel too hard done by.

When he made it downstairs, awake, if not exactly alert, he exchanged the phone for the coffee his wife had made him. He smiled in gratitude and took a quick sip, enjoying the heat as the strong and sweet coffee slid down his throat, giving him energy and switching his brain on.

"Back to work." Melissa's phrasing and tone suggested a question, but they both knew it was more of an observation, one which Nathan responded to with a reluctant nod.

"Afraid so," he said regretfully. He loved his job, loved the challenge of catching criminals and stopping crimes, but he didn't love how often it kept him from his family. It was no consolation that the heart defect his son had been born with had been fixed, or that as a result his wife was better able to cope during those occasions when cases kept him at the office for long periods. He sometimes thought the extra money, and the pride of accomplishment that had come with his promotion to inspector, weren't worth the time he missed with his wife and kids.

The children were too young to appreciate the importance of what he did, all they cared about was that daddy wasn't there when they wanted him, and his wife's patience had a limit, a limit she was sometimes pushed beyond. Fortunately, that happened less now their son was well.

Melissa sighed in frustration. "Robert was hoping you'd help him with his homework."

A pained look crossed Nathan's face at that. He dreaded the day when the homework his children wanted help with was beyond him, but while his son was only seven he could cope, and he derived an enormous amount of pleasure from helping Robert practice his handwriting and his times-tables and the other tasks his teacher set him.

"We might have a lead on the man who killed those two women on Sunday," he said in answer to his wife's unspoken question. "Stephen didn't say what, but he's on his way to pick me up, so it must be pretty good." Taking another sip of his coffee, he pulled open the fridge door and bent to peer at the contents; it wasn't the cooked dinner he had been looking forward to, but he accepted that the hunk of cheese and slice of ham he pulled out to make a sandwich with was the best he could manage just then.

"The ones who were shot?" Melissa asked.

Nathan nodded, and did his best to ignore the concern that showed in his wife's eyes. With his sandwich in one hand, and his coffee in the other, he left the kitchen and made his way along the passage to the living room, where he found his daughter on the sofa, playing with a stuffed toy, and his son on the floor, using the coffee table as a desk. He was supposed to sit at the table while he did his homework, but Nathan wasn't surprised to see his son on the floor; for some reason Robert preferred the floor to a chair and using the coffee table to the dining table.

"Daddy!" Robert said, his voice alive with delight when he saw his father enter the living room. "Help me."

Nathan smiled at his son. "Just a second, Robert." He crossed to the window and peered out to see if his partner had arrived; it was a warm evening, but the early darkness made it clear that autumn was dying, and winter was approaching. When he saw no sign of his partner, he turned from the window and joined his son. "I'll help you for a bit, but I've got to go to work when Uncle Stephen gets here."

Disappointment filled Robert's face when he heard that. "Why?" he asked in a voice that was almost a wail. "I want you to stay."

"I wish I could," Nathan said, meaning it. "But I can't, I have to go to work."

"Are you going to catch a bad man?" That was as much as Robert understood of what his father did for a living, that he caught bad men, and that doing so kept him away from home. "A very bad man?" he asked when his father nodded.

"Yes, a very bad man."

Robert accepted that. "Okay." He liked that his father was a hero who caught bad men, but it wasn't enough to make up for his desire to have his father home and helping him with his homework. "First you help me."

Nathan nodded and bent to help his son with a smile - in truth, the helping required little more than saying something approving when Robert did something right, and encouraging him to try again when he did something wrong. To his relief, there wasn't much writing to be done, and he was able to sit with his son and assist him in reading the book he had been given by his teacher for about five minutes before the doorbell announced Burke's arrival, and the end of father-son time.

"Be good for mummy," Nathan told his kids as he got to his feet. He bent to kiss his son on the top of his head and then moved over to the sofa, where Isobel allowed herself to be picked up for a kiss and a cuddle before being set down again. "Night night. I'll see you both in the morning."

"Be careful," Melissa admonished her husband as he opened the front door. "Don't take any unnecessary risks."

"Don't worry, Melissa, I'll keep him away from trouble," Burke reassured her.

Nathan kissed his wife goodbye and then followed his partner to the car. "So, what's going on?" he asked once they had pulled away from the kerb.

"A group of boys decided to explore the old industrial estate on Greenwell Street after school, looking for whatever's been left behind apparently, and got attacked by someone they think is squatting in one of the buildings there. One of them had to go to hospital for stitches."

"How does that connect to the Bhaskar murders?" Nathan asked. To him, stitches suggested the boy had been injured with something other than the shotgun used on the two Mrs Bhaskars.

"Wells responded to the initial call and called me, he said the description the boys gave matches what we have for the killer from the CCTV footage, and one of the boys said he saw a Honda as he was making his escape."

"A blue Civic?"

Burke shrugged. "No idea, Wells just said the boy saw a Honda. Anyway, the estate and all those empty buildings, makes for a perfect hiding place, no-one's used them in at least a decade, unless you count teenagers looking for fun and privacy, and Collins has decided it's where our killer is - I say was, I doubt he's still there, I imagine he scarpered after his encounter with the boys, if it was the guy we're after - so he's called in the armed response guys, just to be on the safe side."

"I'm glad about that." Nathan didn't fancy being the one to search the dozen or so buildings that made up the industrial estate for a possible killer; even if the man who had attacked the boys wasn't the killer they were after, he was still someone who had shown a willingness to attack people, which made him not the sort of person Nathan fancied searching for in buildings he knew were without power, and consequently light. "Was Collins going to contact either of us about this? The Bhaskar murders is our case."

"Not as far as I've been able to tell," Burke said. "I phoned the station after hearing from Wells, but Collins was busy. If you ask me, he wants to exclude us, so he can take the credit for catching our killer. Wells hinted as much."

Nathan shot his partner a knowing look. "Are you really surprised? You must have heard the rumour that the chief super is retiring next year, if that's true there's going to be a lot of re-shuffling.

Collins' wife is pushing him for the superintendent's position, and he's going to need an arrest like this if he's going to get the job."

NATHAN AND BURKE REACHED the industrial estate on Greenwell Street and discovered that the road on either side of the entrance had been blocked by police patrol cars. In addition to the cars blocking the road, and the civilian vehicles that had been stopped by the barricades, there was the van that both detectives recognised as belonging to the armed response team.

Burke parked his car half on and half off the pavement, as close to the gates of the estate as he could get, and hurried after Nathan. He didn't catch up to his partner until he reached the entrance, where Nathan was attempting to find out what the situation was. He stopped a pace or two behind his partner and stood quietly while Nathan spoke to the DCI, who didn't look at all happy to see his subordinate.

"...think he's already gone," Collins said. "The gates were open when we got here and, according to a couple of the drivers we've spoken to, that's more than unusual, none of them remember seeing the gates open before. I've got officers going up and down the street to see if they can find witnesses, and a couple of the armed response guys watching the entrance, just in case he's still here and he makes a break for it, while the rest of the team is checking out the buildings. None of us," he gestured around, taking in Nathan, Burke, himself, and the other officers who were waiting by the cars blocking the street, "goes in there till I'm sure it's safe."

That was good news for Nathan, who had been afraid Collins would do something reckless, like send in unarmed officers with the armed officers to speed up the search of the estate. He could only guess at how long it was going to take for the armed officers to complete their search of the dozen or so run-down buildings that made up the estate, but he was sure it would be long enough for Collins to become frustrated. He couldn't blame his superior, there was every chance that it would be late before the search was over, and until it was the regular officers and forensics specialists couldn't move in to do their work.

"Have you cleared any of the buildings yet?" Nathan's eyes went to the closest of the dilapidated buildings, which was little more than a silhouette against the dark sky.

"Three so far, they're checking the fourth one now."

"Nathan!"

Nathan felt his heart sink into his stomach, where it sat like a lead weight. He didn't need to turn and search the crowd of onlookers to know who was trying to get his attention, neither did Collins, they both recognised Louisa Orchard's voice, and they were both of the opinion that she was the last person they wanted to have there just then.

"What's she doing here?" Collins asked, determinedly keeping his back to where the journalist's voice was coming from so he could pretend to be unaware of her presence, and so avoid answering whatever questions she had.

"Her job, I imagine, just like us," Nathan said mildly, more amused by the stupidity of the question than he was annoyed by the fact of Louisa being there.

"How did she know to be here? If anyone's talked out of place, I'll have their hide."

Nathan listened to the threat, and found himself wondering how it was that his superior could have changed so much simply through getting married. Collins had always been a tough boss, but he had also been a fair one, until he got married for the second time, to a woman with ambition, a woman who wished to be the wife of the chief constable. Now he was the sort to steal credit for other people's work, and to show more interest in making himself look good than in ensuring his subordinates did their job properly.

"Take a look around, sir. Any one of the people here could have called her. Hell, I'm surprised we haven't got the local news here as well, they must be on their way. There's no way you could have kept this quiet."

Collins grimaced, and looked as if he had swallowed a particularly bitter pill as he accepted the truth of that. He looked around for a moment, his eyes sliding quickly past Louisa before settling on Nathan. "You get on well with her, go keep her out of my hair," he ordered. "And make sure she finds out nothing unless I've approved it."

"Yes, sir." Nathan nodded, though he had no idea how he was supposed to prevent Louisa learning things, she had eyes to see and ears to hear, plenty of people willing to give her information, and the brain of a detective to help her put it all together.

"What do you want me to do?" Burke asked as he followed his partner away from the DCI. He didn't fancy waiting around for the firearms officers to finish their search, or listening to Nathan verbally joust with Louisa.

Nathan thought about things as he dawdled on his way to distract and deceive the journalist. "Find out where the boys who started all this are," he said finally. "See if they can tell you anything that Frank didn't already pass on."

Burke nodded and left his partner.

"Hello, Louisa," Nathan said pleasantly when he reached the journalist. "How are you?"

Amusement twinkled in Louisa's eyes as she returned the greeting and said, "Does Collins really think I'm going to believe he didn't hear me?"

"I wouldn't presume to know what the DCI thinks," Nathan said. He might have a good working relationship with her, but he had too much sense to give any hint of what he thought of his superior to Louisa, especially when Collins was nearby, and there were so many civilians around to overhear him. "Should I bother asking how you know about this?"

"Only if you want to waste your breath," Louisa told him. "You know I don't reveal my sources. So, what instructions did the DCI give you before he sent you over here? To keep me busy and out of his hair?"

"Why don't we talk over there, where it's quieter," Nathan suggested, indicating a spot away from the crowd with a nod of his head.

"Come on then, did he tell you to keep me out of his hair?" Louisa repeated her question once they were far enough from the crowd not to be overheard.

"Of course he did."

# 18

In the darkest and most private corner of The Anvil pub, Kurt sat and sipped at his pint. His eyes shifted rapidly between the television above the bar and the people nearest him. He was taking a risk, being somewhere public, but he felt confident he was safe for the time being, while he considered what he was going to do next.

He wished he knew what was going on at the estate he had fled only a short while before, so he knew what sort of danger, if any, he was in. Since there had been nothing on the local news, which had aired only ten minutes ago, and he had heard only one person mention the industrial estate during his time at the pub, he didn't think he had anything to worry about, at least not for the time being. That left him free to think more fully about where he was going to hide while he punished the last of those who had sent him to jail - there were four to go, but one mattered more than the others, and he planned to take care of him first.

It took him until he reached the bottom of his third pint to think of somewhere he could hide that was as good as the industrial estate had been. He could only hope nothing had happened to the place during his time in jail; that was the problem with having been away for so long - though much about the town had remained the same, there was enough that had changed to confuse him and cause problems. The problems arose mostly from his desire not to draw attention to himself, which made him unwilling to go to anyone for assistance.

His decision made, Kurt got to his feet. He lit a cigarette as he made his way round to the car park at the rear of the pub. He wouldn't ordinarily have driven after drinking three pints, but just then he didn't think it mattered, his hands were steady, his mind clear enough, and he was sure the majority of the police would be focused on what was happening at the industrial estate, not on stopping people for possible drink-driving.

He turned to his right as he pulled out of the car park and reached the main road - the hiding place he had thought of was off to his left, but he had somewhere else to go first, and something else to do. His eyes moved constantly from the road ahead to his mirrors as he watched for any potential trouble, while obeying all the traffic laws he could remember.

His first destination was a house on the outskirts of town. He took a circuitous route to get there, not because he was concerned that anyone might be following him, but because he wanted to avoid going near his former hiding place. The house stood dark, and seemingly empty, in grounds that were a mix of wildly overgrown grass, weeds and bushes, and recently dug over flowerbeds that looked ready for planting as Kurt drove past on his way to the end of the road.

He could see no reason for concern, but was determined to show as much caution as possible after the surprise he had received earlier that evening. His eyes moved constantly, checking the surrounding darkness for anyone who might be paying him too much attention - the houses were spaced well apart, and the road did not suffer much through-traffic, so it was no surprise that he saw no-one.

Having assured himself that he had nothing to worry about, Kurt pulled off the road and onto the drive of his destination. He climbed out, leaving the keys in the ignition in case he needed to make a quick getaway, and headed for the front door of the house.

The smell of decay and corruption assailed his nostrils the instant he pushed open the door - left unlocked since his last visit - and entered. His nose twitched, and his gorge rose in his throat as he took shallow breaths, trying to limit his exposure to the stench, which permeated every molecule of air in the house. Not wanting to add to the difficulty he was having keeping his last meal where it was, and where it belonged, he kept his eyes averted on his way past the living room door, which stood open; he could guess what he would see, he didn't need to actually see it.

Once he reached the kitchen at the end of the passage he made straight for the back door. Things would have been much easier if he could have gone straight down the side of the house to reach the rear garden; the gate was locked, however, and he didn't want to do anything that might draw the attention of the neighbours.

The garden at the rear of the house was a tangled mess, giving clear evidence that no-one had bothered with it in a while, which Kurt knew was the result of the house standing empty for more than a year before finally being bought. Only where the path ran from the back door to the shed in the far corner, partially - mostly - concealed by the overgrown privet hedge that bordered the garden on three sides, had the garden been cleared.

The owner no longer had need of the tools, or anything else for that matter, neither did Kurt, but he did need the shed. The interior was dark, dusty, musty, and full of spiders, none of which bothered him; he ignored it all as he stepped inside and bent to feel around on the floor. He had marked the spot he was after for just the eventuality he was faced with then, so he had no difficulty finding it.

He lifted the section of planking he had removed the week before, and then used the trowel that had marked the spot to scrape away the thin layer of dirt covering the bag he had hidden. Once he had extracted the bulky sports bag from the hole he left the shed, without bothering to replace the planking; he did close the door, since he didn't want to make it too obvious that anyone had been there.

Forgetting his determination not to do anything that would reveal his presence there, he turned the light on the moment he was back in the kitchen, so he could check the bag. He didn't take the time to count the money - it would take him all night to get to one hundred and seven thousand pounds, no matter how quickly he counted the notes - but he was sure it was all still there. He felt a warm glow spread through him as he gazed at the money; he could have reduced the sentence he received at any time by revealing where the money from the robbery was, but he considered a hundred thousand pounds to be a fair trade for a decade of his life.

He had hidden the money in the shed the week before to keep it safe, but after what had happened that evening he wanted it close. If he was found again, whether by the police or anyone else, by accident or by design, he would have to abandon his plans to punish those who had sent him to jail and simply flee the country. If that became necessary, he didn't want to have to delay and make a detour to retrieve his money.

# 19

"Frank," Burke quietly drew Sergeant Wells' attention, and then gestured with a nod of his head to indicate they should move away from the group surrounding the bed.

"What's the situation?" Wells asked the moment they were far enough from the group not to be overheard. "Have they caught him?"

Burke gave an ironic laugh. "I was just going to ask you the same question - what's the situation here? As far as I know, they haven't caught him," he answered Wells' question. "The armed response team was still searching the estate when Nate and I got there; he's been detailed to keep Louisa Orchard out of Collins' hair, and I was sent here to see if I can get anything more out of the boys."

Wells accepted that equably, knowing that Burke wasn't implying he had done a deficient job.

"So, what's the situation here?" Burke asked. His eyes strayed to bed one, where he examined its occupant for a moment before moving on to those sitting and standing around it. The crowd, including the healthy-looking patient, numbered an even half dozen: the boys Wells had told him about when he called, two women he presumed were mothers to two of the boys, and a girl of about eleven or twelve, clearly the sister of the boy in the bed given the resemblance they shared.

"Just what I told you on the phone," Wells said. "The three boys decided to explore the industrial estate on Greenwell Street, they were looking around one of the buildings when they were surprised by a rough-looking guy, their description, who attacked them with a knife. The one in the bed, Aaron Dixon, was injured, and the three of them ran for it; when they reached one of their homes they called nine-nine-nine. The ambulance made it there before we did, so me and WPC Beck talked to the other two before we brought them here; Aaron's mum and sister met us here."

"How badly hurt is he?" From the way the teen looked, calm and relaxed, Burke was sure his injury wasn't too bad.

Wells rocked his hand back and forth. "The cut is pretty deep, it needed half a dozen stitches, but it's not all that serious according to the doctor. They're keeping him in overnight for observation, just to be on the safe side - the doctor said they cleaned the wound thoroughly before stitching him up, but given where the guy who attacked him was living, they want to be sure there aren't going to be complications." He gave a quick grimace. "God knows how dirty that blade was, it could have had all kinds of crap on it."

"Did you speak to the boy who was injured?" Burke asked.

"Not so far, I haven't had a chance, Mrs Dixon is proving to be something of a barrier, she's a bit of a worry-wart; though, truth be told, I didn't try too hard. After speaking to the other two, I didn't see the point in pressing the issue," Wells said when he received a questioning look from Burke. "They told us where to search, I figured that was good enough to get things started."

"I guess I'd better go and see what I can get out of them then. If he had any sense, the guy left the moment he realised the boys were gone, whether he's our killer or not, but they might have seen or heard something that will help us find him again." Leaving Wells, Burke joined the group around the bed. "Excuse me, sorry for interrupting," he apologised, though there was little in the way of conversation going on for him to interrupt. "I'm Detective Sergeant Burke, if you don't mind, I'd like to speak to the three of you." His eyes moved between the three boys, making it clear who it was he wanted to speak to.

It was the woman by the bed who responded, the woman whose posture and proximity indicated to Burke that she was Aaron Dixon's mother. "Is that necessary? They've already spoken to the sergeant over there, and Aaron needs his rest." She spoke as though he was a little boy who was very ill, and Burke didn't miss the annoyance that flashed across her son's face.

"I'm not a kid, mum," Aaron said in a tone of long-suffering. "He's just doing his job; besides, I never spoke to the cops earlier, Matt and Jamie did."

Burke was glad his partner wasn't with him over the next couple of minutes; as patient as Nathan was under most circumstances, he would have found himself tried by Sally Dixon's efforts to prevent Burke talking to her son, for no better reason, it seemed, than because she was overly protective and had a hard time accepting that her son was a teen who was capable of speaking for himself.

"Right boys," Burke said when he had finally persuaded Sally Dixon to let him speak to Aaron, and to take her daughter off to the hospital's cafeteria for a drink; it had been much easier to get rid of Tamara Halliwell, Matthew's mother, though she too was unhappy with the thought of her son talking to the police. "If you don't mind, I'd like you to tell me what happened this evening, every detail you can remember, no matter how trivial it might seem. First, though, could you give me your names." Taking out his pad and a pen, he looked expectantly from one boy to the next.

"Jamie Leeson."

"Aaron Dixon."

"Matt Halliwell." They answered in turn.

"Thank you. Now, what happened at the Greenwell Industrial Estate this afternoon?"

It was Jamie, as leader of the trio, who spoke. "We were after some fun after school and were mucking about on the wasteland behind Matt's place when we decided to have a look around the estate, see if anything good's been left behind."

"We're not in trouble, are we?" Matt asked worriedly. "Mum said we were trespassing and broke the law, and we're all going to end up with criminal records, we're not, are we?"

Burke was tempted to suggest that they could avoid trouble by cooperating with him, but since they already were, he didn't see the point in doing that. "You are guilty of trespass, that's true," he said, and was rewarded with a look of panic and fear. "But since no-one has made a complaint, I see no reason for any of you to worry."

The relief on Matt's face was almost comically exaggerated.

"You decided to explore the industrial estate," Burke prompted Jamie.

"Yeah, we climbed the fence and broke into the first building we came to. It was really dark, almost pitch black, but we found our way to the offices on the first floor, so we could have a look around. Matt was all excited about the stupid shit he found, and Aaron was bored and wanted to do something else."

"And you?" Burke asked, sure that everything they did, good or bad, was done at Jamie's instigation and for his pleasure.

Jamie shrugged. "I was disappointed. I hoped the place would be more exciting; it was boring, though, until the rat turned up that is."

Burke's curiosity was piqued, he couldn't figure out how a rat fitted into what had happened. "What rat?"

"The rat that scared the crap out of Matt," Jamie said, grinning broadly at the memory.

"It did not," Matt protested vehemently.

"It did," Jamie said, while Aaron nodded his agreement from the bed. "It was a big bugger, must have been almost a foot long, longer with the tail, and it scared the shit outta you. You sounded more like a scared little girl than Ariana does when she watches a horror movie."

"Ariana?" Burke asked; he didn't suppose it mattered who Ariana was, but he preferred knowing to not knowing.

"My sister," Aaron answered. "She was here with my mum."

Burke accepted that information with a nod, but didn't write it down. "Okay, a rat turned up, what happened then?"

"You mean after Matt did his impression of Ariana?" Jamie asked, directing a malicious smile at his friend. "Aaron suggested we go looking for a nest, he figured there had to be one somewhere nearby. I thought it was a good idea, so we did. We didn't find the nest on the first floor, though we kept seeing and hearing the rat, so we headed downstairs. When we got there, we saw a foot sticking out from behind one of the machines in the light from Aaron's phone.

"We called out to the person, and then made for where he was so we could see who it was, that's when he attacked us. Aaron got cut and dropped his phone, which made the place as black as anything - we could barely see a foot in front of us - and we ran. We didn't stop until we were back over the fence, across the wasteland, and through the alley to Cromwell Avenue. I think we all expected to find that he was still chasing us when we stopped, but he wasn't there. Thank god! That knife he had was a big bastard." Both his friends nodded in agreement of that statement.

"Can you describe the man who attacked you?"

"Not really." Jamie admitted. "We only got a brief glimpse of him. He was taller than us, about six foot I'd guess, and big, muscly, he had stubble, I remember that, but mostly I noticed the knife."

While that description did match what they had for the killer of the two Mrs Bhaskars, it was also vague enough to match a significant number of people.

"Did you see anything else that might help?" Burke asked. "A vehicle perhaps." His pen poised, he waited to see if any of the teens were going to mention the Honda they had told Sergeant Wells about. He didn't have to wait long.

# 20

Collins left the scene the moment the armed response team reported that the last building was clear. With no headline-grabbing arrest, there was no reason for him to remain.

Nathan was sure his superior, who had passed responsibility for finishing the operation to him, was already doing everything he could to distance himself from it. Fortunately, Nathan was not the sort to be bothered by credit or blame, his interest was solely on doing the best job he could.

"Everything alright, sir?"

Nathan tore his gaze from the two buildings in front of him and focused on the constable, who had appeared silently from the shadows. "Which building is which?"

"Sir?" the constable asked.

"I was told one building is where the attack took place, and the other is where the attacker has been hiding out; which is which?" Nathan looked from one building to the other, hoping to see some clue that would identify them, but they were both identical in the air of abandonment they wore. He didn't fancy wandering around the wrong dark building if he could avoid it, not when it was already getting late, and he could imagine how easy it would be to injure himself on something that would leave him needing a tetanus booster, if not something more serious.

The constable's expression cleared. "This one is where the attack took place," he said, pointing over his shoulder to the building behind him, whose shadow he had appeared from, "and that's where he had his hideout." He pointed to the other one. "You'll find the response team on the other side, I believe they're keeping watch by the busted door."

"Thanks."

Nathan had to stop the moment he entered the building. Someone had sensibly thought to rig up portable lights to illuminate the interior, but the change from the darkness outside was such that he had to give his eyes time to adjust before he could move beyond the door.

Once he could see, and was no longer in danger of either tripping over or walking into something, he made for the stairs at the far side of the building. He ascended cautiously, concerned with every step that the stairs were going to give out under him, only to find that the bigger danger came when he reached the top. The muzzle of the MP5 sub-machine gun that was pointed his way made him freeze, and he had to fight the urge to put his hands up in a gesture of surrender - unlike his partner, who had qualified for the armed response team but decided he preferred to remain a detective, he had never liked guns and avoided them whenever he could.

"Sorry, sir," Sergeant Vernon White, who was in charge of the armed response team, apologised, shifting the gun in his hands so it was no longer pointed at his superior.

"No worries." Nathan was relieved to hear that his voice was steady, and gave no hint of his sudden fright, though he wasn't sure the same could be said of his face. "Is this the place?" he asked when he reached the armed sergeant.

"Yes, sir. From what we saw during our search, the only rooms he used are this one and the bog." White pointed vaguely down the passage behind him in the direction of the toilets. "We did our best not to disturb any evidence, but I can't guarantee anything."

That didn't surprise Nathan, the team's focus would have been on checking the darkness for the knife-wielding man who had attacked the teens - they would have been doubly cautious given the suspicion that the man they were looking for was in possession of a shotgun, and had already killed two people - not on looking for evidence to be sure they didn't damage or destroy it.

Nathan stopped in the doorway with a muttered curse; the room was a black pit, the lights that illuminated the rest of the building didn't penetrate the office.

"What's the matter?" White asked, turning sharply at the profanity, a move which made the beam of light dance crazily across the wall opposite before it settled and fell on Nathan's face, forcing him to squint to avoid being blinded.

"I forgot my torch," Nathan said, holding out a hand to shield his eyes from the light.

"No problem, sir."

Nathan accepted the torch the sergeant held out to him, not the one attached to the muzzle of the MP5. "Thanks." He turned the torch on, and was pleased to see that it had a powerful beam which cut through the darkness, revealing that the room had been, as he had thought, an office at one time. Glad that it was not a large room that would take a lot of time, he began his search.

# 21

Huddled in his sleeping bag, Kurt shifted closer to his camping stove, wanting to get a little warmer. His new hiding place was no warmer than the one he had been forced to flee, it did, however, have the advantage of being less remote, and of having something that an optimistic person might call a view.

A graveyard was not everyone's cup of tea when it came to something to see, but it didn't bother him; just then he wouldn't have cared if his view was of open graves and decomposing bodies.

Finding the old groundskeeper's cottage was still empty, not only empty but almost overgrown, was a godsend. He had expected to find that the house had been knocked down, either to be replaced by something newer, or for the land to be used for graves; that was not the case, however, which was his good fortune. He was forced to leave his car in the car park of the Asda two streets away, where he hoped it would sit unnoticed, but he took comfort from the thought that if the car was found, the car park was far enough from the graveyard that it was unlikely anyone would think to look for him there.

His original intention, after making sure of his new hideout, was to take care of another of his targets; he changed his mind, though, once he had fought his way through the growth of brambles that surrounded the small house and broken open the back door. All he wanted to do at that point was settle in with a drink and a takeaway.

When the end credits for the Blackadder episode he was watching began, Kurt put his tablet down and reached for the carrier that held his drinks. He ignored the large bottle of water he had bought, that was for the morning, and the shaving items - he couldn't be certain how clearly his face had been seen by the teens at the estate, or how good a description they would be able to give the police, but he considered it a sensible precaution to alter his appearance; fortunately, that was easy enough, he just had to shave off his beard - and pulled out the bottle of whiskey.

He felt a warm glow spread through him as his first sip burned its way down his throat and settled in his stomach. It was a good feeling, and he quickly took a second sip before picking up his tablet, so he could start the next Blackadder episode. The episode had barely started when he changed his mind and paused it.

Switching from the movie app to the web browser, he began checking the local news for Branton; he didn't expect there to be much online about the incident at the industrial estate, but he hoped there might be something that would tell him if the police were on to him. If the police were on his trail he would have to reconsider his plans, something he didn't want to do.

As he began his search, Kurt reflected that it was good that he had allowed himself to be talked into taking IT courses while in prison. He was not an expert, by any stretch of the imagination, but he could at least surf the internet with some degree of confidence, if not with any speed.

After half an hour of frustration - he found it easier to use the internet on a computer rather than the tablet device he had bought - he gave up and returned to Blackadder. There was a small amount about the industrial estate on the internet, but it was all very general and revealed no details. He wasn't sure if that meant the police knew nothing that could lead them to him, or if it meant that information hadn't reached the internet yet, either way, there was no reason for him to worry just then - he was hidden, his money was close, he had booze, and he had something good to watch. He was as content as he could be.

# 22

Nathan felt like a teacher presiding over a classroom of delinquents as he waited for the briefing room to fall silent. He could have shouted the officers who filled the room into silence, but he chose to wait, using the time to finish off the coffee Burke had made him.

"Okay, settle down," he said when he reached the bottom of his mug and the noise persisted. "Come on, you've had enough time to play, it's time for work. Townsend, don't think I can't see you playing on your phone." That comment produced a few chuckles and a flush of embarrassment from the constable who had been singled out.

It was another minute or so before silence finally settled over the room and all eyes focused on Nathan. He was surprised that Collins had not put in an appearance to see what all the noise was about, but he supposed the DCI was keeping out of the way to distance himself from the previous evening's failed operation, not that he thought of it as a failure.

"Right, we've got a lot to get through, so let's get on." Nathan took the piece of paper Burke was holding out as he approached the board. "Firstly, and definitely most importantly, thanks to DS Burke, we now have a better description of the man we believe killed Amala and Manjula Bhaskar than that gleaned from the shop's CCTV: he is roughly six feet tall, stocky - muscle not fat - and he has shaggy black hair and a beard. This is what the sketch artist came up with, based on what the three boys our killer attacked told him." He used a magnet to secure the pencilled head-shot to the board, where it could be seen by everyone in the room. "All patrols will have a copy, and a copy is going to the Herald and the local news; with luck, a member of the public will see him and report it, though I suspect he's gone to ground in some new lair."

"What makes you so sure this guy's the Bhaskar's killer? They were killed with a shotgun, the guy yesterday had a knife from what I heard."

"That's true," Nathan admitted. "He did use a knife, but we had a stroke of luck; in the building where he had been hiding, we found paint, spray-equipment, and a number of different license plates, including a pair that match the license number of the car seen leaving the area of Mead Street immediately after the murders. Forensics have been at the old processing plant the killer was using for most of the night, they've gathered a large amount of evidence to be worked through, which is likely to take some time; hopefully, our killer is in the DNA database, and forensics will be able to find him for us.

"I want you all to consider places that our killer might now be using as a hideout. Checking everywhere we can come up with is likely to take a considerable amount of time, but we have to do everything we can to find him, and I don't intend simply waiting for forensics to finish their work - if he doesn't currently have a record, which I consider unlikely, they won't be able to identify the guy for us."

"Don't you think it likely this guy's left the area? He'd have to be pretty stupid to stick around now we've found where he was hiding." Several of the other officers in the room nodded their agreement of Mason's comment and looked to Nathan for an answer.

"It's a possibility, certainly," Nathan agreed. "And one that has to be considered, but I don't think it likely. Having re-watched the CCTV footage from Bhaskar's, I'm convinced the murders were deliberate, and the robbery intended as a cover for them; what the motive for the murders is, I have no idea at this time." He was still sure he knew Vikram Bhaskar from somewhere, and that if he could just remember how the shopkeeper was known to him, he would have the answer to why the two women had been murdered and who was responsible, or at least the start of the answer. "If he was going to do a runner, I'm sure our killer would have done so after killing the Bhaskars; sticking around suggests he has a reason to do so, and it can't be because of a family, otherwise he wouldn't have been hiding out where he was.

"I believe he's still somewhere in town, or holed up on the outskirts."

"You think he's going to kill again." This time Mason made a statement rather than asking a question, and Nathan was reminded that the sergeant was a good detective, even if his personality wasn't always the best.

"Yes." Nathan nodded. "I hope I'm wrong, but I don't think I am, which means in addition to trying to find our killer, we need to try and work out who his next victim might be. Reid, I want you to go back over the information you gathered on the Bhaskars and make sure you haven't missed anything; go into as much depth as you can, there's got to be something there to tell us why they were murdered."

"Yes, sir," Reid said quickly, though there was a troubled look on his face, and after a brief hesitation he asked, "Do you want me to carry on checking out the case files from the Fielding case?"

"Yes, I need you to do both. How's it going?" Nathan hadn't seen the result of Reid's checks to date, they were going straight to Mason and Grey, who were checking out those identified as likely suspects - he assumed that no-one had yet been upgraded to the status of either person-of-interest or possible suspect, if they had he should have been told.

"Slowly," Reid admitted reluctantly. "Some of them have been easy to check and dismiss, but others..." His voice tailed off momentarily before picking up again. "I've managed to get through about a quarter of them, and I've come up with roughly fifty people who needed looking into further, which Sergeant Mason has done."

Nathan turned to Mason, a questioning look on his face.

"No luck so far," Mason said. "Everyone we've checked out is in the clear - cast-iron alibis, one way or another." If he was frustrated by his lack of success, he gave no sign of it.

"Okay, moving on; forensics have apparently got a hit on the second blood sample taken from Terry Fielding's shirt, the report should be on its way over as we speak, so that might get us somewhere. In the meantime, Thompson, Keats," the two constables looked up guiltily as though they had been caught doing something they shouldn't be, "since the door-to-door enquiries are finished, I want you both to help Reid."

"Yes, sir," the two officers said in unison, concealing what they thought of the assignment.

"Sir."

"Yes?" Nathan asked of WPC Beck, Sergeant Wells' new trainee, who stood nervously in the doorway of the briefing room.

"I'm sorry for the interruption, sir," Beck apologised, she looked as though she expected to be shouted at for daring to intrude on the briefing, but took heart when that didn't happen. "But there's a gentleman downstairs in reception who's insisting on speaking to you. Sergeant Wells did try and call you," she said quickly, as though to justify her presence, "but there was no answer, so he sent me up to find you."

"Has he said why he wants to see me?"

Beck nodded. "No, sir; he said his name's Mr Bhaskar, though. He's not the Mr Bhaskar from the shop on Sunday, but he looks like him, and he's very insistent."

From the look on the young constable's face, Nathan got the impression that the Mr Bhaskar in reception had been less than polite, quite possibly even rude. That was to be expected, however, if he was related to the two murder victims. "Okay, I'll come down and see what he wants. Take over, Stephen," he directed his partner. Taking a copy of the sketch produced by the artist, he followed WPC Beck from the room.

IT WAS VIKRAM BHASKAR'S brother, Ravi, who Stone discovered in the small reception. He was in the centre of the eight foot by eight foot square, a newspaper rolled up tight in his hand, and anger creasing his face; his eyes bored into Nathan like twin lasers as he walked through the security door.

"Good morning, Mr Bhaskar, I understand you want to see me," Nathan said.

It quickly became clear that Ravi Bhaskar was in no mood for casual pleasantries, or even for common courtesies. He ignored the hand that Nathan held out to him and thrust the newspaper towards the inspector. "Have you seen this?" he demanded angrily, the paper he was holding waving back and forth as his hand shook.

Curious, and with no idea what to expect, Nathan took the newspaper from Ravi Bhaskar, which wasn't easy since his hand was clenched tight and he seemed reluctant to release it. When he did finally manage to free the paper, Nathan unrolled it, so he could read the front page - he assumed what he was supposed to be looking at was on the cover, and he was quickly proved right. The headline 'KILLER SLIPS THROUGH POLICE NET' stared up at him; he scanned the first paragraph and then checked the by-line, he was annoyed to see that the story was by Louisa Orchard.

He had thought, after their conversation last night, and his efforts to ensure she had accurate information, that she would avoid sensationalising things. He certainly hadn't expected her to misrepresent the previous evening's events, though he was aware that it was happening more and more frequently in her stories - he assumed it was the result of interference from her editor, not that that made him feel better about the situation.

"Perhaps we should talk in here, Mr Bhaskar," Nathan said, keeping hold of the newspaper as he gestured for his visitor to precede him to the visitor's room in the corner of the reception.

With a degree of reluctance, as though he wanted his conversation with Nathan witnessed, not only by the two officers on the reception counter, but by whoever entered the station, Bhaskar allowed himself to be led into the room.

"Do you mind if I read this?" Nathan asked as he took a seat across from Bhaskar. "I haven't had an opportunity to look at this morning's edition." A short, sharp, and barely noticeable, nod of the head answered the question, and he laid the newspaper on the table between them, so he could read the rest of the cover story, which was continued on page five.

By the time he got to the end of it, he wasn't sure whether to be annoyed with Louisa or not; he had already suspected the interference of Roger Kelly, and was now sure of it, he had read enough stories by Louisa to recognise her style of writing, and in a number of places there were words and phrases that were at odds with what he was used to.

"Well?" Bhaskar demanded when Nathan's head lifted from the paper. "What do you have to say? Why weren't my brother and I told about this? Why did we have to read about it in the paper?"

Bhaskar's anger was palpable, it radiated from him in waves, but Nathan ignored it. "I'm sorry you learned about this in such a way; it was my intention to come and see you and your brother later this morning after briefing my team." He saw the dubious look on the face of the man across from him but didn't let it faze him.

"The information in here," Nathan gestured to the newspaper, "is no more than fifty percent accurate. Much of it is wrong or exaggerated, though I don't suppose that will make you feel any better."

Bhaskar stared at Nathan for some time, as though trying to determine if he was telling the truth. Finally, he sagged in his chair and said, "So what is the truth? And why didn't you come and tell me and my brother straightaway?"

"I appreciate your frustration and your distress, Mr Bhaskar, I'm sure I'd feel the same if I were in your position. The reason I didn't come and see you and your family last night is that it was late by the time we finished at the industrial estate, and I hoped that by waiting until this morning I would be able to give you more positive news.

"This," he picked up the newspaper, the annoyance on his face a mirror for that which still showed on Ravi Bhaskar's, though that had faded slightly, "was not supposed to be printed until this afternoon's edition at the earliest, and with a great deal more accuracy. Miss Orchard assured me that she would not run the story until I had a chance to talk to you and your brother."

"Ha!"

Bhaskar's derision exploded out of him with sufficient volume to make Nathan wonder if Wells was going to come in to make sure he wasn't being attacked. Wells did not appear, though.

"You really thought she would do that?"

"She's always cooperated in the past. Rest assured, I'll be speaking to her as soon as I can. Now, before I get down to the events of yesterday evening, would you mind having a look at this picture; tell me if you recognise him." He passed the sketch of his suspect across the table.

Bhaskar took the drawing and studied it for several long moments before handing it back with a shake of his head. "No. Should I?"

Nathan shrugged. "No idea, Mr Bhaskar, but we believe the man in the sketch is the person who killed your mother and your sister-in-law. We have no reason for thinking that you, your brother, or indeed any member of your family might know who he is, but we have to consider the possibility. The picture will be in the paper and on the local news later today, so hopefully someone will recognise him, and be able to point us in the direction of where we can find him. Don't worry, I'll be coming to see your brother and his family with the picture before anyone outside of the station receives a copy; I don't want the first time they see it to be in the paper or on the news, that wouldn't be right."

"Thank you." Bhaskar's demeanour changed rapidly, his anger replaced by gratitude.

"Okay, onto the next thing, last night's incident." Nathan paused for a second to see if Bhaskar was going to say anything, when he didn't, Nathan got down to business. "The start of this story is correct, for the most part," he said, tapping the cover of the newspaper. "Three teens were exploring the Greenwell Industrial Estate yesterday evening, and while checking out one of the buildings they came face-to-face with this man," his hand moved from the paper to the sketch-artist's rendering, "who attacked them with a knife. He injured one of the teens, and the three of them made a run for it. Fortunately, he didn't follow them, or if he did he gave up the chase very quickly.

"When they got to one of their houses they called the emergency operator and reported the incident. Since the report mentioned a dark-coloured Honda, a vehicle we have been looking for in connection with the murders of your wife and mother, my superior made the decision to bring in the armed response team. That was both for public safety and the safety of the officers who were to search the estate.

"Unfortunately, the suspect was gone by the time the estate was closed off and the armed officers could make their search. We didn't find the suspect, but we did find evidence to link him to Sunday's incident, and we are confident that the forensics team will be able to identify our suspect from the evidence they are processing, which will lead to an arrest and a successful prosecution."

When he left a while later, Ravi Bhaskar was satisfied that the police were doing everything they could to solve the murders that had torn his family apart, even if he wasn't entirely mollified over the story appearing in the paper ahead of he and his brother being told about the latest events.

# 23

After checking from all the windows on the first floor that weren't covered by the vines that had overgrown the house, Kurt left. He scratched himself on the brambles that encroached on the rear door, but ignored the lines of blood that ran down his arm and hand, a few minor injuries were a small price to pay for a hide-out that just about no-one was going to believe was being used.

The cemetery was as empty as it had looked from inside the house, and he strode away, confident he hadn't been seen. He saw no-one until he was through the wrought-iron gates and on the street, by which time there was no need for him to worry about being seen because he wasn't doing anything that anyone might consider suspicious.

A ten-minute walk brought him to the Asda where he had left his car. He made a quick check of it on his way into the shop, and was reassured to see that it was still there, and showed no sign of having been tampered with or disturbed in any way. He supposed it was possible the police had found it and were monitoring it, but he couldn't see anything to worry about.

The toilets were just inside the entrance, and he ducked in there after glancing around to be sure no-one was paying attention to him. When he left, fifteen minutes later, he had washed, brushed his teeth and, more importantly, rid himself of the beard that was his most identifying feature. Without the beard there was a slim chance that someone might recognise him, but it had been ten years and more since anyone in Branton had seen Kurt Walker, and he was more concerned about being recognised from whatever description the teens from the industrial estate had been able to give the police. With the beard gone, he looked so different from the person the teens had seen that he was confident he could pass them in the street without being recognised.

The last thing he did before leaving the toilets was change his clothes.

Looking far more respectable than he had when he arrived, Kurt made a round of the shop to pick up some groceries. He couldn't cook in his hideout, not without being in danger of either burning the place down around him or of giving away his presence, but he could still get food he could eat cold, and he needed snacks and drinks. He then stopped at the McDonald's to get himself some breakfast to take back to his hideout while he planned the next stage in his campaign of revenge.

24

Louisa was not surprised to see that neither Nathan nor Burke wore welcoming looks as she approached their table, even though it had been Nathan who requested the meeting. Both of them looked as cold as a North wind in Siberia, Nathan even more so than his partner, which she supposed was to be expected under the circumstances.

Resigned to the lambasting she was sure was about to be directed at her, though determined to deflect it if she could, Louisa took a fortifying sip of her coffee and settled into the seat across the table from the two detectives. It was only a small comfort to her that Nathan had chosen a table in the back corner of the coffee shop, where their conversation was less likely to be noticed or overheard by the other customers; the decision had not been made for her benefit, she was sure, but it suited her just the same.

"Before you say anything, Nate," Louisa said, wanting to gain the initiative, "I know why you asked to see me, and I understand why you're annoyed."

"Annoyed, am I?" Nathan asked, his eyes glinting like chips of ice; he was not normally so cold with anyone, and especially not with someone he knew, liked, and generally got on with, but if there was one thing he couldn't stand - excepting criminals who preyed on the weak and those with little enough to begin with - it was a person who went back on their word, especially when doing so hurt a person who was already in pain, as Vikram Bhaskar, his children, and his brother, were. "I wouldn't say I was annoyed. Disappointed, yes, surprised, certainly, definitely wondering if I'll be able to trust you in the future, but not annoyed."

His voice was calm and soft, yet Louisa found that his words hurt all the more because of that. As a journalist, she struggled with the generally low opinion the members of her profession were held in by the public, not to mention those she relied upon as sources for the stories she wrote; all she could combat that low opinion with was the reputation she had worked hard to build as a person who could be trusted. Hearing that she was no longer trusted by one of the people she respected most was like a physical blow.

"It's not me you should be talking to about this morning's story," she said, unable to meet Nathan's eyes. "It's Kelly; I was up half the night writing that story, using what you told me. I emailed it to him when it was finished with a message that it was not to be run until I heard from you. I was asleep when you called, so it wasn't until I saw the front page of the Herald that I knew what was up.

"Kelly butchered my story, it's barely recognisable as the one I sent him. Here, this is the story I emailed him." From her shoulder bag she took several sheets of printed paper, which she thrust across the table. "You know me, Nate, if I agree to do something, I do it. My word is the most important thing I've got."

Nathan nodded, he did know that, which was what made things worse. He accepted the printed pages, and realised almost the moment he began reading that she was telling the truth; the story that had appeared in the morning edition of the Herald was not the one he held in his hands, it was hard to recognise them as the same story. The sections that hadn't been rewritten had been switched around, and to Nathan's mind it was clear that the original version was the superior, it was more coherent, more factual, and much better written.

"Sorry, I should have known you wouldn't go back on your word."

Louisa accepted the apology gracefully, knowing there was no point in making an issue of it; Nathan's reaction to the story was perfectly reasonable under the circumstances, besides which, she knew he was the one with the power in their relationship - he had the information she needed for her stories, some of them anyway, and even if he didn't he was in a position to make it difficult for her to do her job if she got on his bad side. She didn't actually think he would do anything if she upset him, but it wasn't a chance she was willing to take.

"No need to apologise, this isn't the first time Kelly's messed with someone's story, he's pissed off a few people because of it." Her expression made it clear that she was one of those people. "Believe me, when I get to the office, he'll be getting a piece of my mind; what he's done this time was beyond his job description. I've a good mind to go over his head and speak to the owner."

"That would probably be a waste of time," Nathan remarked, toying with the large cup that held the remnants of his overpriced coffee. "From what I know of Malcolm Edwards," he had only met the Branton Herald's owner on one occasion, but Edwards enjoyed the local limelight and most people in town knew a fair amount about him, "he's more interested in profits than anything else, except possibly the Blades; the more money the paper makes, the more money he can pump into them. Kelly has improved sales of the Herald; if Edwards has to choose between keeping you happy and keeping Kelly happy, I suspect he'll go with Kelly, so he can spend more money on his team."

Louisa sighed, she knew the truth of what Nathan said, even if she didn't like it. "So you reckon I shouldn't rock the boat."

"It's generally not a good idea," Nathan remarked.

"At least not unless you've got a lifeboat waiting for you," Burke said, entering the conversation.

"What do you mean?" Louisa couldn't help wondering if Burke had deliberately spoken cryptically to confuse her, she wouldn't have put it past him. Burke spoke to her only occasionally, and more often than not he left her more at a loss than she would have been if he had stayed silent.

Burke lifted his cup to his lips but then set it down again when he realised it was empty. "As the situation stands, you have no real bargaining power, with either Kelly or Edwards, you need to change that."

Nathan was surprised his partner was willing to offer advice to Louisa, Burke usually preferred to have nothing to do with journalists. Since Burke was prepared to give advice, he left them to it while he went to get fresh drinks for himself and Burke.

"Is there time to make the late edition?" he asked when he returned to the table, having given Burke and Louisa enough time to finish their conversation. He was curious about the advice Burke had provided, but not enough to ask him about it, he had more important things on his mind.

Louisa glanced at her watch before nodding. "If I get to the office in the next hour. What have you got for me?" She was surprised Nathan was prepared to give her another story so soon, considering the reason for their meeting that morning.

Nathan took the folded-up picture of his suspect from his pocket and handed it over. "This is the guy we were looking for last night. I'd like it on the front page this afternoon, with the usual 'if you know this man, or have seen him, please contact...' blah, blah, blah, and it definitely needs 'don't approach if sighted, extremely dangerous, and believed to be armed'." He was sure Louisa knew just what to put with the picture to get the right response from the public without putting them in danger.

"Definitely not someone I'd want to meet down an alley on a dark night," Louisa remarked after studying the picture for a couple of seconds. "Or on a crowded street in the middle of the day for that matter." She gave an involuntary shudder. "Those eyes, you can just tell he's a cold-blooded killer."

Nathan had to agree with her assessment, it was just what he had thought when he saw the sketch for the first time; he could only hope the artist had taken some creative license with the description he had been given when it came to the eyes. His hopes weren't high, though; not only was it the artist's job to be as accurate as possible, but there was something familiar about the eyes, he had the uncomfortable feeling he had seen them before, and that their owner was a danger to him.

"Can you get it on the front page for this afternoon?" he asked.

"I'll do my best, but I can't promise anything," Louisa told him.

"Why not?" Burke asked, not sure why there should be a problem with something so important. "What else could you have for the front page?"

"Me? Nothing. But as I understand it," Louisa looked distinctly uncomfortable, "Kelly has a story about the Fielding murder for the late edition."

"What sort of story?" Nathan asked. From the way Louisa avoided looking at him, her gaze was fixed on the large cup of coffee in front of her, he suspected it was one he wouldn't like.

"I don't know the details, the story's been written by Kelly and Marc Wallace, but it has something to do with the barrister Paula Fielding's been having an affair with." Louisa didn't need to look up at Nathan's face to know he was unhappy that the affair had been discovered and was going to be put in the paper. "I'll let you know when I find out the details of the story."

# 25

Surprise, excitement and confusion danced across DC Grey's face, each vying for control, as DS Mason brought the car to a stop in the visitor's car park at the front of the Cole and Rushman Production Company.

He had no idea why they were there; as far he knew they were supposed to be checking out the list of potential suspects in the Terry Fielding murder, which DC Reid had provided them with, and trying to close the investigation into a spate of recent car thefts. Neither of those things had anything to do with Cole and Rushman, at least not to the best of his knowledge.

"What are we doing here?" he asked of his partner. "I thought we were going to speak to Allan Owens." Looking down at the printout in his lap he saw that he was right, and Allan Owens was the next name, after Chris Yew, whom they had left a little over half an hour before without discovering anything, beyond that they could cross his name off their list of possible suspects.

"We'll do that later," Mason told Grey. "Right now we're going to do what seems to have slipped Nathan's mind." He turned off the engine and threw open the door, so he could get out.

"What's slipped the inspector's mind?" Grey asked when he was out of the car and had joined Mason on the walk across the car park to the entrance.

"Terry Fielding's colleagues. Nathan's decided his murder is connected to his wife's work, and he's forgotten about having Terry Fielding's colleagues questioned to see if they know something." Mason didn't try very hard to conceal the pleasure he felt at thinking of something that either hadn't occurred to, or which had been ignored by, the man who got the promotion he felt should have been his. "The only people who've been spoken to so far have been connected to Paulina Fielding, not Terry."

Mason jogged up the steps to the entrance of the plain-looking building, pushed the door open so he could enter, and strode over to the reception counter.

"Good morning. How can I help you?"

"Detective Sergeant Mason, I'd like to speak to someone about Terry Fielding." He held out his warrant card for the receptionist's inspection and Grey, who was trying not to look around in the hope of seeing someone even slightly famous, did the same.

Once she was satisfied the two detectives were genuine, the receptionist said in a voice that almost dripped with sincerity, "It's such a shame what happened to Mr Fielding, he was so nice to everyone; I couldn't believe it when I heard what happened to him. Why would anyone want to kill him? It just doesn't make sense." She brought her attention back to her job with an effort and offered a small smile of apology. "I'm sorry, it's just been such a shock. I'll let Mr Cole know you're here."

While Mason took a seat on the sofa, Grey wandered the reception area looking at the posters for the various TV shows and films the company had produced. It surprised him that he knew so few when the majority were apparently filmed locally.

In the five minutes that passed before anyone came to see the two detectives, Grey discovered that he was not in a hotbed of celebrity activity; not one person entered or exited the building during that time that he knew, though he did hear the receptionist mention three names he recognised. He forgot all about celebrities when footsteps echoed around the largely silent foyer; he turned in time to see a young man stop in front of the sofa.

"Sergeant Mason?"

"That's me." Mason pushed himself to his feet.

"Good morning, I'm John Naismith, personal assistant to Mr Cole, if you'll follow me, I'll take you up to see him."

"Thank you." Mason fell in at Naismith's shoulder as the young man turned and led them over to a lift that neither of the detectives had spotted previously.

Naismith waited until the doors had closed and the lift begun its ascent, then he said, "I understand you're here about Terry Fielding."

"That's right." Mason nodded. "We're here to talk to anyone he might have worked with, and who might have information about his murder. Did you know Terry Fielding?"

"Yes. You're going to have a hard time finding anyone here who didn't know him, even if they didn't work with him. He was a very popular guy, and, of course, he'd been here for quite some time and had worked on some of our most successful shows of the last decade. He was up for best documentary at the regional television awards, fifth year in a row he's been up for an award in one category or another, and there was talk that this time he was in with a shot at a National Television Award."

Mason expressed what he hoped was a suitable level of admiration for such an achievement - documentaries had never appealed to him, except when the subject was crime.

It took a little over five minutes to reach their destination, which seemed to be in the farthest corner of the building. When they got there Naismith ushered them straight through the outer office and into the inner office.

"Mr Cole asked me to apologise for his not being here to see you straight away, he's attending to a small matter and will be here as soon as he can. In the meantime, if there's anything I can get for you, a drink or a snack, just say." Naismith looked expectantly from Mason to Grey, as if he would be only too happy to get them whatever they wanted.

"Coke please," Grey requested, pretending not to notice the look Mason directed at him, a look that could have been disgust or disappointment.

"Tea for me, thank you," Mason said, switching his attention to Naismith.

"Would you like milk, lemon or sugar?" Naismith asked.

"Milk and two sugars, thanks."

Both Mason and Grey had time to finish their drinks, which were brought promptly by Naismith, before Hector Cole arrived. He appeared so suddenly, his movements so quiet, that neither detective realised he was there until he spoke.

"Good morning, gentlemen." Hector Cole closed the door quietly behind him and walked across the office to take the leather armchair by the sofa on which the two detectives were seated. He was an elderly gentleman, his age evident in the greying, almost white, hair that covered his head, and the slow way he eased himself into the chair, his voice was firm, though, and his eyes bright, indicating his mind was still active. "Forgive me for being late, but some things just have to be dealt with by the man at the top."

The door opened before Mason could decide how to respond to that and Naismith entered the room bearing a tray, on which was a cup of tea and a plate of assorted biscuits. Naismith placed the cup of tea in front of his boss, and the plate in the middle of the coffee table, and then left.

"Please, help yourself." Cole gestured to the plate. He didn't speak again until he had taken a sip of his pungent Earl Grey tea, and Grey had taken advantage of the invitation and helped himself to several of the biscuits. "I understand from my assistant that you are here to talk about Terry Fielding, who was murdered so brutally on Monday night."

"Yes, sir, I'm Detective..." Mason was cut off before he could finish introducing himself.

"I know, you are Detective Sergeant Mason, he is Detective Constable Grey, and I am Hector Cole," the old man said briskly. "I'm sure you both have lots to do to find poor Terry's killer, there's no point wasting time with unnecessary things. How can I help you? I promise you'll have the full cooperation of everyone in my company."

Mason was a little taken aback by that, he wasn't used to such immediately and voluntarily offered support and it made him suspicious. "Thank you," he said after recovering from his surprise. "If you don't mind, I'd like to begin our questioning with you."

"Of course. If you'll excuse me a moment, I'll make sure we're not disturbed." Getting to his feet he crossed to his desk, so he could speak to his assistant over the intercom. "Now, what would you like to know?" he asked when he returned to the chair.

"Why don't we start with how long Mr Fielding worked for you."

"That would be about twelve years," Cole said. "I'd have to have the records checked to be sure, but I believe it's been that long."

"Was he always a documentary maker?"

"I think when he first came to work for the company he was a cameraman, then an assistant director, it must have been seven or eight years ago that he started making his own documentaries. He was an award winner pretty much from the start."

"I imagine some people must have been resentful of his success; did Mr Fielding have any enemies?"

"Enemies," Cole said with a shake of his head. "That's the kind of thing that happens in the TV shows and films we make, not in real life, in real life people don't have enemies, they have professional rivalries."

"Okay, so I take it, since he has been successful, Mr Fielding has some professional rivalries." Mason waited until Cole nodded and then he continued. "Are any of the people those rivalries are with the sort who might go to the extreme of murder to remove competition?"

"Not in my opinion, but maybe someone else will know more about Terry's competition. I know he was in the running for another regional award, but I can't see what good it would do anyone to murder him now, that wouldn't stop his documentary winning. If it's going to, and we all hope it does, it would be a fitting epitaph."

Mason knew it was cynical, but he couldn't help thinking that Terry Fielding's death was probably going to put him in with a very good chance of winning a final regional television award, even if it was given more out of sympathy or pity than because it was deserved.

"What about the people Mr Fielding has worked with, any problems there?"

"I'M TOLD THAT MR FIELDING got on with everyone he worked with," Mason said. "It's unusual, in my experience. Is there no-one that he had a problem with? Maybe someone he had a difference of opinion with that might have got out of hand, or someone who's work he wasn't satisfied with."

"No, nothing like that." Olivia Branch, who had been the senior camera operator on Terry Fielding's last documentary, shook her head. She was the last of the people Terry Fielding had worked with from the list that John Naismith had provided. "Terry worked with a small team, one he put together over the past seven years; it's easy to get on with everyone when you only work with a few people."

"I guess that's true, if he only worked with a few people, it's doubtful any problems would have remained secret for long." That didn't help the investigation any, Mason reflected; he was looking for possible suspects, not people who could be discounted as suspects. "I understand Mr Fielding was in the running for a Regional Television Award, possibly even a National Television Award," he said. "That sort of thing can inspire envy and rivalries; can you think of anyone who might have felt like that?"

Branch considered the question for several long moments before answering. "There's Walter Hunter, over at East Coast Productions, I know he was annoyed with Terry - he seemed to think he should have got the last spot in the documentary category; I don't know why he blamed Terry for him not getting nominated and not any of the others, though." She shrugged. "If you ask me, he didn't stand a chance anyway, his documentary was very ordinary, nothing original or imaginative about it at all."

"Could he have been annoyed enough to kill Mr Fielding?"

That question amused Olivia, who couldn't keep herself from laughing; she cut the laughter off as quickly as she could, but her amusement remained in her eyes. "I'm sorry," she apologised once she had herself more or less under control, "it's not a laughing matter, I know that, but if you'd ever seen Walter, you know why the idea of him killing anyone, especially Terry, is so funny."

"Perhaps you could explain it to me," Mason suggested.

"Of course." Olivia became sombre and serious again. "Walter Hunter is short and scrawny; he's only about five foot, and if he weighs more than seven stone then I'm an elephant. He couldn't fight his way out of a wet paper bag, let alone kill anyone."

"People can surprise you, Ms Branch," Mason told her. "Just because someone is small doesn't mean they aren't capable of overpowering a larger person, especially if they have the advantage of surprise. And there is evidence that suggests Mr Fielding was caught by surprise by his killer."

"Oh, I know that, sergeant, but Walter is a germaphobe, he's not crazy about it but he does hate getting dirty, and he faints at the sight of blood; I mean he literally faints - I remember one occasion when he saw a cut, fainted and broke his nose, then fainted again when he woke up and saw the blood from his nose. Just the mention of blood makes him woozy and nauseous. It's why his documentaries are always so bland and boring, he's not willing to get down and deal with the nitty-gritty."

Mason nodded, he had once known someone who reacted like that to the sight of blood. "I'll still have to check him out. You never know what strong emotions can lead a person to do."

The interview continued for a while longer, but Olivia Branch wasn't able to offer anything else that might solve Terry Fielding's murder. She had worked with him on a number of occasions, and been happy to do so every time, regardless of whether he was directing, producing, or behind the camera. Finally, when he was sure that he was going to get no more from her, Mason allowed her to go, leaving him alone with Grey in the small conference room Hector Cole had allowed them to use for their interviews.

"Well," Mason turned to his partner, "either Terry Fielding was the nicest guy who ever lived, or he was very good at concealing what he was really like," he said. "I can't believe that every one of the people we interviewed really liked him and had nothing bad to say about him; it doesn't seem possible he could have been that nice, or that he managed to interact with so many people without upsetting or offending any of them - not even once apparently. That's not natural. Even a saint couldn't manage it."

"It's possible Mr Fielding was as nice and well-liked as everyone suggests," Grey said, a dubious note in his voice, "but I doubt it. Even Jesus had enemies. More likely they're either covering involvement in Terry Fielding's murder or, more likely, they just don't want to bad-mouth him now he's dead. I'm sure if we had asked about him last week we'd have got different answers."

The comment was cynical, but Mason recognised the truth of it. "That's certainly possible," he agreed as he put a line through Olivia Branch's name on the piece of paper Naismith had provided them with. "But if that's the case, they've all taken it to extremes. Normally we'd have had at least one person willing to tell us something negative, even if it's only that he liked to steal company stationery, or he was knocking off one of the interns. The trouble is, I can't see them all being involved in his murder, that's just too unlikely, he's only a small-time documentary maker, it's not like there would be much for them to gain.

"Whatever the truth, we're going to have to take a closer look at Terry Fielding's life, and the people in it."

# 26

"Let me see if I've got this straight." David Salter, the owner and managing director of Salter Gaming, leant forward, his elbows on his desk as he fixed DI Stone with a penetrating gaze. "You want me to let this gang," he made the description an epithet, "rob me just so you can arrest them."

Nathan shook his head. "That's not quite what I was saying, Mr Salter," he said, unsurprised by the reaction of the man across from him; he didn't imagine that any business owner would be willing to cooperate if the plan was actually as David Salter had described it. "We have no intention of allowing anyone to rob you."

"I can't tell you how relieved that makes me feel." The sarcasm magnified Salter's accent, a gift from his Jamaican parents. "Why don't you explain what you do intend, so I can be sure I'm understanding you."

"As I said, we have intelligence that the gang who robbed Jennings' Electrical is intending to rob you on Sunday night."

"Then why don't you arrest them? If you know who they are, why haven't you arrested them?"

"I wish it was as simple as that. We have the names of those involved in the Jennings' robbery, and the fact that your warehouse is their next target, but we have no evidence against them. Without evidence, arresting the gang will simply tip them off and make it harder for us to catch them. We have them under surveillance, and are investigating them as discreetly as we can.

"We hope to be in a position to make arrests before the weekend, before they attempt to break into your warehouse, but this kind of investigation takes time and patience." Nathan got the impression Salter, like many people, had to work at being patient. "If we aren't able to make arrests before the weekend, we'll have to set a trap for them at your warehouse. I realise that's something you'd rather avoid, so would we, but I hope you'll cooperate."

Salter's gaze intensified for a moment, seeming almost to burn into Nathan, then he turned his chair to stare out the window. He was silent for more than a minute as he watched the pedestrians walking along the pavement on the other side of the High Street.

Finally, he turned back to the room, and the detectives on the other side of his desk. "What exactly is it you intend doing, if I give you permission to make use of my warehouse?"

"We'd need to take a look at your warehouse, I believe it's on Stafford Trading Estate, before making any definite plans, but in essence we would want to let the gang break in and start loading their vehicle with your goods. That would make sure we have them bang to rights. We'll have surveillance equipment in place to record everything, and once they're inside we'll block the exits, so they can't get away." Nathan saw the concern in Salter's eyes and correctly interpreted the cause of it. "You'll be compensated for any damage or inconvenience."

Salter didn't appear entirely convinced, but his concern did lessen at that news.

"You could look at it this way, Mr Salter," Burke spoke up. "By helping us catch this gang, who will most likely strike again and again until they are caught, you'll make yourself look pretty good with other local business owners." He figured David Salter was either a Rotarian or aspired to be one, and would do anything to get in good with those who ran the local circle. "Think of the publicity you'll get when the report of the arrests appears in the paper."

"You think it'll make the papers?" Salter asked, not quite able to conceal how much that idea appealed to him.

Nathan nodded, pleased that his partner had thought of a way of gaining Salter's cooperation so quickly and so easily. "I'm confident that not only will the Herald do a story on the attempted robbery of your warehouse, and on your selfless, civic-minded willingness to assist in the capture of dangerous criminals, but I believe I can arrange for you to be personally interviewed by the Herald's top reporter." He knew he was laying it on a bit thick, but it seemed to be just what David Salter wanted to hear. "I shouldn't be surprised if the story ends up on the front page on Monday."

After several long moments, during which Salter's eyes gleamed greedily at the thought of the publicity for himself and for his company, he said, "When would you like to take a look at my warehouse?"

"As soon as possible, if that's alright with you," Nathan said, recognising the question for the agreement to cooperate that it was.

"How about now? There's no point putting things off."

"I hope you won't mind if I don't go with you, Mr Salter, only I have something else I must take care of. Rest assured, Sergeant Burke is excellent at planning tactical operations. He is more than capable of working out the best way to protect your warehouse, and will ensure we are able to contain and arrest the gang." Nathan saw that Salter was less than pleased to hear he wasn't going to be there, but he couldn't help that, with multiple investigations underway he couldn't be everywhere he wanted.

# 27

The reports of 'clear' came in quickly as the armed response team moved through the house, checking each room in turn. It was less than five minutes before the final radio call came in from Sergeant White.

"The house is clear, sir," White said. "There's no sign of the suspect. We do have a problem, though..." He hesitated for a few moments, and then continued, "We found a body in the living room."

Nathan was left speechless by that. He had expected a few things from the raid on the house belonging to the man whose blood had been found on Terry Fielding's shirt, but a body was not one of them. "Could it be the suspect?" he asked when he found his voice.'

"No, sir," White's voice was definite.

While the officers with him secured the area, Nathan entered the house. The moment he crossed the threshold his nose was assailed by the stench of corruption, the unmistakeable, nausea-inducing smell of something that had been dead for some time. It explained White's certainty that the body didn't belong to their suspect; for a smell to reach the level his nostrils were being assaulted with, the body must have been there for a significant amount of time.

The stench gave Nathan some warning of what he was going to find in the living room, but he was still unprepared for just how bad it was. The body was on the floor by the sofa, dressed in jeans and a dark green t-shirt, stained with blood and Nathan knew not what else; blond hair surrounded the man's head like a shrunken halo, and flies crawled over the exposed face and hands. He saw all of that in the momentary glimpse he had before he was forced to turn away and hurry back outside, where he sucked in several lungsful of fresh, uncontaminated air in an effort to subdue and control his rebellious stomach.

"He's a bit ripe, isn't he."

The comment made Nathan look around. Sergeant White was in the doorway, he looked a little green, but otherwise seemed in complete control of himself, or at least more in control than Nathan was. "How can you stand it without looking as if you want to throw up?" he wanted to know.

White shrugged. "I just don't think about it." He made it sound as if it was as simple as that to manage. "You forget, sir, I was in the army before this, so I've seen and smelled plenty of bad things. He's not a pretty sight, and he sure doesn't smell good, but he's not the worst thing I've ever had to deal with." He smiled as he glanced over his shoulder down the passage that led to the rear of the house. "If it makes you feel better, you're coping better than some of my boys. O'Brien and Ryan are out the back puking their guts up; for a moment I didn't think Ryan was going to make it outside before he lost it."

Somehow that did make him feel better, Nathan realised; White's team were trained, and meant to be tough, yet he had been able to control the urge to empty his stomach, while two of the team hadn't. The thought heartened him, and he took another deep lungful of the clean, fresh air that surrounded him before straightening up and re-entering the house.

The stench assailed his nostrils again the moment he was inside; along with the sight of the body, it mounted a determined attack on the control he had over his stomach. It required every ounce of self-control he possessed to subdue his rebellious stomach as he walked into the living room, and he almost lost the battle as he opened his mouth to speak into his radio and got his first taste of the air.

He swallowed reflexively, which only made more of the unpleasant air swirl around his taste-buds, making him gag. He forced his rising gorge back down and focused on what he had to do, request the doctor, and someone from the coroner's office - the doctor was a formality, no-one could look at the body and think he was still alive, but the coroner, or his assistant, were necessary to handle the body.

"Who do you think he is?" Mason asked from the doorway. He had been making sure the officers forming the perimeter were doing their job properly, but now that was done he could join Nathan.

Nathan was pleased to see that Mason was having just as much difficulty controlling his reaction to the body as he was, but he didn't let it show. Instead he returned to his examination of the body. He waved a hand to disturb the flies that were blocking his view, but it didn't make all that much difference; however long the body had lain there, it was enough time for the face to swell up and obscure the features.

After a period of silence Nathan stood and moved away from the body so he could look around the living room. He paused a couple of times to examine photographs that showed a blond man on holiday in various parts of the world, and each time he looked back at the body that was now being scrutinised by Mason. Finally, he gave up his wandering and rejoined his subordinate.

"I think," he said slowly, as if unsure of his words, "that this is the man we were looking for, our suspect, Will Henman."

Mason considered that without taking his eyes from the body at his feet. "There is a resemblance to the file photo you showed at the briefing," he said. "But if this is the guy whose blood was found on

Terry Fielding's shirt, we're up shit creek. I have no idea how long he's been dead, but it's clear it's been long enough that he couldn't have killed Fielding, which means the killer is still out there, and we don't have the first clue who he or she is."

Nathan had to agree with that. The blood sample the forensics department had taken two days to identify had been their only clue. Now they had a second murder, linked by blood to Terry Fielding's, and they had to find out what other links there might be between the two men. The only positive that Nathan could see in the situation was that a new crime scene raised the possibility of forensic evidence being discovered, evidence that might lead them to the killer. A slim hope, given the lack of evidence found at the scene of Terry Fielding's murder, but a hope nonetheless.

"Are forensics on the way?" he asked.

"Not unless you called them. You're in charge here, I wouldn't dream of making a call like that without your say so."

Nathan ignored the smile that played about Mason's lips, knowing he was trying to get a rise out of him. He had no intention of giving him the satisfaction. Instead he radioed the control room to ensure the forensics team was on its way, and that DCI Collins would be told about the discovery of the body; he knew virtually nothing about the situation at the house, but Nathan knew Collins wouldn't be happy if he wasn't made aware of the body as soon as possible.

DCI COLLINS TOOK HIS time reading the preliminary report from the raid on Will Henman's house, not that it was very long. When he was done he closed the folder and set it down on his desk. It was obvious from his body-language that he wasn't happy; the last thing he needed was another murder - four murders in the space of a week was unprecedented, and that, combined with the racial tensions caused by the Bhaskar murders and the irate phone call that had been directed to him just a short while ago, left him concerned not only for his future promotion prospects but for his current position.

"He's been dead for a week?" Collins asked finally.

Nathan shrugged uncertainly. "Doc Jones made a brief examination of the body, from which he concluded he's been dead for a week, but we won't get anything close to a definite time of death until the P.M.'s been done. Even then it's unlikely we'll get the kind of accuracy we'd like. We'll know how many days ago he died, but we probably won't have an hour of death, which'll make it tough when it comes to nailing down any suspects."

His experience with murders was limited, but better than Nathan's, so Collins was not surprised by the possibility that the time of death would be more of a time-frame. "It's definitely murder, though?"

"Definitely murder. The initial examination indicates he was stabbed five times, that, of course, will be confirmed by the P.M., which might also give us some idea of the type of weapon used. I don't imagine we're going to learn anything we didn't already know from Terry Fielding's P.M., though, since at first glance it seems clear the same knife was used in both murders."

"That would explain how this guy's blood ended up at Fielding's murder scene," Collins remarked. "Motive?"

Nathan could only shrug unhappily. "No idea at the moment. We haven't found a motive for Fielding's murder yet, and beyond the fact that they were both killed by the same guy, as the blood makes clear, we don't have any idea what might link them. I think when we figure out what the motive for one of the murders is, we'll have the answer to both."

Collins looked dubious at that, and Nathan was tempted to tell him that he believed he knew Will Henman from somewhere -

he had got the same sense of recognition from the photographs of the suspect as he had when he attended the scene of the Bhaskar murders and met Vikram Bhaskar - and that he suspected there was a connection between all four of the recent murders. He didn't think Collins wanted to hear that until he had proof to back up his suspicions, however.

"Are you sure there's a connection?" Collins wanted to know. "Isn't it possible that Fielding and Henman have no links, and were killed during robberies? Wasn't some jewellery and a few other things stolen from the Fielding place?"

"Yes. Paulina reported the theft yesterday evening as soon as she discovered it, but we don't yet have details of what was stolen; she promised to get the details to us today, including copies of the photographs of the jewellery she took for the insurance company, but so far I've heard nothing."

"How about the Henman place, was anything taken from there?"

"That's impossible to say at the moment," Nathan said. "We have no-one we can ask, and I wasn't there long enough to see if anything obvious is missing." He had been called away from the house the moment Collins heard the news that a body had been found. "I'm not even sure there's going to be anyone we can ask; if the house has been robbed then it stands to reason that the body belongs to the owner, which is Will Henman, and given the fact that it wasn't found for a week or so, I don't think we're going to come up with any friends or family in a position to tell us if anything is missing.

"The alternative possibility is that the body isn't that of Will Henman, if that is the case then nothing is going to be missing from the house, not stolen anyway."

"If it isn't Will Henman, who the hell is it?" Collins asked sharply. "And what the hell is he doing at the house? For that matter, where the hell is Will Henman?"

Nathan smiled at the questions, though there was no humour in the upward lift of the corners of his mouth. "Truthfully, I think the body is that of Will Henman, the basic characteristics match photos from the house, but it's going to take a DNA test to be certain given the state of the body and how long it's been lying there. Unfortunately, it doesn't help us any to prove it's Will Henman because that leaves us with the question of who killed him."

Collins sighed unhappily; whatever the identity of the body, the situation was complicated, more complicated than he liked, and he decided to change the subject to his other problem. It wasn't as serious as what they had been discussing, but it was connected.

"Have you seen the Herald this afternoon?"

Nathan hadn't, there had been no time for him to go to the shop and buy the latest edition of the paper, and the only copy he had seen around the station was from that morning, nonetheless he could take a guess at why his superior had asked the question. "You're on about the article about Paulina Fielding's affair with Kevin Michaels, aren't you."

Collins nodded, his jaw tensed as he held back the urge to snap at Nathan for not warning him about the story when he clearly knew it was going to be in the paper. "I had Mr Michaels on the phone a short while ago, as you can imagine, he was very unhappy about the article."

"I'm not surprised. He told me he wanted to keep his affair with Paulina quiet until after his divorce was final; I imagine he didn't want his wife to find out and screw him." The barrister's annoyance over the story was understandable, what Nathan didn't understand was where he had chosen to vent that annoyance. "Why did he call you? Surely it's Kelly over at the Herald he should be complaining to. Not that I think it's likely to do him much good; with the murder of Terry Fielding, his affair with Paulina Fielding is a matter of public interest, though I don't suppose Kelly thought of that when he ran the story, he was just interested in selling papers."

"Mr Michaels believes we are responsible for the story appearing in the Herald. Apparently no-one knew about the affair with Paulina Fielding until he spoke to you and Burke; since that's the case, he feels that the only way anyone at the Herald could have found out about it is if they were told by someone here. The obvious suspects, of course, being yourself and Stephen." He held up a hand to forestall Nathan's denial. "I don't believe for one moment that either of you would have told anyone at the paper, not even Orchard, about the affair; you're both too aware of the consequences, and too sensible to risk them. The same, however, cannot be said for many of the other officers around here.

"I have assured Mr Michaels that no-one working here would have given the story to the paper, but he's made it clear that if he discovers someone from this station is responsible, he'll be suing."

Nathan didn't doubt that if Kevin Michaels found enough evidence to sue, Collins would make sure the person responsible was punished severely, perhaps even with the loss of their job. He couldn't bring himself to worry about that, however; he had more important things to be concerned about, like solving four murders.

# 28

Kurt couldn't believe it. He hadn't wanted to believe it when he heard about it in the shop, and he still didn't believe it now he saw it. How had the police found out about Will? He had left nothing at his other crimes scenes that could connect them to this place, had he?

As he leant casually against a wall down the road, Kurt thought back over his murders. No, he could think of nothing he had done, or not done, that would have led the police from either the Bhaskar murders or his murder of Terry Fielding to Will Henman. It must have been nothing more than bad luck that led the police there.

He didn't feel any better after coming to that conclusion; if bad luck could have resulted in the discovery of his former partner's body, then it might also enable the police to connect all the murders he had committed, not only to one another but also to him.

From his vantage point, Kurt could see the two uniformed officers who guarded the front door and, through the living room window - he had pulled the curtains after killing Will, but now they stood open - the white-suited forensics team. He couldn't tell what they were doing, which concerned him since he no longer felt as confident that there was no evidence to be found, but the occasional flashes of light told him that someone was taking photographs, recording the scene for later analysis.

He could also make out the silhouette of someone moving around in the bedroom at the front of the house. Why anyone should be looking around in there, he didn't know; if there was any evidence to be found at the house, and he fervently hoped there wasn't, it certainly wouldn't be found there. The only rooms in the house he had spent any time were the one that contained the body of his ex-partner-in-crime and the kitchen.

After watching the house for a little longer, Kurt pushed away from the wall and departed. There was no point in him hanging around; the longer he stayed there, the greater the chance of him being spotted and someone becoming suspicious of him.

When he reached his car, which he had parked a street away to keep it from being spotted, he started the engine. Instead of driving away, though, he sat there and thought about the problem presented by the discovery of Will's body. He might not like to admit it, but he couldn't deny that the police were capable of connecting the murders he had committed and linking them to him, given enough time, and they were likely to do so quickly now that they had the body of his former partner.

What he needed, he decided, was something that would distract them from their investigations. Distract them for long enough to let him complete what he was in town to do and then escape out of the country. It would have to be something big, he realised, to draw their attention away from four murders.

It didn't take him long to come up with something that would not only distract the police, but also further his own plans. It was something he had already been planning, so he wouldn't have to waste much time on research and groundwork, he just needed to modify things slightly to make it a little more spectacular.

# 29

"You think they're all connected?" Burke asked in a quiet voice. He was at the dining table in the living room of Nathan's house, drinking coffee that disagreed with his taste-buds while Melissa watched the TV in the living room.

Nathan nodded slowly. "I do."

"Why? What's the connection?"

A half-smile played about Nathan's lips as he shrugged. "I wish I knew. Right now I don't have the first clue what the connection is; I'm certain there is one, however. I'm positive I know both Vikram Bhaskar and Will Henman, and from the same place, but how and why, I don't know. It's locked away in here somewhere," he tapped the side of his head, "but I'll be damned if it wants to come out into the open."

Burke studied his partner's face for several long moments. "So the murders are all connected," he said, accepting his partner's theory. "Four bodies, one killer, and no motive at present; why haven't you told Collins? He's still got us looking at them as separate cases; the Bhaskars on one side and Terry Fielding and Will Henman - assuming that's who was found in his house - on the other, that's splitting our resources, and diminishing the effectiveness of both investigations."

"I know," Nathan said with a look over at his wife to be certain she was still focused on the television; she appeared to be, but he was sure she had at least half an ear on his quiet conversation with Burke. "But Collins has forgotten what it's like to listen to his instincts. Unless I can give him proof, he's not going to accept that the two cases are connected. And after the phone call he got from Kevin Michaels this afternoon, the last thing he wants to hear is that we might be dealing with a serial killer."

"I think technically this guy would be considered a spree killer, or maybe multiple-murderer, rather than a serial killer."

Nathan rewarded his partner's comment with a sour look. "I don't think it really matters what the correct description is for this guy, Collins isn't going to want to hear it until we've got proof, and right now we don't."

"I take it you want to keep this as quiet as possible for the time being."

Nathan nodded. "If we tell anyone at the station, it'll just be a matter of time before it reaches the Herald, and then we'll have a panic. That's the last thing we need with Kelly doing everything he can to stir up racial tensions."

"Not only that, we'll have Collins all over us. Heads will roll, most likely ours." Burke knew as well as Nathan that if the DCI lost his chance to secure the promotion his wife coveted he would take it out on anyone and everyone he could, regardless of whether they were involved or not. "So how do you want to go about proving the murders are all connected and we're looking for one suspect not two?"

It was almost a minute before Nathan answered that question for he wasn't certain himself. "We already have Reid, Thompson and Keats looking into the Bhaskar and Terry Fielding cases; I think we should have them look into Will Henman as well. He was identified through the criminal database, so he must have been arrested for something. It's possible that whatever he was arrested for is the link we're currently missing; depending on when it happened, and if it went to trial, Paulina could have been either the prosecutor or his defence barrister."

"And the Bhaskars the victims or witnesses?" Burke asked, following his superior's line of thought. "It doesn't fit, though; if the connection is something Henman did, why is he one of the dead? I could understand if he was out for revenge and killing those who put him away; that theory goes straight out the window if he's one of the victims though and it leaves the question, if he and whatever crime he committed is the reason for the murders, who's killing everyone and why?" He immediately answered his own question with a theory. "Perhaps Henman had a partner, someone who, so far, has managed not to be connected with the crime.

"Why would he wait until now, though?" Nathan asked as he tried to puzzle his way through the problem. "If I don't remember him, or whatever crime he committed, and you don't either, then it must have happened years ago. It doesn't make sense that he would suddenly decide to do something about the situation." Despite what he said, he thought Burke might be onto something; the mention of a partner rang a barely audible bell in his mind.

"Perhaps something's happened recently that has made Henman's partner afraid his participation is about to be revealed, and he's taking steps to prevent it. Or he got caught, went to jail, and is now out and looking for revenge."

That possibility made another synapse in Nathan's brain twitch.

"There is another possibility..." Burke said.

"What's that?"

"That the body at Will Henman's house isn't Henman, just someone who has the same general appearance; Henman could be the murderer we're looking for, and he's using the body at his house to throw us off the scent."

Nathan considered that notion briefly before dismissing it with a shake of his head. "No, I don't think that works. We only found the body at Henman's because of the blood on Fielding's shirt, and we know the blood is Henman's. If the body is supposed to be a decoy, I don't think Henman would have left the discovery to chance."

"Maybe it wasn't left to chance," Burke remarked. "It might be that Henman intended us to find the body, eventually, and to assume that it's him; the longer it took us to find it, the harder it would be to identify, and the better his chances of getting away."

Nathan had to admit that that made a horrible kind of sense, though he sincerely hoped his partner was wrong. The notion that they were dealing with someone willing to kill a person merely to throw them off the scent did not sit well with him; it begged the question, how much further would the killer be prepared to go to accomplish his goal and get away with it?

# 30

Nathan kept his eyes shut as he groped on his bedside cabinet for his phone. When he found it, he opened his eyes briefly so he could see to accept the call that had woken him; the phone vibrated one final time in his hand and then it was still.

"Stone," he grunted. He didn't know what the time was, and he wasn't sure he wanted to know; it was the middle of the night, that was enough for him. He hoped the reason for the call was a good one, and his sleep hadn't been disturbed for something trivial.

"Detective Inspector Stone?" The question was asked in a low, rough voice.

Nathan's eyes snapped open and he sat up quickly. There were not many reasons for someone to call him in the middle of the night, and fewer still for that person to try and hide his identity, and all of them made it a good idea for him to pay attention to the call.

"That's me," he said, pushing himself up to one elbow. He kept his voice as low as that of his caller, though in his case it was because he didn't want to wake his wife. "Who is this, and how can I help you?"

The voice ignored the questions and instead asked one of its own. "You the cop looking for the guy killed them two Muslims? The ones got shot on Sunday."

Nathan's first instinct was to correct his caller and tell him that the Bhaskars were Hindus, not Muslims, but he quickly stopped himself; it was more important that he find out what his mystery caller knew about the murders than it was to correct his racial and religious misconceptions.

"I am, do you know something about the murders?"

"I know where you can find the guy what did 'em."

If he hadn't been awake before, Nathan certainly was now. He slid out from beneath the covers and crossed barefoot to the door, so he could continue the call in the bathroom where, he hoped, his voice wouldn't disturb his wife. "How do you know where he can be found?" he asked.

"None o' your business, pig!" the voice snapped. "I know, that's all you need to care about, d'you want to know what I know or not?"

It had been a long time since anyone called him a 'pig', but Nathan realised the epithet made it likely his caller was a criminal of some sort, which explained why he hadn't revealed his name or how he knew the killer's location - talking to the police frequently caused trouble for criminals with their fellow lawbreakers. With that in mind, Nathan ignored the insult, and the anger with which it was uttered, and focused instead on the more important matter, that of finding out what his caller knew.

"Yes. Where can I find him?"

"He's hiding out in the woods near the old ruins up by the Brant; you know the place?"

Nathan nodded automatically as he answered, and immediately felt foolish for doing so. "I know the place." He couldn't imagine why the killer would have chosen to hide there, it was a favoured picnic and dog-walking spot and come dawn he ran the risk of being discovered by a dog let off the leash for a good run.

Once he had everything his informant was willing to tell him, which was virtually nothing, and the call had been ended - abruptly - Nathan returned to the bedroom. Guided by the sliver of light that shone through the crack where he had left the door ajar, he crossed the room to his wife's side of the bed. He bent to gently shake her shoulder, and then hurriedly leant back out of the way as one of her hands came up to swat him - he had received more than a few bruises from his wife's flailing hands where she reacted to being woken unexpectedly over the years.

"Honey, wake up." He reached out cautiously to shake her shoulder for a second time.

"Huh. What? Nate?" Melissa's voice was filled with sleep as she reached for her glasses, so she could see her husband better. "What time is it?"

"A little after two."

"What's up?" Melissa sat up quickly. She knew Nathan wouldn't have woken her in the middle of the night without a good reason, and her first thought was that something was wrong with one of the kids. Nathan's voice lacked the urgency it would have carried if there had been a problem with either Robert or Isobel though.

"I've got to go to work."

"Is it important?"

Nathan nodded. "Very. I've just been given a lead on where to find the guy I've been looking for."

"The one you were talking to Stephen about earlier? The one who's been on the news?"

From the way his wife's face went pale in the dim light, Nathan assumed she had heard enough of what he and his partner had been talking about to worry. It was understandable, he was a little concerned himself, more than a little if he was honest.

"That's the one," he said, keeping how he felt out of his voice to stop his wife worrying any more than she already was.

"You will be careful, won't you. Don't go being brave or stupid."

"I'll be alright," Nathan said reassuring. "I'll have the armed response team there, Collins doesn't want us taking any chances with the arrest, besides, you know me, I'm never brave if I can help it."

"But you can be stupid."

That made Nathan smile. "Don't worry, I'll get Stephen up in a minute, he'll make sure I don't do anything stupid. You go back to sleep, honey, with a bit of luck I'll be home before you get up. Love you." He kissed her quickly, and then straightened up, so he could get dressed and make the necessary phone calls to get everyone moving, before their unnamed suspect left his hiding place and disappeared again."

KURT SMILED AS HE WATCHED the car drive down the road and then disappear around the corner. The phone call had worked, just as he had been sure it would; it made him glad he had gone to the effort of finding DI Stone's mobile number - it hadn't actually required much effort on his part, he had simply paid someone he met in prison, someone who knew a lot more about computers than he did.

He waited until Stone's car was out of sight, and then he waited for another five minutes. When he was confident Stone wasn't going to be coming back in the immediate future, he got to his feet and left the garden where he had been hiding. It took him less than a minute to reach Stone's house, and once there he set about the next step in his plan for revenge on those responsible for the loss of his family, and for the ten years he had spent in jail.

First of all he examined the lock on the front door; he could pick it, he decided, but not quickly, and not easily, and he would be visible to anyone who happened to look out of their house while he worked on it - the odds of that happening were slim, but it was still possible, and he had no desire to take such a risk. With that danger in mind, he made his way round the side of the house. A padlocked gate barred his way to the rear of the property, but not for long.

The door at the rear of the house was a little tougher to get open than the front door would have been, but at least he could work on it without being in danger of being witnessed.

After nearly two minutes of quiet swearing he conquered the lock and was able to enter the house. He carried his supplies into the kitchen, and left them there while he made a quick tour of the ground floor. It took him almost no time; apart from the kitchen there was only the living room and a cupboard under the stairs.

Unscrewing the cap from the first of his petrol cans, he began pouring the contents over the floor and carpet as he backed out of the kitchen and made his way along the passage. There was enough petrol in the can for him to douse the passage and a decent portion of the living room; the fumes made his nose twitch and his eyes water, but he ignored the discomfort as he worked.

When the can was empty he put it aside and opened the second. He used the contents of that can to soak the carpet on the stairs - with each step he took up to the first floor he expected to hear a squeak from a floorboard that wasn't properly nailed down. He was both surprised and relieved when he reached the top of the stairs without being betrayed by the house he intended destroying.

He puddled the last of the petrol from the can at the head of the stairs, in front of the two doors he assumed opened onto bedrooms; that done, he put the can down and began to remove the jars from the bag on his shoulder.

A clinking sound, made when two of the jars knocked together, made him freeze and strain his ears for any indication he had been heard. He was ready to leave at the first sign that someone was coming to investigate the noise he had made, he wasn't finished with his preparations, but he was far enough along that it would be more of an annoyance than a disaster if he was detected.

When a minute passed without the sounds of someone stirring or of approaching footsteps, Kurt relaxed a little. He returned to the business of positioning the jars and bottles of petrol he had filled earlier along the upstairs passage; each item was placed on its side with the makeshift fuse he had prepared as close to the carpet as he could get it.

He was not, by nature, an arsonist, he had never before done what he was setting up then, but he was confident that things would work out the way he wanted them to. He supposed it was easier for him than it would have been for another arsonist, because he didn't care about hiding the fact that he was committing arson.

Once he had the last of the jars in place, as close to the door of the front bedroom as he dared get, he retreated back the way he had come. He paused when he was at the head of the stairs, halted by a sudden thought. His eyes lifted to the ceiling above him, searching the darkness until he found what he was looking for; the smoke-alarm was positioned almost directly above him, fortunately within reach when he stood on tiptoes and stretched up. He took it down quickly, so he could remove the battery, the last thing he wanted was to have the family woken by the alarm before the fire could take hold, that would give them a chance to escape, and he didn't want that.

Kurt kept an eye out for any other smoke-alarms as he made his way out of the house; he found one at the foot of the stairs, and another in the kitchen, and dealt with them. The fumes from the petrol-filled house burned the back of his throat and nostrils, and he was glad when he made it outside and could once again breathe fresh air, though he didn't allow himself too much time to stand around and enjoy it.

He took a lighter from his pocket as he closed the front door. It was only a cheap and disposable Bic, but it was reliable, and that was all that mattered. He produced a flame at the first try, and used it to light a length of string left over from what he had used to create his fuses.

It was the one piece of his plan he hadn't given much thought to, figuring it was the easiest part, and where he was least likely to have a problem, unfortunately he was wrong. After he pushed the string through the letterbox it burned out before it could ignite the fumes from the petrol-soaked carpet.

He tried again with a second piece of string and got the same result. Frustrated, he looked around for something he could use that would get him the result he wasn't getting from the string. He spotted the recycling box at the end of the path and moved to check it; as he had anticipated, the box had been filled in readiness to be put out for collection first thing. He took a newspaper from the top of the pile and returned to the front door, where he rolled the newspaper up, tight enough to go through the letterbox, and set light to it. He waited until the flames were evenly spread along the paper, and he was confident it wasn't going to go out, then he shoved it through the door and stepped back.

A muted 'whoosh' signalled that the petrol fumes had been ignited and flames were racing through the house.

He turned away and strode quickly down the path, so he could head for the corner. The part of him that still suffered the loss of his children wanted to stay and watch as the house burned, to listen to the screams of pain and cries for help. He knew that wasn't a good idea, though. If he wanted to remain free he had to leave straight away, before the fire he had just started woke the neighbours and drew their attention to the street.

A COMBINATION OF HEAT, smoke and noise woke Melissa Stone and she sat up abruptly, coughing and choking as the smoke that filled the room also filled her nose and mouth, flavouring every breath she tried to take.

Panic swept through her, making her heart race, as she realised the house was on fire. It magnified when she realised the smoke alarm she could hear was the one in her daughter's bedroom. Throwing back the covers she hurried to the door, where she barely noticed the heat as she grabbed the handle and yanked the door open.

A cloud of smoke, thicker and darker than that which had already filled the room, rushed in to engulf her. She resisted the urge to fall to her knees and cough her lungs up, instead she groped her way through the doorway and out into the passage, where an orange glow told her the stairs were on fire, and that the flames, which were spreading along the passage towards her were fiercest in the area immediately in front of the doors of her children's bedrooms.

Without a thought for the danger to herself, Melissa leapt through the orange and red flames that reached up through the smoke, groping for her. She hit her daughter's bedroom door with a heavy thud that would have made her gasp in pain, if she wasn't already crying out from where the flames were attacking her legs. She fought the urge to turn and run, and instead took hold of the door handle, ignoring the pain as it burned into her, so she could open the door.

The skin beneath her burning pyjamas felt as though it was melting as she made her stiff-legged way across the bedroom to the barely visible cot. She reached down for her daughter when she got there, but it wasn't until she picked Isobel up and felt how still and silent she was that she realised something was wrong. Isobel should have been making some kind of noise, coughing and spluttering, or otherwise fighting for air through the smoke.

There wasn't time for her to wonder why her baby was so still and quiet, though, she still had to rescue her son, who was worryingly quiet in the room opposite.

Without thinking about the fact that she was moving towards danger, she made for the doorway as rapidly as her burned and blistered legs could manage. She tried to jump the flames that were advancing into the room when she reached the doorway, but that did no good because the flames were everywhere. She stumbled and fell when she landed, twisting so she would fall on her side and not on Isobel.

The flames caught at her hair and her pyjamas and she beat at them as she went up like a Roman candle. With the flames attacking every inch of her they could reach, she struggled to her feet while protecting her daughter. Every nerve screamed with pain as her skin blistered and melted until her brain overloaded and she could no longer tell where the pain was coming from.

# 31

Its siren blaring loud enough to wake those neighbours who weren't already aware of what was going on, and its lights illuminating its surroundings in sudden flashes of blue, the fire engine raced along the street. It came to a hurried stop outside the blazing house, which had been visible from a distance away, and the men and women who made up its crew disembarked with practised haste.

The watch manager moved away from the truck to speak to the crowd of neighbours who had gathered a short distance away - he needed to know who, if anyone, was inside so he could give his officers the appropriate orders; he also needed to make sure the occupants of the neighbouring houses were safe. While he did that, his crew setup the hoses and started the process of tackling the blaze.

In less than thirty seconds, Calvin Hart had determined that none of the family had yet made it out of the house as far as the neighbours were aware, though the husband's car was missing from the drive. The neighbour to the right was positive the car had been there at midnight when he went to bed, but hadn't heard it leave.

The apparently absent car gave Hart some hope that the family was safe, but he knew he couldn't operate on that basis, he had to assume that the family was still inside and in need of rescuing.

"We need to get in there," he told his second-in-command after he finished with the neighbours. "Could be the family is still inside: husband, wife, and two kids, boy of seven and a girl of two."

"Yes, sir." Jackson turned to his officers. "Turner, Williams, family to rescue," he called out. "Two adults, two kids."

"Yes, sir," both officers responded in unison. They hurriedly grabbed breathing equipment from the truck and made for the front door, so they could break it down and enter the property.

Three quick, powerful blows with an axe and the door flew open; smoke billowed out and the sudden influx of oxygen fed the flames. The two firemen moved aside quickly as the hose was redirected to pour water through the doorway and douse the flames in the passage; after about a quarter of a minute the hose was returned to the upstairs of the house.

The ambulance that responded to the emergency call arrived as Turner and Williams disappeared into the house to begin their search for the family. The paramedics were as well trained as the fire-fighters, and a single glance at the burning house was enough to tell them what to expect, it also told them what the chances were of there being survivors, but neither man allowed that to interfere with their preparations.

The worst fears of everyone - fire-fighters, paramedics, and neighbours alike - were realised after almost five minutes when Turner and Williams reappeared from the smoke, each of them carrying a small, unmoving, and pathetic-looking figure. They moved hurriedly over to the ambulance, where they surrendered their burdens to the paramedics; both men were sure there was nothing that could be done for the children, but the effort had to be made, in case some miracle could be achieved.

Neither Turner nor Williams waited to see if any miracles were forthcoming, they had another person to bring out, and another person to look for.

# 32

Everyone was tired, as was to be expected of people who had been woken in the middle of the night, and not confident of success, given the circumstances. They were determined to do their job, and do it to the best of their abilities, though.

A pair of patrol cars and the armed response team's van were positioned so they blocked the dirt road that ran through the woods alongside the Brant. If their target was where the mystery caller had told Nathan he was, they didn't want him able to escape, not by car, escape on foot was something they couldn't prevent; the size of the woods that lay on either side of the river, and encircled the Roman ruins by the picnic area, made it impossible for anything short of a full-blown army with overhead surveillance to secure the area completely.

They did have overhead surveillance, but one helicopter, even one with the ability to search the area with infra-red, couldn't do a thorough job of scanning the woods, at least not in a timely fashion.

"How do you want to handle this?" Sergeant White asked as his team made a final check of their equipment.

Nathan considered that for several long seconds. He could understand why White was asking him, searching a wooded area for a suspect who was almost certainly armed was a little different from the team's normal field of operations, but that didn't make him feel any better about the question.

"I think the best course of action is for you and your team to clear the ruins first," he said. "The chopper has done an infra-red scan and found no sign of him, and there's no sign of a vehicle in the area either, but you guys might find something the chopper missed. While you're doing that, the chopper will sweep the woods; if they find anything they'll guide you in to check things on the ground."

White nodded. "And if we find nothing in the ruins and the chopper comes up empty?"

"You'll need to make a physical search of the woods." Under other circumstances Nathan would have been amused by the lack of enthusiasm White showed for that idea.

"You realise there's very little chance of us finding anything," White said. "Even if your source is right and the killer is here somewhere, the chances of us finding him are somewhere between slim and none; a physical search of this area will take days, and unless the chopper spots him on infra-red, or he turns out to be an idiot - unlikely given the way things have gone so far - it'll be all too easy for him to slip away and avoid being found."

Nathan nodded. "Believe me, I'm aware of that. This search is almost certainly a waste of time, but we can't ignore the possibility that the guy who called me is right, and our suspect is hiding out in this area."

"Look at it this way, Vernon," Burke spoke up as he did up the bulletproof vest he had taken from the van, "the problems you've mentioned make this quite a good hiding place for him, and if we're lucky he's not only here, but so confident we won't find him that he's asleep, and your team can catch him unaware."

NATHAN STOOD AT THE corner of the Roman fort closest to the trees, waiting for the news he knew was going to come soon - the search had to be abandoned; the chopper had found no sign of anyone in the woods, and it simply wasn't practical for Vernon White and his team to continue - and thinking about the last time he had been there, when he and his family celebrated his son's seventh birthday with a picnic.

He was lost in his thoughts, and only peripherally aware of his surroundings, when his phone rang, breaking the peace and quiet of the night. The noise was so unexpected that it was a few moments before either he or Burke realised where the music was coming from. The moment they did, Nathan's hand dived into his pocket for his phone, while Burke looked round at his partner; both of them wondered who the call was from, wondered if it could be the man who had sent them out to that isolated spot, and what the reason for the call was.

"Stone," he answered the call after a glance at the screen revealed it came from the station.

Burke watched as Nathan's face became steadily greyer in the pale moonlight. He couldn't imagine what might have caused such an abrupt change in his partner's demeanour, but he realised it must be something bad for him to take on the deathly pallor he had.

Suddenly the phone slipped from Nathan's fingers as he turned and ran from the ruins. His friend's reaction to the phone call caught Burke by surprise, he couldn't imagine who could have called, or what they could have said, that might have caused Nathan to react in such a way. He stooped to snatch up the dropped phone, which he saw now had a scratch across the screen, and hurried after his friend.

He caught up to Nathan at the path that led through the woods to where the vehicles were parked. "What's going on?" he asked, pulling his friend to a halt. "Nathan, what's going on?" he repeated his question when Nathan showed no sign of having heard him.

It was a few moments before Nathan recovered the ability to speak. "There's been a...a fire at...at my place," he said, every word coming out haltingly, as though it required an effort.

The news appalled Burke and made his blood run cold as he thought of Melissa Stone and the kids. Looking at his partner he knew instinctively what he had to do, it was so obvious he didn't need to think about it; lifting his radio to his lips, he contacted White, who was somewhere in the middle in the woods, and explained the situation, as briefly as he could, while he followed Nathan, who had resumed his hurried pace along the path.

When they reached the vehicles, he guided Nathan to the passenger seat, he didn't think it a good idea for his friend to be in control of a vehicle just then, and slid behind the wheel. With the portable siren plugged into the lighter socket, magnetically secured to the roof, and providing a bright blue warning to anyone who might be on the streets to get out of the way, Burke raced from the woods at well above the speed limit. The late hour was to the benefit of the two worried detectives since traffic on the roads was virtually non-existent, which meant Burke's less than perfect control of his friend's car didn't endanger anyone.

The smoke that reached for the heavens was visible from streets away. Burke's hands tightened on the steering wheel when he saw it, but his partner seemed oblivious to it. As far as Burke could tell, Nathan was unaware of anything but the dashboard in front of him, he had slipped into an almost catatonic state the moment he was guided into the passenger seat; it wasn't until they reached Carnarvon Street, where Nathan lived, and they had parked, that Nathan again showed signs of life.

Burke threw open the driver's door and got out quickly, he was beaten by his partner, though. Nathan managed to make it halfway to his house in the time it took Burke to get to his feet.

Nathan made it as far as his drive before anyone but Burke was aware he was there; the attention of everyone on the street was focused on the burning house, where the fire-fighters fought to extinguish the last of the flames. It was Hart who saw him, saw him and reacted quickly to intercept him before he could run into the house, where he would be in danger from the smoke that filled every room and billowed out of the windows, from the flames that stubbornly refused to die, and from the powerful jet of water being used to douse them.

So intent was Nathan on reaching his house and his family, whom he was sure were still inside, that he was caught by surprise when the fire-fighter grabbed him and spun him away from his objective. Automatically he fought against the restraining grasp.

"Let me go!" he screamed. "Let me go! I have to get in there. I have to save my family." A fresh burst of adrenaline gave him the strength to wrench himself free and shove aside the man holding him, so he could start towards the house again.

The delay caused by the fire-fighter gave Burke the chance to catch up, and he almost rugby-tackled his partner in his desperation to prevent him risking his life. What he hadn't anticipated was just how frantic Nathan was; he was caught by surprise when an elbow smashed into his face, stunning him. It was all he could do to maintain the grip he had on his partner.

"Calm down, Nate," Burke said as he struggled to restrain his friend, a job that became easier when the fire-fighter Nathan had broken free of caught hold of him as well. "Nate, you have to calm down." He kept his voice as moderate as he could in the hope that his calmness would get through to his partner.

"Get off me." Nathan wriggled, writhed, twisted, and wrenched at the hands that held him. "Get the hell off me. I have to get in there. I have to get to my family."

"Your family isn't in there," Hart told the man on the ground. "They were brought out a while ago."

The words didn't immediately penetrate Nathan's frantic efforts to escape those subduing him; even when they did, it took him a while to comprehend their meaning and their import. Once comprehension dawned on him he stopped fighting and sagged in relief, going as limp as a rag doll.

"They're safe?" he asked in a weak voice as the adrenaline that had flooded his system drained away, leaving him exhausted, and with barely enough energy to speak. "You got them out alright? Where are they?" He twisted his head this way and that, searching for his family.

"They've been taken to hospital. The ambulance left about a quarter of an hour ago."

Cautiously, Burke released his friend and helped him to his feet. Despite the reassurance of the fire-fighter's words, he couldn't help feeling that there was something not said, something important, something that might just send Nathan over the edge. He studied the face of the fire-fighter briefly, the expression on it was serious, even grave, and that told him just how bad what hadn't been said was. Instinctively he knew that his friend was going to need him at the hospital for support, first, though, he wanted more information.

"Go back to the car, Nate," he said in a gentle voice. Pointing his friend in the right direction he gave him a gentle shove to get him started. "I'll be there in a minute to drive you to the hospital." He waited until his partner was out of earshot to turn his attention back to the watch manager. "Okay, what's the situation?" he asked in a tone he normally reserved for interrogating suspects.

"I can't say, sir," came the answer. "All I can tell you is that this is a serious fire, which we have almost succeeded in putting out. It will be up to the fire investigator to determine the cause of it; he will make his report when he's finished his investigation."

Burke responded to that by taking out his warrant card, certain it would get him the answers he was after. If he was going to help his friend through things, he needed to know just how bad they were. "Do you think you can tell me now?" he asked in a voice that suggested, despite their working in different branches of the emergency services, it would be a bad idea for him not to get an answer. In an effort to further influence him, Burke said, "He's a DI, this could be connected to a case we're working on. "He didn't really think that was true, though the moment he said it he realised it might be; it was too much of a coincidence that Nathan received a phone call that got him out of the house not long before a fire gutted it.

Hart accepted the identity of the man before him with a nod after giving the warrant card the briefest of looks. "Hart, Watch Manager. It's bad," he said with a grim look. "Very bad. We got the family out, as I said, the wife and both kids, but the kids weren't breathing."

Burke went even paler than he already was at that news, which was worse than he had feared.

"And the wife has very serious burns over a large proportion of her body. The paramedics did everything they could here, and then took them all to the hospital. If they were successful in reviving the kids, I haven't heard anything, but I don't suppose I would."

"There's more, isn't there," Burke said, correctly reading the look in the eyes that had a hard time meeting his. "What is it?"

"The fire was arson."

"Are you sure?" Burke asked. While he knew, intellectually, that Nathan's position put him at risk of retribution from criminals he had either put behind bars or investigated unsuccessfully, he had a hard time imagining anyone actually wanting to hurt his friend. Nathan had always been a very reasonable, honest, and decent person, who had never once abused the power his position gave him.

"The investigator is the one who will have to make the final determination on that, but my officers reported smelling petrol throughout the house and finding several petrol cans. The conclusion seems pretty obvious, but it won't be made official until the investigator finishes his report," Hart said. He liked what he knew of the cause of the fire no more than did the sergeant before him.

"Then it will be up to us to catch the guy who did this." Burke felt a hot flush of anger sweep through him, burning away the coldness that had filled him since the phone call telling Nathan of the fire; under normal circumstances he was neither a violent nor a vindictive person, but just then he thought how nice it would be to have a bit of time alone with the man who thought it okay to set fire to a house with a woman and children in it. The notion was both unprofessional and a dangerous way of thinking, and he quickly forced it down, locking it away in the deepest recesses of his mind, where he hoped it would remain.

Once he had his feelings under control, Burke thanked Hart and then left him to his work, so he could take his friend to the hospital.

BURKE BROKE ALL RECORDS, not to mention a significant number of traffic laws, on his way to the hospital. The result of which was that he made it there in barely ten minutes. He parked in the first vacant spot he found, and then chased after his partner as Nathan raced across the car park to the accident and emergency department's entrance, heedless of the few vehicles that were moving around and how close he came to being knocked down.

Nathan was already at the counter by the time Burke caught up to him, loudly and angrily demanding to see his family, while the other occupants of the waiting room looked on in astonishment. The nurse was trying to handle the situation as calmly and as properly as her training had taught her to, without success; Nathan was having none of it.

Showing no sign of being aware of, let alone responding to, the nurse's efforts, Nathan repeated over and over again that he wanted to see his family, that he knew they were there and he wanted to see them.

"Calm down, Nate," Burke said, laying a hand on his friend's arm. "I'm sorry about this," he apologised to the nurse. "He's a little distraught right now." That was a gross understatement, but he was sure if it had been his family that was rushed to hospital from a serious fire he would be just as panic-stricken. "We're looking for his family: wife and two kids. They were brought in from a fire on Carnarvon Street about fifteen minutes ago."

The nurse nodded. "Yes, sir." She typed something into the computer before her, and it quickly became clear from the look of annoyance that flashed across her face that she had failed to find what she was looking for. She offered a quick smile of apology. "I'm very sorry about this, but it seems that your friend's family isn't on the system. If you could provide me with a few details, I can locate their medical records, the doctor will need them, then I can see if there's anyone available to talk to you."

Burke's hand on his arm calmed Nathan for a few moments, but upon hearing that the nurse could tell him nothing, and that she wanted him to just hang around, he flared up again. "I want to see my family, now!" he said in a loud voice that could be heard by everyone in the waiting room, as well as by those smoking just outside.

It required all of Burke's persuasiveness to calm Nathan and get him to take a seat and stay there. Nathan was all set to break down the doors that led from the waiting room to the treatment area, and to attack anyone who got in his way or tried to stop him. Burke was just thinking that he would have to handcuff his friend to keep him in the seat when he abruptly stopped fighting and went still. What caused his sudden capitulation, Burke didn't know, and it worried him more than the frantic efforts to find his family had.

With a wary eye on his partner, in case his stillness was nothing more than a ruse to lull him, so he could make another attempt to get into the treatment area, Burke returned to the counter. Every time one of the doors swung open, either to let out a nurse or doctor, or to admit a patient, he expected to have to chase after Nathan as he made a break for it.

Once he was finished with the nurse, which didn't take long, he crossed the waiting room to the vending machine that sat in the corner. It needed a good clean, and he was sure the drinks available from it were far from his usual standard, but he ignored his concerns; there were more important things to worry about just then than his distaste for vending machine coffee.

# 33

Kurt took a circuitous route back to his hideout, though he doubted anyone would have seen or noted him, and, as he had previously, left his car at the Asda a couple of streets away. He walked the rest of the way, before struggling through the growth that made the house such a good hiding place, at the expense of several new scratches on the exposed areas of his skin, which he ignored.

The first thing he did upon reaching the bedroom where he had made his lair was take a bottle of cider from his supply and pop the top off. He took a long swallow of the drink, which had been kept at a reasonable temperature by the chill air of the room, then put the bottle down so he could pick up his tablet.

He was still a little buzzed by the thought of the revenge he had taken on Inspector Stone that night, a revenge he felt was more than appropriate given what he had cost him, as he searched the internet for local news and listen to the news on Rock Radio. He found nothing, but that didn't surprise him; given how late it was, he imagined it would be at least a few hours before anything about the fire appeared on any of the sites he had checked, or on the radio.

He wished he could hear or read something about the fire before morning, he wanted some idea of how successful his act of revenge had been. By the time he reached the bottom of his bottle of cider, though, he realised that his idea of staying up to wait for news regarding the fire, and the fate of Stone's family, was stupid. It was unlikely that anything of importance would be posted before dawn, so he would be wasting his time, and the battery power of his tablet, which he couldn't recharge at his current location. It was better if he got some sleep; he would be better able to deal with anything that resulted from his arson once he was rested and his brain was no longer fogged by tiredness.

Rolling his now empty bottle into the corner of the room, where it chinked against the others he had emptied previously, he wrapped himself up in his sleeping bag and closed his eyes. As he drifted off to sleep a smile touched his lips at the thought of how much Stone was going to hurt when he learnt of the fire; he couldn't decide it if would be better for the kids to die or be seriously hurt - seriously hurt he decided after a moment's reflection; if they were dead, Stone could put the pain of their loss behind him, but if they were seriously hurt he would feel it every time he looked at them.

The smile disappeared abruptly, driven away by the memory of his own children; he missed them every single day, and wondered where they were, and if they still went by the names he and his ex-wife had given them. Even if he found out, he didn't think he would do anything about it; Amelia had been four, and Patrick just three, when they were taken away - he didn't suppose they remembered him now.

# 34

Burke was startled out of his doze when the alarm on his phone went off, announcing that it was six a.m.. Yawning, he stretched and took out his phone, so he could silence it. The sudden lack of sound was as jarring as the burst of music that had disturbed him.

Yawning for a second time, he got to his feet. A glance at his partner revealed that Nathan hadn't moved, he was still on the chair he had pulled close to the bed when they were shown to the room, his eyes on his son's face, and his son's hand in his. The tears that had cascaded down his cheeks when the doctor finally came to see him were no longer falling, Burke guessed his friend had no more tears to shed, but they had left a glistening trail down his cheeks, a clear indicator of the grief the night had brought.

Burke wished his friend's grief was at its limit, but he doubted Nathan was going to be that fortunate, not given what the doctor had said. Things were going to get worse, probably that day, and as strong as his friend was, Burke doubted his ability to cope if things got as bad as he thought they were going to. Nathan was going to need his support to get through the next few days, and probably the next few weeks as well; there were things he had to do, though, things he couldn't put off.

"Nate." He kept his voice soft, not wanting to intrude. "Nate." He shook his friend's shoulder to get his attention when he showed no sign of having heard him. "I've got to go and take care of a few things, I'll be back later; do you want me to bring you anything when I return?"

It didn't surprise Burke when Nathan shook his head without taking his attention from his son. Having got his answer, he collected his jacket from the back of the chair on which he had dozed; he paused in the doorway to look back into the room for a moment, he wanted to say something to give his friend hope but there was nothing to say, so he left.

The first thing he did was look for the doctor; he wasn't sure he would be able to get any information from him, but he had to try. Once that errand was completed - he wasn't happy with the information he got, but at least now he knew the situation as well as the hospital staff did - he departed the hospital, driving away in Nathan's car since it was the only vehicle he had available to him. He didn't suppose it was going to matter to Nathan that he was using his car, Burke doubted his friend was going to leave the hospital unless he was dragged out of there.

MORBID THOUGH IT WAS, not to mention pointless, Burke couldn't help detouring past Nathan's house on his way to his own place.

The house was a wreck, whoever had started the fire had done a good job of it. He could only wonder how any of the family had made it out of the smoke-blackened house alive; he couldn't bring himself to even try to imagine how Melissa and the kids must have felt at waking to discover the house on fire and filled with smoke. With a heavy sigh, he turned his attention away from the house and carried on down the road.

A little over ten minutes later he reached his own place. The moment he entered his flat he stepped into the kitchen, so he could switch on his coffee machine which was, as always, filled and ready to be activated. While the most important appliance he owned got on with its work, slowly filling his small flat with the delicious aroma of an Arabica blend, he headed for the bathroom for a shower.

He finished up a longer than usual shower, most of which he spent allowing the steaming hot water to ease his tired and stressed muscles, and got out to dry himself off. He shaved quickly, and then dressed in a fresh suit before returning to the kitchen, where he was in the middle of making breakfast when his phone rang.

KURT CAME AWAKE WITH a sudden shock when his hand came into contact with the cold metal of his camping stove. From the angle of the shadows created by the small amount of sunlight that made it through the window it was not long after dawn, early enough that his immediate thought was to roll over and go back to sleep. He changed his mind when he remembered why he was so tired.

Sitting up, he reached for the bottle of water that was with the rest of his box of cider, so he could take a couple of swigs to wash away the dryness in his throat and mouth. Once he felt a little more hydrated he put the water aside and picked up his tablet.

Almost the moment he turned it on and connected to the internet he saw a report on the fire he had started. By the time he made it to the end of the story he was satisfied that he had succeeded beyond his expectations. It was inconceivable, based on what the news report had to say, that Nathan Stone was anything but an emotional wreck.

A part of him wished he could see the man who had caught him, who had put handcuffs on him and sent him to jail. He wanted to see just how much Stone was hurting, and have him know who was responsible for his pain and why. He quickly dismissed that idea, however; no matter how satisfying it would be, he knew it wouldn't be worth the risk such an action would engender.

It was better if he left Stone to wonder who had torn his life apart and why; with luck the lack of knowledge would torment the detective as much as, if not more than, the damage done to his family.

He read through the story a second time to be sure he hadn't missed anything, and then he listened to the seven o'clock news. There was nothing new in the report, but the way the radio presenter read the news added a fresh dimension to it, and Kurt smiled anew as he listened to the result of his actions. He felt a twinge of remorse over what had happened to the children, but it vanished quickly as he remembered the tears of his own children as they were taken away - he hadn't been there to actually see the tears, but he had been told about them by his ex-wife and could easily imagine them - and his own tears, and the urge to kill himself when it finally became clear that he would never be allowed to see them again.

What he had done would no doubt be seen by many, most in fact, as an horrific act from a brutal person, but in his mind Stone's children had suffered less than his own had. Their pain had been over quick, his children's had lasted.

When the news report finished, with nothing mentioned that gave him cause for concern, he put the tablet away, turned off the radio, and took out his phone. He was almost finished with his revenge, two days or so and he would be done, which meant it was time for him to make arrangements to get out of the country. He had already made some arrangements, but now he needed to check on them and put the last few things in place.

He didn't want to remain in town any longer than necessary, he wanted to get away and start a new life with the money he had waited so long to get his hands on.

LOUISA ORCHARD CRAWLED from her bed with great reluctance ten minutes after her hand banged down on her alarm clock, silencing its hated, horrifically loud, beeping. It was the same every morning, her alarm went off, she woke with a groan and groped for the clock, so she could turn it off, and then she pulled her duvet tight around her while she tried to pretend the world didn't exist.

With an enormous effort, she threw back the duvet and got to her feet to head along the passage to the bathroom. Once she was done there, she made for the kitchen to put the kettle on and drop some bread into the toaster.

While she waited for her breakfast to be ready, she turned on the radio in the living room. Ally Grantham, the morning DJ, was just announcing that there was six minutes until the seven-a.m. news. Louisa turned the volume up before returning to the kitchen to wait for the kettle and the toaster, neither of which took long.

She made it back into the living room with her breakfast just in time for the start of the news. She didn't like hearing about events from the news - it was her job, wherever possible, to report on events before anyone else - but it simply wasn't possible for her to be on top of events twenty-four hours a day, not unless she wanted to go without sleep.

Sitting on the sofa, her feet tucked up under her, Louisa took a big bite of her toast while she listened to the start of the news report. The toast turned to ash in her mouth when she heard the lead story; she couldn't believe what she was hearing, and she sat there, frozen to the spot, while she listened to the rest of the story, hoping she had heard wrong. The incident was bad enough, a fire at a family home was always a tragic event, but knowing one of the people involved made it many times worse.

Abandoning her breakfast, she retrieved her phone and dialled DI Stone's number. She drummed her fingers impatiently against her leg while she listened to the phone ring, and ring, and ring; when it switched over to the answer machine she ended the call and tried again. Three times she tried to get hold of Stone, and each time she got the same result. Finally, she gave up and called another number in the hope of getting information.

BURKE WAS SURPRISED to hear Louisa Orchard's voice when he answered the phone. Of all the people he might have anticipated the call coming from, Louisa was almost at the bottom. He couldn't imagine why she was calling him, and it was a few moments before he thought to ask.

"Good morning, Louisa, how can I help you?" he asked, keeping his voice as polite as a sleep and caffeine deprived system would allow. He could do nothing about his lack of sleep just then, but he could rectify his caffeine deprivation - he poured himself a cup of heavenly, aromatic Arabica coffee, and then left the machine running while he wandered into the living room.

"I've just heard the news report on the radio," Louisa said, her voice distressed. "How's Nathan? Are he and his family alright?"

"Nathan's alright, physically at least, emotionally he's a wreck," Burke told her after a few moments' thought. He wasn't going to say anything, until he realised that Louisa could have found out pretty much everything there was to know about the fire from her sources; she hadn't though, she had chosen to call him. He was sure that before calling him, Louisa would have tried to get hold of Stone, which suggested her interest was more in Stone and his well-being than in a story. "His family's a long way from being alright, though. The fire was bad, very bad." He didn't want to say much more than that; he knew Louisa and Nathan were friends, on some level, but he wasn't sure they were close enough for him to tell her what had happened to Nathan's family.

"The news report said it was arson, is that right?"

"That hasn't been confirmed yet," Burke said quickly before taking a long sip of his coffee. A sigh of pleasure escaped him as he was hit by a jolt of caffeine. "The watch manager at the scene said it was, but you know the procedure, until the fire investigator has finished and announced the cause of the fire, it's all speculation."

*'Who's behind the fire?'* The question rose automatically to Louisa's lips, but she resisted the urge to ask it; the question was that of a journalist, not a friend, and she knew which one she wanted to be just then. "The news report also said the kids..." Her voice broke a little even though she had never met Nathan's children. "That the kids..." She couldn't finish.

Burke knew what Louisa was trying and failing to ask - he could well imagine what the news report had said, and her reaction to it sent her up in his estimation; it was clear that she was thinking and acting like a human being, rather than a journalist with a story to write. "Isobel died before they could get her out of the fire, that's the little girl, and Robert is in a bad way - they're hopeful he'll pull through, but his heart could be an issue."

"Is that still a problem? I thought they fixed his heart."

It surprised Burke to hear that she knew about the operation Robert had had to fix the hole in his heart. "They did, but his heart is still weak, it's always going to be weaker than it should be, which means he's vulnerable to things like smoke inhalation, which put a strain on the heart."

"What about Melissa? How is she?" Never having been married, and not having kids, Louisa had a hard time imagining the hell Nathan must be going through - to lose one child to a tragic event was bad enough, but to still be at risk of losing the second, she shook her head; worse still to have the tragic event be a deliberate act.

"She was still in surgery when I left the hospital - she suffered serious burns."

"Is there anything I can do?"

That question startled Burke more than any of the others had. "No, I don't think there is. I don't think there's much that anyone, except the doctors and nurses, can do right now. Thank you for the offer, though, I'm sure Nathan will be grateful when I tell him."

The moment the call was ended, Burke got to his feet and headed into the kitchen for a second cup of coffee. As well as the coffee, he poured himself a generous bowl of muesli to quiet the grumbles from his stomach. He turned the television on when he got back to the living room, and was relieved to see that his Playstation 3 was still running, and his second attempt at the Le Mans 24-hour race remained paused at three hours and thirty-eight minutes.

He raced for about ten minutes, between sips of coffee and spoonfuls of cereal, before a thought occurred to him. It was such an obvious thing that he was surprised it hadn't occurred to him before, he supposed the very obviousness of it was why it had taken until then for it to occur to him.

After finishing another lap he paused his game and moved to the table in the corner of the room, where his laptop sat, taking his breakfast with him. It only took a few moments, once the laptop had booted up, for him to type his partner's name and the other names into the web browser, he then hit enter and lifted his mug while he waited. He didn't even manage to get the mug to his lips before his browser came back with the results of his search.

His eyes ran down the list of results as he considered which one to check out first. In the end he decided that none of them looked more likely to provide him with a good answer than any of the others, so he clicked on the first one.

# 35

"Stephen."

Burke had barely made it through the door of Branton Police Station when he was hailed by Sergeant Wells, who had desk duty that morning.

"Frank, how's things this morning? Anything going on?"

Wells ignored the question and asked one of his own instead, "How's Nate? Is it as bad as I've heard?"

"I don't know what you've heard, but yeah, it's pretty bad," Burke told him. "I wouldn't expect to see him for a while."

"That's what I figured." Wells' normally cheerful face was sombre. "Collins is looking for you," he said, changing the subject. "He wants to see you as soon as you get in. I think he wants to know about the fire."

"I'm sure he does." Burke didn't relish the prospect of reliving his partner's nightmare for the benefit of his superior, he didn't imagine he was going to be able to avoid it, however, and he was sure Collins didn't just want to know about the fire. Fortunately, he had his own reason for wanting to see the DCI, the summons meant he would be able to deal with that without delay.

Once through the security door he made his way upstairs and along to Collins' office. Every officer he passed took the time to ask how Stone was, a testament both to how widely news of the fire had spread and how popular his partner was. Many of them had clearly heard the rumour that the fire had been started deliberately, several times he was told how much they would like a bit of time alone with the arsonist. As a result, it took him almost ten minutes to reach his superior's office, where he knocked on the door, and then entered quickly following the call of 'come in'.

"Good morning, sir," Burke said the moment he was through the door.

"Stephen, have a seat. Would you like something to drink, tea or coffee?" Collins asked as Burke took the seat across from him.

"Coffee please, thank you, sir."

The coffee arrived after just a couple of minutes and Collins immediately got down to business. "Tell me about last night," he instructed.

It took better than ten minutes for Burke to relate everything that had happened, and he was glad when he got to the end of events. Experiencing everything had been one thing, but hearing it detailed, even if it was by his own lips, made it seem even worse.

Collins was silent for a long time following the conclusion of Burke's narration. "You said the doctor doesn't think Melissa is going to pull through," he said finally, his expression blank.

The tone made it seem a question, but Burke got the impression he was more interested in giving himself extra time to think.

"Yes, sir. They were still operating when I left the hospital at just after six, but given the level of smoke inhalation, and the amount of her body that suffered burns, third degree - which I believe is the worst level you can get - they don't have high hopes." Burke took a few sips of his coffee, which was not a patch on what he had had at home, and then said what had been preying on his mind since he first spoke to the doctor upon his arrival at the hospital. "I think, though the doctor didn't say, that the operation is something of a desperate act, and one that probably won't work."

Collins' face showed something then, it showed how appalled he was by the thought of doctors operating on Melissa Stone when they didn't think it was going to do any good. It seemed cruel, and an unnecessary source of additional anguish for Nathan, who had already lost his daughter and still stood to lose his wife, and perhaps his son as well.

"What about Robert?" he asked. "What do they think his chances are?"

Burke shrugged, it was all he could do. "I don't know," he admitted. "Given how weak his heart is, I'm amazed he's lasted this long; the watch manager from the fire crew told me he had stopped breathing when he was brought out of the house, thankfully the paramedics were able to get his heart going on the way to the hospital."

"You think it's just a question of time. Jesus!" Collins swore when Burke nodded slowly, reluctantly. "Nobody deserves this kind of bad luck, least of all Nate. You said the fire was arson?"

"Almost certainly according to the fire crew at the scene, but we don't yet have confirmation from the investigator. That's not likely to come until this afternoon at the earliest, even if it is as obvious as I was told."

"Who'd want to kill a woman and two kids?" Collins shook his head in disbelief; even after his years on the police force he had a hard time understanding - he couldn't accept - the cruelty that people inflicted on their fellow humans. Something occurred to him then. "You said Nate received a phone call from someone claiming the guy who killed the Bhaskars was hiding out in the woods near the old fort."

Burke nodded

"And that the fire must have started not long after Nate left the house, given how soon the report was called through to him by the duty sergeant." Another nod. Do you think there's a connection?"

It was the opening Burke had been waiting for. "I'm positive there is."

Collins was taken aback by Burke's certainty. He wasn't used to hearing him so positive unless there was hard evidence to back up whatever he believed. "So, who would have wanted to trick Nate out of the house and then set fire to it to try and kill his family?" For the first time in a long time he was more interested in closing a case because he wanted the suspect caught than because it would be good for his career.

"If I'm right, then his name is Kurt Walker, and he's the guy who killed Amala and Manjula Bhaskar, Terry Fielding, and Will Henman, and he's also the guy who attacked the three boys at the Greenwell Industrial Estate." Burke was not surprised to see disbelief on his superior's face.

"Are you trying to tell me that everything that's happened over the past week is the result of just one man?" Collins asked dubiously. He couldn't help thinking that it would be better, in one respect, for everything to be the result of one man's actions, but the notion was so out there he had a hard time accepting it, not least because each incident was different, and criminals tended to be creatures of habit who weren't likely to change, or even alter, their 'modus operandi'.

"Yes, sir, I am."

"Explain."

"Nate and I were talking yesterday evening, he told me he believes the Bhaskar murders and the murder of Terry Fielding are connected, as well as that of Will Henman, and that he was sure he knows Vikram Bhaskar from somewhere. He believed if he could remember where he knew Vikram Bhaskar and Will Henman from he would have the solution to the case." Burke saw Collins' next question in his eyes and answered it before it could be voiced. "He didn't want to say anything until he was more certain, and he had some proof. He thought it better if he didn't disturb the way the separate investigations were going, or put the idea into anyone's mind, in case he was wrong, and it got them looking in the wrong direction.

"When I got home this morning, it occurred to me that a simple Google search might be the quickest and easiest way to see if there is a link between the murders."

"I assume you found something."

Burke nodded.

"Okay, tell me what you found. Who is this Kurt Walker, and why has he been killing all these people? I especially want to know why you think he set fire to Nate's house," Collins said. "I assume there's history between them."

"Very definitely. One of the first cases Nathan investigated after becoming a detective was a robbery at the Oak Hill Post Office; it was a major case according to what I found online. A guard was killed by the two masked and armed robbers before they got away with a little over one hundred thousand pounds."

Collins couldn't suppress the whistle of amazement that drew from him, it was the biggest haul he had heard about from the local area, bigger even than what was stolen from the Rock Radio Musical Festival earlier in the year. "I think I remember, vaguely, being told about the case at some point, it happened about a year and a half before I got transferred here, that must make it eleven or so years ago. That would explain why Nate had difficulty remembering the case." He realised he had interrupted and quickly apologised. "Sorry, go on, you were saying."

"Kurt Walker and Will Henman are the two who robbed the post office..."

Despite having just apologised for doing so, Collins couldn't help interrupting again, "They were partners? So why did Kurt Walker kill Will Henman?"

"I have no idea on that score, sir, I was going to see if I could find their records and the case file in the system as soon as I got in to see if the answer is there," Burke said. "I know that Vikram Bhaskar was a witness to the robbery, Paulina Fielding was the barrister who prosecuted the case, and Nate was one of the detectives - DS Worthing was in charge, but he's been retired for five years, and dead for three, so I can't imagine there would have been any point in trying to punish him. The article I found, from an old issue of the Herald, said there were two other witnesses to the robbery."

"So there could be another couple of victims out there, just waiting for us to find them." That was a notion that appealed to neither officer.

"Maybe, but it's also possible he hasn't gotten around to them yet. If that's the case we might have a way of catching him; we don't know why he killed his partner, and right now we don't have a clue where he's hiding, but it seems to me he's after revenge against the people who put him behind bars, and he's getting it by going after their families.

"If I'm right about that, and the other two witnesses are still alive, then Walker is going to be looking to hurt them by killing someone close to them."

Collins figured out what was in Burke's mind then. "We put surveillance on the witnesses and their closest family, and then move in when he makes his move. At the same time, we do everything we can to try and figure out where he's hiding." He nodded and gave a small smile. "That could work. So, what's the names of the witnesses, and where can we find them?"

"I don't know the answer to that right now. Their names weren't in the article I found; they'll be in the case file, though, and I can find out where they live once I have the names, as well as the names of their family members, then we can set up surveillance.

"It's going to be a big surveillance operation," Burke said, aware that Collins was not a fan of such operations, and he preferred them to be as small as possible when they couldn't be avoided. "We're going to have to put officers on every close family member we discover, just to be on the safe side."

"In that case I'd better not delay you any longer. With Nate now indisposed, I'll be taking charge of the case, but for practical purposes you'll have to manage the actual running of it; do you think you can handle that?"

Burke nodded. "Yes, sir. As soon as I've found the witnesses, I'll let you know so we can plan the surveillance."

# 36

Exhaustion was etched into every line of Burke's face as he slowly made his way along the corridor to the room where he had left Nathan. He was bone-tired, and wanted nothing more than to find a corner in which he could curl up and sleep for the next day, if not longer; that option was not available to him, however, there was too much for him to do.

All he could hope was that now they knew - perhaps not with a one hundred percent certainty, but with enough for the purposes of the investigation - who was responsible for the murders, they would be able to catch him and close the case soon, perhaps even today; it wasn't much of a hope, but it was something to cling to.

He hesitated when he reached the door of the room that Robert Stone had been put in, reluctant to enter and discover that the worst had happened. After a few moments he forced aside his concerns and pushed open the door.

Burke quickly saw that his fears were unfounded, Robert was still alive, though he showed no sign of having improved, and Nathan was still at his bedside, clasping his hand in his own. As he entered the room and looked more closely at his friend, Burke got the impression that something was wrong, his eyes were red and there was evidence of fresh tears on his cheeks.

If everything was okay with Robert - as okay as it could be under the circumstances - then there was only one thing that could have happened. Burke felt his blood run cold as the thought occurred to him.

He didn't like adding to what his friend was going through, but he had little in the way of choice. One of the reasons he was there was to find out if Nathan knew anything that could help them catch Kurt Walker before he could attack anyone else.

"Nate, it's Stephen." His voice was gentle as he approached his partner. "How's Robert doing? Has there been any improvement?"

It was a long time before Nathan lifted his head from the bed, where he had his cheek pressed against his son's hand. He looked round at Burke, but it wasn't until he blinked his eyes a few times to focus them that he recognised his partner.

"Hi, Stephen," he croaked, his voice rough from grief and, Burke guessed, a lack of fluids.

"Hi, Nate." Burke fetched his friend a cup of water from the pitcher on the cabinet by the head of the bed. "How's Robert doing?"

Nathan looked down at his son, and then back up at his friend. "No change," he said sadly. He took the cup, but showed no interest in lifting it to his lips. "They say it's a good thing, and if he makes it through the day his chances of recovery are good, but he's so weak." His voice caught in his throat. "He's having such a hard time breathing. It's like when he was a baby, and they didn't know if he was going to make it."

"He's a fighter, he'll pull through," Burke said with all the confidence he could muster as he laid a comforting hand on his friend's shoulder. "How about Melissa, how's she doing?" He regretted the question the moment he asked it for it prompted a flood of tears as his friend collapsed visibly.

Nathan's hand tightened its grip on his son's as tears poured down his cheeks and he was wracked by sobs. In moments he had become a shadow of his former, already diminished, self; he seemed to have shrunk until he was nothing more than a husk of the robust and capable figure he was normally. The cup of water tipped in his hand, spilling its contents, which splashed to the floor, soaking his feet, before it fell from his grasp.

In between sobs Nathan's mouth opened as if he was trying to say something but no sounds made it past his lips.

"She didn't make it."

The quiet, female voice made Burke remember what it was he had intended doing when he left the hospital that morning, and what he had forgotten. It wasn't Nathan's sister who had answered his question, it was Louisa Orchard, who was sitting in the corner of the room watching Nathan with concern written on every line of her face. Burke was surprised, not just that she was there but that he hadn't realised it until then; it wasn't like him to not spare a glance for a room when he entered it, no matter what was on his mind.

"How long have you been here?" he asked, unable to keep either his surprise or his suspicion from his voice. He couldn't think why the journalist would have come to the hospital, and he certainly couldn't fathom why she had chosen to stay and keep Nathan company.

Louisa gave an uncertain shrug, as if she wasn't certain of the answer herself. "A while. I only meant to pop in to say...well to tell him..." She couldn't seem to finish what she was trying to say, and after a few seconds she gave up and said something else. "When I saw that Nathan was here on his own, I figured you were at the station or something, I decided I should stay, in case he needs anything. It's not like I've got anything better to do today." When she saw Burke's surprise she said, "Kelly wanted me to cover this story, but I told him Nate's a friend and I wouldn't do it, even if I thought he'd print the story as I wrote it.

"I don't think he liked that, he threatened to sack me if I don't write the story." If that prospect worried her, she didn't show it.

If anything, she looked relieved, as though she was glad of the confrontation with her editor.

It was almost half a minute before Burke found the words to respond to that; he was astounded that Louisa had in effect thrown away her journalistic career because she didn't want to write a story that would hurt her friend. "I'm sure Nate will be thankful you're not writing a story about the fire."

Louisa shrugged, as if that didn't matter to her.

Burke approached the journalist and lowered his voice, he didn't want to disturb or upset Nathan any more than he already had. "You said Melissa didn't make it? What happened?" He glanced round to see if his friend had heard him.

Louisa also looked over at Nathan, she watched him for a few seconds and then turned her attention back to Burke. "She made it through the surgery," she said in a voice that was as quiet as Burke's had been, "but after about an hour something happened. I don't know what. They gave Nathan the news about three quarters of an hour ago, told him the usual, 'they did everything they could, they're very sorry, complications, blah, blah, blah.'" The disgust on her face made it clear what she thought of the platitudes offered by whoever had delivered the news of Melissa Stone's death. "Does Nate's sister know what's happened?" she asked in an abrupt change of subject.

Burke grimaced as he shook his head. "Not unless someone else has let her know," he said. "I meant to call her when I left here earlier but..." He hesitated for a moment, then shrugged. "I got a little distracted. Excuse me, I'd better make that call before I forget again."

The phone call lasted for a very uncomfortable five minutes - Burke had only met April Stone a handful of times, and he had never before had cause to call her - and then he returned to the room. He still had something he needed to do, even if it was likely to upset his friend.

"I'm sorry about this, Nate." He squatted at his friend's side. "I know this isn't a good time, but I think I know who's responsible for the murders, and for the fire, and I'm hoping you know something that will help us find him before he kills anyone else." He ignored Louisa, who had perked up at his words, unable to conceal the journalistic curiosity they inspired. "Do you remember a Kurt Walker?"

Nathan showed no reaction to the name, he gave no indication he had heard anything of what his partner had said, and Burke reached out to take him by the shoulder. He hoped the contact would get his attention.

"Nate," he said softly, his voice gentle and filled with remorse for the necessity of what he was doing. "Can you hear me? Do you remember Kurt Walker?"

The name triggered a memory, a ten-year-old memory of an incident he had almost forgotten - had forgotten until then. "An eye for an eye."

"What was that?" Burke asked. His friend's voice was so low he wasn't sure he had actually said anything.

"An eye for an eye," Nathan repeated. "That's what he said at the trial. He said he was going to make us all pay, he was going to make us feel the pain we had put him through. He didn't care how long it took, he was going to make us suffer."

"Based on recent events, it seems as if he's almost accomplished what he threatened to do," Burke said, not at all happy that a threat made a decade ago was being fulfilled and he hadn't, so far, been able to prevent it - the fact that he hadn't known about the threat till then made no difference to his thinking. "So far he's gotten his revenge on Vikram Bhaskar, Paulina Fielding, and you." The moment he said that he regretted it and expected Nathan to collapse again; to his surprise, and the surprise of Louisa, he didn't. "He's also killed his former partner, though we don't know why right now."

"I do," Nathan said. He became more animated, until he seemed almost like his old self, as if the discussion was giving him the energy to fight off the depression and lethargy that the night's events had left him with. "Will Henman sold him out. One of the witnesses, Mrs Blenkinsop, was able to identify him as one of the robbers, and when we brought him in we offered him a deal - he could either go down as an accessory to murder, along with armed robbery, or he could give us his partner and cop to a lesser charge.

"He chose the deal - told us where to find Walker, testified against him, and got seven years, he was out in three and a half. Because of that, Walker swore he'd get revenge on him along with the rest of us. Henman didn't have any family, so all Walker could do is kill him."

"Well that explains that," Burke said, glad he now knew the reason behind that murder, which hadn't fitted in with the others, though it didn't really advance the case any, especially in the area of catching Kurt Walker. "I've been through everything I could find on the case, and as far as I can tell there's only two people left he might be after; we're arranging for officers to keep watch on them, though we don't really expect Walker to do anything about Mrs Blenkinsop." He saw his partner's questioning look. "She's old, alone, and dying; Collins agrees with me that there would be nothing for Walker to gain by killing her. So far, with the exception of Will Henman, he's targeted the families of his victims." He blanched as he remembered that Nathan was one of those victims. "Mrs Blenkinsop has no family for him to target, and it would be too much of a risk for him to try and get to her given how many people he would have to get past at the nursing home."

"Why has he waited so long to come after us?" Nathan asked, sure he should know the answer, he couldn't chisel it out of the mess his brain was in just then, however.

"He only got out of jail two months ago," Burke said. From the moment he arrived at the police station to when he left to come and speak to Nathan, he had been working to find out everything he could about Kurt Walker, while drinking mug after mug of coffee to keep himself awake. "He got out without any problems; apparently he behaved himself in the run-up to his release." He snorted at that, sure it had been an act. "And was cooperating with probation; then his probation officer went on holiday a fortnight or so ago and Walker disappeared."

"And no-one thought to tell us?" Nathan asked in amazement. "Where was he living?" If Walker had moved back to town after leaving prison, he was sure he would have heard about it, even if only indirectly.

"Southampton, he's got family there apparently. As for why we weren't told he had gone missing, it's the usual story," Burke said. "Until I called this morning to find out what I could about him, Southampton probation didn't even know he was missing. His probation officer broke his arm on holiday and hasn't returned to work yet, and no-one in the office realised Walker was supposed to have an appointment during the last week, so he wasn't looked for.

"He hasn't been seen by his family in a week and a half - at least that's what probation told me after they did some checking - but they didn't say anything because it was none of their business. I imagine they either didn't want to get him in trouble, or didn't want to risk pissing him off. Either way, it looks as though he's probably been planning this since he got out, if not longer; he's managed to find out enough information to get himself this far, and now he's only got two targets left, one of whom we don't think he's going to bother with. That leaves him with one.

"We're setting up surveillance on Irene Painter to catch Walker when he comes after her, but we'd rather catch him before then if we can. Can you remember anything from when you arrested him that will help us find him now?"

Robert stirred then, distracting Nathan from his partner and the question he had asked. Nathan's attention became focused on his son's face as he searched for some sign that Robert was going to wake, that he was going to recover from his ordeal. Apart from the slightest of changes in his son's breathing, though, there was no indication that he was going to wake. Finally, his eyes moved from his son's face to the machines that were monitoring him; there was the slightest of blips in the otherwise regular up and down line that traced the slow beating of Robert's heart, but no other sign of a change in his condition.

Burke gave his friend some space, though he knew he couldn't leave him for too long - he hated pushing his friend under the circumstances, but he needed whatever information he might have. He could have handed the job off to DS Mason, but he didn't feel his colleague capable of being appropriately compassionate, too often he was rougher and cruder than necessary. Aside from that, Burke felt it was his duty to do what had to be done.

"I'm really sorry, Nate, but I need to know anything you can remember about Walker that might help us catch him."

As if Burke's words were a trigger, Robert's breath rattled in his throat, and all the machines monitoring his vital signs went haywire, filling the small room with noise as they sounded alarms. Robert continued to struggle for air, and his body convulsed violently as if he had received a massive electric shock. His back arched, his hands clenched and unclenched, looking more like the claws of an animal than the digits of a young boy, and his eyes flew open, bulging unseeing from their sockets.

The change in his son came so suddenly that Nathan froze in shock; he had no idea what to do, and could only stare helplessly, his eyes moving rapidly between Robert and the machines monitoring him. It was hard for him to watch as his son battled for life, all the more so because he wanted to help, to do something, but he didn't have a clue what he could do, or even if there was anything he could do.

Unlike his friend, Burke wasn't frozen by shock; he found the panic button and used it to summon help.

# 37

DC Grey glowered at the phone as he put it down. This was the third time he had tried to get hold of Sergeant Burke without success. He had no idea where Burke was, or what he was doing, but since he couldn't get hold of him, and there was no way he was going to try getting hold of the inspector under the circumstances, there was no other option available to him - he didn't like it, but what else could he do.

"Grey," Collins said in a voice that was less than welcoming when he saw who had disturbed him. "What do you want?"

If Grey hadn't been nervous before, the far from friendly greeting from his superior would have given him pause. He was there with a purpose, however, and he steeled himself. "I'm sorry to disturb you, sir. I've been looking through the information Sergeant Burke found on Kurt Walker."

"And?" Collins prompted impatiently when the young DC paused.

"I think Sergeant Burke has missed a possible target," Grey said.

"Really? I've been through the information myself, and I can't think of anyone Sergeant Burke might have missed. We have officers at the Beresford Nursing Home to keep an eye on Mrs Blenkinsop, and Sergeant Mason and DC Reid are on their way to check on Irene Pointer and her family."

The dubious look on his superior's face made Grey even more hesitant, but he summoned his courage and spoke anyway. "I know that, sir, but I believe the social worker is in danger as well; she might even be in more danger than the other two."

Collins was caught by surprise, and for a few moments all he could do was stare at Grey. Finally, he asked, "What social worker?"

"Nell Petrocelli, she's the one who took Walker's kids away. Social services got involved with the family while Walker was on remand, they determined the children weren't being properly cared for by Walker's wife, so just before the trial they were taken into care. It wasn't part of the investigation or the trial, so it wasn't in the case file, but I found a story online from the Herald about the trial, it's probably the same one Sergeant Burke found.

"When he found out his kids had been taken away, Walker tried to attack Ms Petrocelli in court; he apparently made some pretty nasty threats while he was being restrained."

"Have you told Stephen about this?"

"No, sir," Grey said before quickly explaining why. "I've tried calling Sergeant Burke several times, but he's not answering his phone; as far as I know he's still at the hospital with Inspector Stone. Since I wasn't able to get hold of him, I thought it best to see you about Ms Petrocelli."

"And you were right to do so," Collins told Grey, dismissing the annoyance that flickered across his face at the news that Burke, as well as Stone, now seemed to be incommunicado; he hoped it was only temporary and Burke would be back in touch soon. "Do you know where to find Ms Petrocelli?"

Grey shook his head. "No, sir, not at present."

"I suggest you find her quickly, before we have another body on our hands." Collins didn't like the thought that there was another potential victim out there, it meant he would have to stretch his already over-extended resources, which was an invitation for something to go wrong. "Once you know where she is, and where she lives, I want to know so I can make the necessary arrangements."

"Yes, sir." Grey recognised the dismissal for what it was and quickly left his superior's office so he could get to work.

# 38

Even after an hour Burke remained struck by the suddenness of it. One moment Robert had been quiescent, breathing shallowly while the monitors surrounding his bed showed his continuing efforts to remain alive, the next he was fighting for air and writhing and convulsing like he was in the grip of a demon that needed to be exorcised.

Doctors and nurses had converged from all directions in response to the alarms, which had filled the room with noise. They had fought valiantly, doing everything possible to try to save Robert, to no avail. After a battle that lasted for a little more than half an hour, they were forced to admit defeat and accept that they could do nothing to keep Robert alive.

The pronouncement, when it came, was a crushing blow for Nathan, who collapsed at the news that the last of his family was gone. In the space of a day, barely twelve hours in fact, he had gone from being a husband and a father to a man without a family, and he felt as though his heart had been cut from his body, taking with it his will to live.

Nathan sat in the passage, occupying a seat between Burke and Louisa, his head in his hands, his eyes unfocused and red from tears.

"Mr Stone."

The fog his mind was mired in made it hard for Nathan to hear the voice that spoke his name, and he paid it no mind; his brain made no association between the name that was spoken and himself - it was as if he had no identity anymore, he was no-one and nothing.

"Mr Stone."

Still Nathan didn't associate the name with him, though something tugged at the back of his mind, telling him he should pay attention to the voice.

Burke eyed his friend worriedly, not sure what he could do to help him through the agonies he was clearly suffering. When it became clear that Nathan was not going to react to his name, Burke answered for him. "Can I help you?" He hoped there wasn't more bad news - he couldn't imagine what else could have happened - his friend had endured about as much as any person could or should.

The doctor, his expression serious, even grave, shifted his attention to Burke. "I just want to offer my condolences and see if there's anything your friend needs."

"The last twenty-four hours back," Louisa said sharply from her position on the other side of Nathan. Her voice held barely concealed contempt for the stupidity of the doctor's words.

"Believe me, if we could give your friend that time back, we would," Doctor Mallard said with complete sincerity. "Unfortunately, we can't. We can, however, provide help to deal with the shock of what has happened. Do you think he would benefit from speaking to our chaplain?"

Burke bridled at the way the doctor was speaking, as if Nathan wasn't even there, but he quickly realised his friend was so oblivious to everything around him that in a sense he wasn't there. Though he supposed it was perfectly natural for Nathan to have withdrawn into himself after what had happened, he worried that the longer he remained like it, the harder it would be to draw him out.

"Nate isn't religious," he said, "at least not as far as I know. I've never known him to be so, but if you think the chaplain will be able to help, or perhaps a psychologist. Anything to get him through this."

"I'll get the chaplain to come down," Doctor Mallard said. "And I'll see if I can locate our grief counsellor. Does Mr Stone have any family who can help him? He's going to need a lot of support to get through this, and that support will be best provided by family, as well as by friends like the two of you."

Louisa looked uncertain, but Burke was able to answer the question. "I've spoken to Nate's sister, she's in Rome at the moment, or she was when I called her, she's getting the first available flight back; with any luck she's already on her way." He had been relieved to hear that April was on a short haul not a long haul flight, and could get back without a long delay. "Aside from that there's Nate's grandmother, but I'm not sure how much help she's likely to be - she's elderly and sick. Given the circumstances, I think it's likely to put too much of a strain on her if she were to try and help to any great degree."

Doctor Mallard nodded understandingly. "Does Mr Stone have anywhere to stay for now? I don't know how badly his house was damaged, but even if it is habitable, it might be advisable for him to stay elsewhere, with someone, for the time being..."

Burke didn't hear all of what the doctor said for his phone rang in his pocket. He excused himself to answer it, and was surprised to see that he had received several missed calls; when they had come in, he didn't have a clue, he had neither heard nor felt his phone ring since he arrived at the hospital, and they hadn't been there when he called Nathan's sister. There was no time to look and see who the missed calls were from, though, for the screen showed that the incoming call was from DCI Collins.

"Hello, sir," he said when he was far enough from Nathan, Louisa, and the doctor not to be overheard.

"Where are you?" Collins asked without preamble. He had too much going on to waste time with pleasantries, not least of which was the phone call he had only recently finished with the superintendent regarding the cost of the ongoing murder investigations; being able to tell his superior that they now knew who they were looking for, and were closing in on him, had helped only a little.

"I'm still at the hospital," Burke answered. "Nate's son died half an hour ago, and his wife died a while before that."

"Jesus!" Collins swore. "How's he doing? Is there anything we can do for him?"

"I'm not sure there's much anyone can do for him at the moment," Burke said. "Right now it's like he's in a trance, he's just sitting there, completely oblivious to everything around him. The doctor's getting the chaplain and a grief counsellor down to see him, hopefully they'll be able to help."

"Is there anyone with him?"

"Just myself and Louisa," Burke answered.

"Is that Nate's sister?" Collins didn't think it was, but he couldn't recall her name just then.

"No, it's Louisa Orchard. Nate's sister is on her way back from Rome. Did you call for a reason, sir?" Burke asked.

"Yes." Collins couldn't help wondering why the journalist was there, the only reasons he could think of were negative, but he pushed them from his mind and focused on the reason for his call. "It seems you may have missed a potential victim when you went through the Walker file. DC Grey came to see me, he said that Kurt Walker attacked a social worker at his trial, or tried to, and he made a number of threats against her."

"That's good work from Chris," Burke said, showing no concern over the censure implied by Collins' words. "Do we know the name of the social worker?"

"Nell Petrocelli, at least that was her name at the time of the trial. She's married since then, and it's now Nell Dewson. I've got Grey watching her house, a couple of uniforms watching Irene Pointer's house, and Mason and Reid are trying to find Mrs Pointer. I've also got all the officers that can be spared checking out Walker's known associates and haunts; Southampton are doing the same down there." Collins hesitated for a moment. "I know you want to stay with Nathan, and I wish I could let you, but I need you to track down Mrs Dewson and her family and make sure they're safe. Based on what Reid told me, it looks as if Mrs Dewson is the logical next target for Walker; she and Nathan seem to be the two he hates the most."

"Yes, sir." Burke disliked the thought of leaving his friend at such a time, but he was sensible enough to realise that there was little he could do for Nathan just then, while he could help save Nell Dewson and her family, and help catch Kurt Walker. Aside from those considerations, there was the fact that he couldn't disobey an order from a superior officer, at least not without a very good reason.

"Once you've made sure Mrs Dewson and her family are safe, I want you to take charge of the search for Kurt Walker. I'll be coordinating everything from here, making sure there are uniformed officers and armed response officers close enough to respond quickly if he shows up anywhere, but I want someone I trust to handle the search for him, someone who won't take unnecessary risks."

# 39

Grey wasn't happy, if he was honest, he was pissed off; he had discovered a potentially fatal and embarrassing gap in the information on Kurt Walker and his targets, yet his reward was to sit in his car and watch an empty house.

Though he knew it would be dangerous, given everything he had done, Grey secretly hoped Walker would show up; he wasn't normally inclined towards being stupidly brave - the normal level of bravery was usually quite enough for him - but having a large role in the capture of such a dangerous criminal was bound to go a long way towards getting him off the DCI's shit list.

If he had had any clue what the outcome of such thoughts would be, he would have prayed fervently for just about anything else, including his immediate posting to the Outer Hebrides.

Cars had been driving up and down the street at regular intervals throughout the afternoon, so Grey paid no particular attention to the one that drove past just before three p.m.. It wasn't a Honda Civic, which was the make of car Walker was believed to be driving, and Grey spared it no more than a passing look. Only when the red Citroen turned off the road and pulled into the drive of the house he was watching did Grey realise who it must be.

Grabbing his radio from the dashboard, he threw open the door next to him and got out of the car. "DC Grey to control, over," he said into the radio as he strode briskly up the road.

"Control to DC Grey, go ahead, over."

"I'm at the Dewson house, Mr Dewson has just arrived home with the kids. I'm heading to the front door now." For a heartbeat that seemed to last for an eternity, Grey froze as he caught sight of movement in the window of the upstairs room at the front of the house, which he assumed was a bedroom; somehow, he knew who it was straightaway, though he couldn't quite believe it.

"Control," he said urgently, picking up his pace until he was running. "I need backup here asap, armed backup. I think Walker's here at the house."

KURT HEARD THE CAR pull into the drive and swung his legs round so he could get up from the bed he had been relaxing on. He moved to the window, where he stood to one side while he looked out to see who he had heard; as he had thought, it was Tim Dewson and the two children, and he quickly grabbed up his bag and his shotgun on his way out of the room.

He stopped at the head of the stairs, out of sight of the front door, while he listened; he didn't want to reveal himself too soon and risk losing any of his victims, so he waited until he heard the door bang shut behind the last of the trio.

He swung round the bannister and started down the stairs, taking them fast and noisily. The volume and rapidity of his descent provoked a scream from the young girl who appeared on the stairs. He was sure the shotgun in his hand contributed to the terror in the girl's face, but he didn't care, by the time he was finished she would have far more reason to be terrified, not that it would do her any good.

WHY HE DIDN'T CALL out a warning to Nell Dewson's husband and their two children, Grey didn't know, perhaps it was because making his radio call to control while running had taken all the spare breath he had. He was less than a dozen feet from the front door when it shut, and closer still when he heard a high-pitched scream, the sort that could only have come from a young girl.

Without slowing his pace or thinking about what he was doing, Grey threw himself at the door. Thankfully, the door, while solid, was not strong enough to stop him, and his momentum proved sufficient to smash it open, though the impact did leave him feeling as though he had just shattered every bone in his shoulder. In addition to generating an enormous amount of pain, the impact slowed him down significantly and he stumbled across the threshold before falling to the floor at the feet of Tim Dewson.

"Control to DC Grey, come in, over." After a few seconds the radio crackled again. "Control to DC Grey, come in over; can you confirm, suspect, Kurt Walker, at your location, over?"

The voice was muffled, coming as it did from beneath Grey's body, but it was still audible.

Kurt didn't know how the police knew he was there, and just then he didn't care. The only thing that mattered was what he was going to do about the situation. He had just decided that he should kill her family there and then, instead of waiting for Nell Dewson to get home, when the sound of sirens reached him.

There was more than one police car approaching, he could hear them converging from opposite directions. They were close, and Kurt realised he would not be able to get away easily, whether he killed the Dewsons or not. By the time he could get to a car - his own was out of the question given where he had parked it, a decision he now regretted - the police would be there.

Since escape was out of the question, he had only once choice open to him, he had to make use of the people who were cowering under the menacing twin muzzles of his sawn-off shotgun. A hostage situation was not something he had ever envisaged himself becoming involved in, and he didn't have the first clue what he should do or expect, but he intended making the best of it.

A groan from the floor as the cop - DC Grey according to the radio call, not that he cared what the guy's name was - began to push himself to his feet spurred Kurt into action. Springing forwards he brought the butt of his shotgun down on the back of the cop's head with as much force as he could muster, instantly the young man slumped back to the carpet, where he lay, unmoving.

"Get in there," Kurt ordered Tim Dewson and his children, indicating the living room with his shotgun - a malicious grin split his lips at the way Tim Dewson's eyes fearfully followed the black holes that threatened to reward disobedience with horrific violence.

"Come on, little man," Tim said comfortingly to his son, who he saw was so afraid he had wet himself, as he took his hand and led him into the living room.

"You too." Kurt grabbed the girl, who was sobbing on the stairs, and all but threw her through the doorway and into the living room. Ignoring the girl, who stumbled into the arm of the sofa and bounced away to the floor, he grabbed the unconscious detective so he could drag him into the living room; he wanted him where he could see him in case he woke.

"Put the phone down," he snapped sharply, dropping his burden he used both hands to steady his gun as he aimed it at Tim Dewson, who had the receiver of the portable phone to his ear.

Kurt waited until he had seen Dewson put the phone down, then he shoved the girl on the floor out of the way with his foot. He was about to grab the detective again and finish the job of dragging him into the living room when he thought better of it, there was no reason for him to exert himself when there was someone who could do so on his behalf.

"Bring him in here," he ordered Dewson. "And you," he nudged the girl, "pull the curtains." Since the police clearly knew who he was, and that he was there, he was sure it was only a matter of time before the armed response team got there; he didn't want them to be able to see into the living room. He had seen enough films involving hostage situations to know that it was not a good idea to let the police marksmen have a clear sight of him. If they couldn't see him or what he was doing, they would have to be cautious about taking action.

Moving further into the room, Kurt took up a position by the television in the corner, where he could see the whole room and keep an eye on all three members of the Dewson family and the unconscious detective.

With one eye on his hostages, he twitched aside the corner of the curtain so he could look outside. Both the police cars he had heard approaching had now arrived, they were parked diagonally so as to block the road in front of the house, and their flashing lights told the whole street that something was going on.

"WHAT'S THE SITUATION?" Collins asked of Burke when he reached him. Looking around he saw that the street had been completely blocked, and that uniformed officers were keeping the curious, mostly the street's occupants, but there were others there, including journalists and reporters, at a safe distance.

"Not good, sir," Burke answered unhappily. "Information is sketchy at present, but as far as we can tell Walker is in the house with four hostages: DC Grey, Tim Dewson, and the two Dewson children, Sonia, nine, and Calvin, six. There's been no communication with either Walker or any of the hostages as yet, at least nothing constructive."

"What does that mean?"

"The last communication we had from Grey was the radio call to control in which he stated his belief that Walker was in the house. We've had nothing from him since, and all attempts to contact him have gone unanswered. His car is parked just down the road, and he told control he was after Tim Dewson and his kids; there's no sign of him around, so I'm working on the assumption that he's being held hostage in the house. It's the worst case, but I think it best to operate on that basis."

Collins nodded his agreement. "If he's in there, that's not good, but you're right, best to assume he is and plan with that possibility in mind. He's got the living room curtains pulled," he noted as he stared at the house. "I imagine that's so we can't see where he is, what he's doing, or where he's got his hostages; is there anything we can do about that?"

It was Sergeant White who answered that question, since he was best equipped to do so, it being his job to handle the tactical side of the situation. "I'm having an infra-red camera set up," he told the DCI from his position at Burke's shoulder. "It won't tell us everything we want to know, but it will enable us to determine how many people are in the house and where they are."

"Can your team take him out?" Collins wanted to know. He was uncomfortably aware of the camera crews which were taking up positions as close to the barriers as they could get to ensure they missed none of the unfolding drama. If things went well and it was captured on camera then he and his department would look good, but if things went badly he suspected he would have to forget all about his hoped-for promotion to superintendent.

"Not without risking the hostages," White answered without hesitation. "We don't have anywhere near enough information about the situation. We'll know more when the infra-red setup is ready, I've also got an officer trying to get close enough to plant a mike." He pointed out the darkly-dressed figure moving stealthily along the side of the Dewsons' Citroen. "So we can hear what's going on in there, but it'll still be a risk for us to go in."

"Can't your sharpshooters do anything?" Collins looked round at the two officers armed with rifles who were using police cars for support as they trained their weapons on the living room windows.

White shared a look with Burke; neither officer could quite believe that Collins thought the sharpshooters could do anything when they couldn't see into the house. They also couldn't believe that the DCI was already thinking of ending the situation with gunfire; the armed response team was intended as a last resort in a hostage situation, to be used when everything else had failed.

"With the curtains closed, they wouldn't have a clue what to shoot at," White told Collins. "Even with infra-red assistance it'd be risky. Someone's going to have to negotiate."

Burke fixed his gaze on his superior, making it clear who, in his opinion, should do the negotiating.

KURT'S FOOT HAD JUST collided with Grey's body for a second time, venting his frustration at being trapped with the people he had gone there to kill, when the phone rang. So nervous was he that the shotgun in his hand lifted automatically, and his finger tightened on the trigger, as he spun away from the unconscious detective on the floor. He managed to stop himself before he shot the phone, but the movement of the weapon forced a squeak of fright from Sonia, who struggled to contain the urge to scream.

He ran his eyes over the trio huddled on the sofa - Tim Dewson sat in the middle of his children, an arm around each as he tried to comfort them; his voice murmured reassuringly, though the distressed looks on his children's faces made it clear his words were not working - and decided that none of them had the gumption to try anything. They weren't likely to try and attack him, not that the kids could have accomplished much if they had tried, and none of them even glanced at the door.

For good measure Kurt kicked the bruised and battered figure on the floor in the face, as a warning of what they could expect if they tried anything. He then took a quick look out the window before crossing to the phone.

FOR A MOMENT COLLINS wasn't sure there was anyone on the other end of the line as he stood at the rear of the surveillance van, the phone that was connected to the van's recording system pressed to his ear. Only when he heard breathing did he realise someone was there, they just weren't saying anything.

"Kurt Walker," he said. For the first time in a long time he wished there was someone more senior who could take charge - the lives of four people, three of them civilians, and two of those children, rested in his hands; it was a responsibility that made him very uncomfortable. "I'm Detective Chief Inspector Collins; I understand you have four people in there with you: Tim Dewson, Sonia Dewson, nine, Calvin Dewson, six, and one of my officers, Detective Constable Chris Grey, is that correct?"

It was almost a minute before Kurt decided there was no harm in answering the question, since he wouldn't be revealing information the police didn't already have. "Yes," he said simply. He intended keeping his responses as short as possible to avoid being drawn out and giving away more than he meant to.

"Are they alright?" Collins uttered a silent prayer that Walker had enough sense to realise that his best chance of getting out of the house alive lay in making sure his hostages, especially the children, came to no harm.

"They're alive. That can change, though," Kurt said meaningfully.

"I have armed officers out here with me, Mr Walker," Collins said warningly. "If anything happens to those hostages, they'll be forced to take action."

"And if I see anyone closer to the house than the wall at the end of the garden, I'll start killing people," Kurt warned in response. "Starting with the pig."

Collins felt a chill go through him at the casual way in which Walker delivered the threat. Given the fact that he had already killed more than half a dozen people in the last week alone, that they knew of, Collins didn't doubt that Walker would carry out his threat.

"What is it you want, Mr Walker?" Collins had no training in how to negotiate under such circumstances, and he found himself wishing there was an actual hostage negotiator available to him - the golden rule, he recalled from the films and TV shows he had seen, was to keep the hostage-taker talking; so long as they were talking, they weren't killing hostages, and they might be convinced to surrender.

"I want out of here. I want you to pull your people back and let me leave."

# 40

"...Have confirmation of the hostage taker's identity; he is Kurt Walker, a convicted armed robber, who was released from prison just two months ago after serving two-thirds of a fifteen-year sentence for armed robbery and murder. Inside the house on Inkwell Street with Kurt Walker are Tim Dewson and his children, Sonia and Calvin, nine and six, and a detective constable; while outside, Detective Chief Inspector Collins is attempting to negotiate with Walker, and the members of the armed response team continue to watch the house, ready to act at the first sign of trouble..."

The news report, which issued forth from the radio in the corner of the hospital cafeteria, provoked the first response from Nathan in almost an hour. He had said nothing since being guided down to the cafeteria by Louisa and his sister following April's arrival at the hospital. He hadn't even moved since wrapping his hands around the lukewarm cup of coffee that had been set before him by Louisa.

His head lifted as he registered the name given out by the newsreader and connected it with what his partner had told him upstairs before his son...his mind shied away from that thought.

"Isn't that the guy Stephen...?" Louisa started to ask, her voice trailed off as Nathan abruptly surged to his feet. "Nate, where are you going?"

"Nathan?" April called after her brother, as startled by his sudden departure from the table as Louisa. When Nathan didn't respond

211

to her call, showed no sign of having heard her in fact, she hurried after him, with Louisa at her side. "Where's he going?" she asked in surprise when she saw her brother was heading towards the exit.

Louisa didn't know why Nathan's sister thought she might know where the grief-stricken detective was headed; there had been little in the way of conversation between the two of them since April's arrival, beyond a terse recital of what had happened to Nathan's wife and kids, nothing to make April think she had any special insight into what her brother might be thinking.

The truth was, she thought she did know where Nathan was going, and why he was going there, but she didn't like the assumption that she knew. She couldn't help feeling there was a suggestion implicit in the question that she knew Nathan better than she did, perhaps even in a way she shouldn't.

"If I had to guess," Louisa said, not slowing her pace as she hurried after the striding Nathan, whose longer legs gave him a distinct advantage. "I'd say he's heading for Inkwell Street, so he can confront Kurt Walker."

"He'll get himself killed," April said, afraid for her brother. His quiet passivity, the way he had seemed unaware of everything that was happening to or around him, was so unlike him that she didn't know how to deal with it, didn't know what to say to him, even after speaking to the grief counsellor; his sudden activity, though, especially since it seemed to have a self-harmful motivation, worried her more.

"Let's hope not." Louisa was as worried as April, though she did have one bit of knowledge that gave her hope that they could stop Nathan before he could do anything that would fall under the headings of crazy, stupid or suicidal. She knew from Burke that Nathan didn't have his car there, which meant he would either have to find a cab or a bus to get him to his destination, unless he was going to do something really stupid, like steal a car.

Fortunately, Nathan wasn't stupid enough to try and steal a car, or any other kind of vehicle. Unfortunately for Louisa and April, he was lucky enough to find a cab the moment he stepped out of the hospital; it had just discharged its passengers at the hospital entrance and he immediately slid into the back and slammed the door. By the time Louisa and April made it outside it was too late to stop him.

"Where's your car?" Louisa asked of April as she dug in her pocket for her mobile phone.

"It's this way," April said, leading the way to where she had parked.

While April drove, Louisa spoke rapidly into her phone, apprising Burke of the situation. If Nathan was heading for a confrontation with the man who had murdered his family, she hoped his partner would be able to stop him before he could put himself in harm's way. A part of her could understand the impulse that was almost certainly driving Nathan at that time, but another part of her knew that what he was planning - she thought - was tantamount to suicide, something she didn't imagine he would ever consider if he was thinking rationally.

WHEN THE TAXI STOPPED, having travelled as far along Inkwell Street as it could, Nathan paid the fare and got out without waiting for his change.

He strode briskly down the street towards the barricade that was keeping back the onlookers, and was immediately let through when he was recognised by the uniformed sergeant in charge of the officers there.

He had an urge to head straight for the house where Kurt Walker was holding his hostages - he didn't need anyone to tell him which house it was - but his intellect pushed him in the direction of the surveillance van that was parked across the street from it.

Burke hurried over the moment he spotted Nathan, glad that Louisa had warned him his partner might be coming there; he had no intention of letting him go through with whatever he was there for.

"Nate, how are you feeling?" He took his arm, so he could guide Nathan away to a quiet spot, where they could talk without being disturbed, and hopefully without being observed, though he suspected the cameras belonging to the news crews would have already picked him out, and the reporters would be making what they could of his arrival.

Nathan paid no attention to his partner, or his efforts to guide him, he simply pulled his arm from his grasp and continued on to the surveillance van. He found Collins there, his attention focused on the house across the street, though his eyes flickered often to the phone that was connected to the computer in the back of the van - the computer automatically recorded every call made to or from the phone and traced it - as if he expected it to ring at any moment.

"What's the situation?" Nathan asked, speaking for the first time since he told the cab driver where he wanted to go.

Collins was startled by the appearance of his inspector, whose imminent arrival he hadn't been warned about, and it was a moment before he responded to the question. "You shouldn't be here, Nate," he said finally, wondering why Stone was there. He had a bad feeling about his subordinate's presence, and his mind raced as he tried to think of a way to get him to leave without creating a scene that would be aired repeatedly on the local evening news.

"What's the situation?" Nathan repeated his question. "The news said Walker is in there with four hostages." His eyes remained on the house, and in particular on the curtains across the living room windows, which twitched as someone, most likely Walker, kept an eye on what was happening in the street.

"They're right," Collins said. "He's got DC Grey, Tim Dewson, and Sonia and Calvin Dewson, that's the husband and kids of the social worker who took Walker's kids into care. Thanks to the infra-red setup we've got, we know that all five of them are in the living room. We can't be certain which figure is which, except for the children, obviously, but an educated guess makes the person on the sofa with the kids their father, and the figure on the floor Grey - I'm concerned about him, he hasn't moved since we got the infra-red camera focused on the room, though Walker hasn't said anything about his condition.

"Lastly, we've got Walker, he's clearly nervous, he hasn't stopped pacing the room, except for when he's peering out the window."

"You said Walker hasn't said anything about Grey's condition, you've had contact with him then?" Nathan felt as though his brain had been split in two, and that each half was operating separately, and with opposing goals; one half wanted him to rush into the house and confront Walker, regardless of what happened to the hostages as a result; the other half was thinking both rationally and professionally, and doing its best to figure out how to resolve the situation without loss of life, preferably without even injury to any of the hostages.

How he could be so empty of feeling, other than the desire for revenge on the man who had robbed him of his family, yet still be so concerned about the lives of people he hadn't met and didn't know, he had no idea.

Collins nodded. "I called him to establish the situation and get what information I could, and he called us about twenty minutes ago to demand that we pull back and provide him with a fast car. "We've got," he checked his watch, "another forty minutes to do so. If we don't do what he wants, he's going to kill one of the hostages."

"Do we know anything else about the situation in there?"

"We've managed to plant a microphone under the window, so we know Walker is watching the news, which means he has at least some idea of what is going on out here because we haven't been able to get rid of the news crews yet. Beyond that," Collins shook his head, "we know nothing."

"Have you tried to persuade him to release any of the hostages?"

"He was uncooperative," Collins said, which was a massive understatement, the suggestion had been answered with a stream of profanity.

"Why don't I talk to him," Nathan said.

"What could you say that would change his mind?" Burke asked, a note of suspicion in his voice.

Nathan shrugged. "No idea, but what can it hurt. Right now you've only got a bit over half an hour to produce a fast car and clear everyone out of here or he's going to kill a hostage - the past week says he'll make good on his threat." He closed his eyes momentarily and forced away memories of what the past week had cost him, a cost he might not have had to pay if he had just been able to recall what connected Vikram Bhaskar and Paulina Fielding. "And I bet you haven't even started trying to find a car that is likely to be able to acceptable to Walker."

Collins was reluctantly forced to admit that that was true.

# 41

The moment the phone rang, Kurt snatched it up. "What?" he demanded as he pulled back the corner of the curtain, so he could look out. He could see no sign of the car he had requested, or any sign that the police were pulling back, and he assumed the call was a delaying tactic.

"Kurt, this is Inspector Stone." It required every ounce of self-control he possessed to keep his voice calm and composed; just the one word from the killer was enough to provoke a vivid flashback to the last day of the trial, ten or so years ago, when Kurt Walker had been pronounced guilty and had gone crazy, swearing vengeance on all those who were responsible for him being there. 'An eye for an eye', that was what he had promised, just as it said in the Old Testament; as he suffered, so would they.

It surprised Kurt to hear Detective Stone on the phone, he was the last person he had expected to hear from, and he couldn't resist the urge to taunt him. "How's the family?" he asked, wishing he was in a position to see the response to the question as well as hear it - he was disappointed, despite his hopes, he received no violently explosive reaction.

All the blood drained from Nathan's face at the question, and he pressed the phone to his ear so tightly it was in danger of becoming permanently attached to him. Despite that, his voice was eerily calm as he said, "They're dead. Your fire killed them."

Kurt didn't gloat over that, though it was what he had set out to do, instead he said, "Perhaps now you'll feel some of the pain I've suffered since you cost me my family." He changed the subject then. "Where's Collins? I thought he was in charge."

"DCI Collins is making arrangements for the car you requested," Nathan told him. "We assumed you're after some kind of sports car with your request for a fast car; well, that will take a bit of time to organise - we don't have a supply of sports cars, and I don't imagine you'd accept one of our pursuit cars."

A short, sharp bark of laughter answered that comment. "Do you think I'm an idiot?" Kurt demanded. "I know you can track those cars. You've got half an hour to get me the car, and to pull back everyone you've got out there, or I start killing hostages; if you're after more time, you can forget it."

"No, Kurt, we're not after more time."

"What the hell do you want then?"

"One of your hostages," Nathan told him.

Although the request wasn't unexpected, Kurt was a little startled by the bald way Nathan made it. It was a few seconds before he responded, and when he did it was in his typically abrupt fashion. "Why the hell would I give you one of my hostages? While I've got them, I've got all the power."

"You only have the power while the hostages are alive and well," Nathan said, aware that both Collins and Burke were watching him closely, their expressions hovering on the edge of fearful as they worried he was going to precipitate a disaster. "If you hurt any of them, you run the risk of giving us a reason to send in the armed response team." Sergeant White, who was standing a short distance away, looked less than thrilled at that comment but Nathan ignored him, just as he was ignoring his partner and his superior.

"You'd better not give me a reason to hurt anyone then," Kurt said. "Get me my car and get rid of your people, and everything will be alright."

"You must have some idea how this kind of thing works, Kurt; if you want something from us, you have to give us something in return to show goodwill. This situation is all over the local news, and will probably be on the national news as well soon, releasing a hostage will make you look reasonable; it'll show you're a decent person at heart, and it'll generate goodwill with the public. You're going to need that if you want to get out of this."

"So if I release a hostage, you'll give me the car and move your guys back?"

"One hostage will get you the car," Nathan told him. "You've asked for two things, if you want both, we're going to need two hostages from you."

Kurt's response to that could have been predicted by any one of the detectives who stood around the rear of the surveillance van. "How about I shoot one of the hostages in twenty-five minutes and you can have the body. Will that get me what I want?"

Nathan had to resist the urge to tell Kurt Walker just what killing a hostage would get him, a bullet from a police marksman that was unlikely to be stopped by a curtain. Instead he said, "If you release a hostage now, as a show of good faith, we'll get the car here. When we have it, and we've proved that we are prepared to keep our word, you release the second hostage; then we'll move everyone back, like you want. Is that acceptable to you."

The phone went dead in Nathan's hand, but he got his answer when the front door opened a couple of minutes later. It didn't open all the way, just wide enough for Calvin Dewson to squeeze through without showing any part of Kurt Walker's body that might provide the marksmen with a viable target.

The little boy looked back at the house as the front door slammed closed; the confused look on his face made it clear he didn't have a clue what was going on. He took a hesitant step towards the door, as if he expected it to open again so he could go back inside and rejoin his father and sister, then he looked uncertainly down the path to the street and the crowd of police cars and officers.

It was only when his mum, who had been found and brought there by Burke before the situation became the circus it currently resembled, called out and he saw her that Calvin moved. He hurried down the path as quickly as his legs would carry him, tears that were a mix of fear, confusion, and relief running down his cheeks.

"Mummy!" he sobbed as he stumbled along and all but threw himself into his mum's arms when he reached her.

The phone at Nathan's elbow rang as Calvin walked along the path and he snatched it up.

"You've got the boy, now, where's my car?" Kurt wanted to know.

"It's coming," Nathan told him. "It'll be here shortly."

"You've got ten minutes." Kurt was about to hang up when he stopped. "What have you got me?"

"A Porsche," Nathan answered, as surprised as those around him by how calm and in control of himself he was remaining - he could feel the grief, and the rage it inspired, bubbling just beneath the surface, but he was determined not to let either out; if he did he was sure he would only be giving Walker what he wanted, and he wasn't prepared to do that. He might give in to what he was feeling when it was all over, in fact he was sure he would, but until then he was resolved to keep a tight rein on his emotions.

He knew that Collins could, and probably should, take charge of the negotiations again, but Nathan felt a stubborn desire to see things through till the end - he had been there at the start, with the murder of Vikram Bhaskar's wife and mother, and if it was at all possible, he intended being there when it was over, so he could be the one to put the cuffs on Kurt Walker. Protocol might say that since he had been targeted by the killer, he should no longer be involved with the case, but he was damned if he was going to let anyone remove him.

"Don't ask me what make or colour it is, though," he said. "I don't have a clue."

"As long as it's got a full tank, I don't give a damn."

Nathan turned to his partner after Kurt hung up. "How long 'til the car gets here?"

Burke checked his watch. "It should make it in time," he said. "It can't be more than a few minutes away now."

"Good. You'd better get ready to clear a path for the car," Nathan said, "and get ready to clear everybody out of the way once Walker releases the next hostage."

"You're not planning on letting him leave, are you?" Burke asked, not sure what his partner was thinking.

Nathan shook his head. "Of course not. We'll pull everybody back until they're out of sight of the house, and we'll move the marksmen to somewhere that gives them a view of the house, and the car when it gets here. Walker's going to have to come out in the open to get to the car, which should give the marksmen an opportunity to take him out."

Burke wasn't pleased with the thought that his partner seemed to be planning for Walker to be shot rather than arrested - like most officers, he felt that something had gone wrong, or he had failed in some way if it became necessary for a suspect to be shot - it wasn't like him. He could see that under the circumstances, what Nathan was thinking probably represented the best way for them to get Walker without risking the lives of the hostages, if Walker couldn't be persuaded to surrender, but it didn't make him feel any better about it.

Pushing aside his concerns, he set his mind to coming up with an alternative to what Nathan was thinking. While he did that he moved away from the surveillance van so he could arrange a path through the onlookers for the car Walker had requested. Nobody was pleased about being asked to move, there were audible complaints from a number of people, but they did as requested; unsurprisingly, it was the news crews, with their cameras, that voiced the loudest protests.

When the car arrived Nathan was surprised, Collins had managed to get hold of a brand-new Porsche Carrera.

He waited until the driver, he wasn't a police officer so Nathan assumed he worked for whatever dealership the car had come from, had parked the car and made a hasty retreat through the avenue of onlookers, only then did he pick up the phone.

"The car's here," Nathan said the moment Walker answered. "It's parked right out front."

Kurt twitched the curtain aside so he could look out and inspect the car. "I'm impressed," he admitted grudgingly when he saw the vehicle that had been provided. "I figured you guys would try and fob me off with some beat up old thing. Has it got a full tank?"

"Yes, there's even a bag of MacDonald's on the passenger seat. Collins must be in a good mood," Nathan remarked.

"What's that?"

"Nothing, just speaking to myself," Nathan said, embarrassed, he hadn't meant to say that out loud.

Kurt considered that for a moment, he wondered if Stone was trying to conceal something from him, but he couldn't imagine what, so he pushed it from his mind and said, "I suppose you want the girl now."

"Yes. I want Grey as well," Nathan said, knowing he was pushing his luck. He anticipated an explosive reaction, and he wasn't disappointed.

"What the hell are you trying to pull? We had a deal; you get the boy and I get the car; you get the girl and you pull everyone back out of the way. Now you're trying to change things. Are you trying to get someone killed?"

"No, not at all," Nathan said hastily. "It's just Calvin Dewson told us DC Grey is injured; if that's the case, it would show additional goodwill on your part if you let him go so he can be treated."

Kurt looked down on the detective on the floor as he considered that; it was true the man was injured, he had vented his anger and frustration on him, kicking him repeatedly in whatever part of his body presented the most readily accessible target when he felt the need. His nose was a bloody mess where it had been smashed by a particularly vicious kick, and Kurt was sure he had done for at least a couple of the unconscious detective's ribs; not only that but the way his arm was positioned suggested the elbow had been fractured, an injury that was almost certainly made worse by the fact that his hands were cuffed behind his back.

It was possible, Kurt supposed, that he had caused enough damage for his life to be in danger - that wasn't something he cared about, at least not beyond how it might affect him, but he realised it was a problem for him just then. If the detective died of his injuries he would lose a hostage, without gaining anything, and he would be left with only one hostage, at that point the armed response team might consider it worth the risk to assault the house.

"I'll give you the pig instead of the girl," Kurt told Stone.

"No deal," Nathan said firmly. "We agreed on the girl. If you want me to pull everyone back, we want the girl." He was determined to get Sonia Dewson out of danger, even if it meant leaving Grey where he was for the time being.

"You'll have to make do without your guy then, unless..." Kurt paused as a thought came to him, a thought that appealed to him a great deal.

"Unless what?" Nathan asked cautiously, wondering what Walker was thinking.

"If you want something from me, you have to give me something," Kurt declared. "I'll give you the girl in exchange for moving everyone back, but if you want your guy, you're gonna have to trade him for someone else."

"What do you mean?" Nathan was sure he understood but he wanted clarification, and some time to think. Walker seemed to be offering him what he had hoped for, but not expected to get, and he needed to decide if it was really what he wanted.

"I mean, if I give you your detective, I want someone to take his place. I'm not giving you someone without getting someone in return." Kurt thought the idea was a good one, one that had no downside for him as far as he could see. "You want your cop, you take his place."

Nathan waited a full thirty seconds before responding, so Walker would think he had to consider the offer. "Okay, I'll take Grey's place," he said finally, making it sound as if he was doing so only reluctantly. "Send the girl and I'll start getting everyone moved out here, then I'll trade with Grey."

It was another couple of minutes before the front door opened to allow Sonia Dewson to leave the house. As before, the door opened just far enough for the small figure to slip through; like her brother, Sonia paused on the path to look back at the front door, but when she was called she didn't hesitate to hurry to where her mother was waiting to make sure she was alright.

A paramedic was there as well to make a professional assessment, though there was no sign of injury; apart from the distress that was visible on her face even from a distance, there was no outward sign of the ordeal she had been through.

Nathan waited until he received a thumbs-up from the paramedic to say Sonia Dewson was alright, then he began moving everyone back from the house. He left it to Burke to handle the news crews and the civilians, who he was sure would protest every step they were made to retreat, and once he was on his own again, Nathan spoke to the two marksmen.

"Are we really pulling back?" Paulson asked without taking his eyes from the scope, through which he was watching the living room.

"Yes." Nathan nodded. "At least everyone else is. I've agreed to trade places with Grey, so he can get treated for whatever injuries he's got, and I want the two of you to find alternative vantage points, somewhere out of sight, but with a clear view of the target. Can you do that?"

Paulson looked around so he could assess the area. "Are the vehicles being moved as well?"

"Yes. They'll be moved to block the road further back, out of sight out of the house." Nathan didn't want to give Walker an opportunity to get away, but he did have to comply with what the killer wanted, up to a point.

"Shouldn't be a problem then," Paulson said confidently. "When do you want us to move?"

"Now. I want the two of you in place before I go in," Nathan told him. "How long will it take you?"

"About ten minutes. Harry'll go first and get set up while I cover the house, then I'll move," Paulson explained.

"Okay, get it done as quick as you can." He left the two marksmen to do their job while he got the crowd on that side of the house moved.

"What's going on, Nate?"

Nathan was in the middle of explaining what he wanted to the sergeant in charge of the uniformed officers at that end of the street when the shout drew his attention. He was tempted to pretend he hadn't heard his sister, but he suspected she would keep calling as long as he was within earshot. It was better to talk to her quickly and then get on with what he was doing, he decided.

"What's going on?" April repeated her question when her brother reached her. "Why are you moving us further away?" She wanted to ask why he had rushed out of the hospital, but was afraid he had come to do something crazy, and that asking him about it would encourage him to do whatever he was thinking - she didn't want to be in any way responsible for him risking his life.

"We're working to secure the release of the last two hostages," Nathan told her. "To get the girl released we had to agree to move everyone back to where they can't be seen from the house." Aware of the crowd that surrounded his sister, filled with people eager to hear what he was saying, while doing their best to make it seem as if they weren't, he kept his voice low, low enough, he hoped, so that his sister and Louisa were the only ones who could hear him.

"So you're going to give him what he wants," April said angrily. "He killed your family, and you're giving him what he wants, a chance to escape." She didn't understand the intricacies of a hostage situation, the give and take it required, but she did understand that she had hurt her brother; the moment the words were out, she wished she could take them back. "I'm sorry, Nate. I'm sure you know what you're doing."

"It's okay," Nathan said once he had recovered from the shock of his sister's anger. "We're not giving him a chance to escape. Trust me, I wouldn't do that. But we do need to get him to let his guard down and trust us, so we can convince him to surrender."

"Do you think he will?" Louisa asked, curious on both a personal and a professional level since she could never fully turn off her journalistic brain. "Given everything he's done so far, he doesn't strike me as the sort to compromise."

"We're hoping so. I don't think he's actually prepared to die to get what he wants." Nathan excused himself then, so he could return to the job of getting everyone out of sight of the house. How Walker intended to get from the house to the Porsche, and then to leave the area, without exposing himself, he didn't know. He was curious to see what Walker had in mind, but he didn't expect things to get that far; he was sure he could get the situation resolved, one way or another, before it reached that point.

The phone was ringing when Nathan got back to the surveillance van and he snatched it up. "Stone," he said, forcing his voice into the calm and pleasant tone he had been using with Walker since the first call.

"I thought you wanted your guy," Walker snapped. "What's up, changed your mind?"

"No. I've been making sure everyone's getting moved back like you want." The moment he was off the phone Nathan lifted the radio from his belt. It didn't take long to make sure the two marksmen had moved to new positions and were again set up, so they could cover the front of the house and watch for Walker.

"Okay, I'm heading to the front door now," Nathan told Walker once he was ready. He felt a flutter in his stomach at the thought of what he was about to do, but whether it was caused by fear or anticipation, he didn't know.

"Get rid of your radio and your phone first," Walker instructed; he didn't entirely trust Stone not to have something planned, but he already knew what he was going to do to ensure that whatever the detective had on his mind it would fail. "In fact, empty your pockets, get rid of everything you've got with you; the only thing I want you to bring is your handcuffs."

It took Nathan a few moments to divest himself of everything, and when he was done he took off his jacket and tossed it into the back of the van with his things.

"You can get out of here now," he told the officers in the van before slamming the door and starting across the road, so he could walk up the path.

"What the hell is he doing?" Louisa asked of no-one in particular when she saw Nathan heading towards the house.

"What?" April asked, looking around as she tried to work out what her new friend - under the circumstances it seemed the most appropriate description to use - had seen. It didn't take her long. "Oh Jesus!" she gasped. "You don't think he's planning on going into the house, do you?"

"It looks like it," Louisa said, worry creasing her features and making her voice crack and waver. "I definitely wouldn't put it past him, given what's happened." She reached into her purse for her phone and dialled Nathan's number; it didn't surprise her that she got no answer. Not wanting to waste time with another attempt at contacting her friend, she dialled Burke's number instead.

"Yes?" Burke answered his phone more abruptly than he would have usually. He was doing his best not to show it, but he was becoming increasingly frustrated with the news crews, who were protesting every foot they were asked to take.

"Stephen, it's Louisa." She ignored Burke's tone, which she correctly guessed wasn't aimed at her, and asked, "What's Nathan doing?"

"What do you mean?" Burke asked. He had been so focused on what he was doing, he didn't have a clue what his partner was up to.

"He's heading up the path to the house," Louisa told him. "It looks like he's planning on going inside."

Burke spun away from the crowd he was trying to control. "Shit!" He swore as his eyes homed in on his partner. Forgetting all about the phone in his hand, he ran towards the house; he was sure even before he started that he stood no chance of reaching his partner before he made it to the front door, but he hoped that somehow he would make it in time.

He was at the end of the path when the front door opened so Nathan could enter the house and he skidded to a stop. He was tempted to run up the path and force his way into the house to save his friend, but he knew it would be foolish in the extreme; he had no idea what awaited beyond the door, except that Kurt Walker was almost certainly armed with a sawn-off shotgun, and he wasn't about to risk himself when there was no guarantee of him being able to help.

# 42

Nathan felt a degree of trepidation as he stepped over the threshold, at the same time he felt a sense of relief; one way or another, the situation would be resolved soon. While he couldn't say he was eager for things to be over, given that he anticipated a degree of violence before Walker was stopped, he did want to reach the end of the worst day he could either remember or imagine.

He saw Walker the moment he entered the house, the killer was halfway down the passage towards the kitchen, a sawn-off shotgun in his hands. Nathan did his best not to react to the weapon, but even with the indifferent attitude he currently had towards his life and his health, he couldn't help feeling as though a hole the size of the gaping black chasms that stared at him from the muzzles of the shotgun had opened in his stomach.

"Where's Grey?" he asked, amazed that his voice was steady, without even a trace of a quiver.

"In there." Kurt gestured to the living room with his shotgun. "He's unconscious, so if you want him, you're gonna have to drag him outside. Be quick about it."

Nathan hesitated for a moment, a little nervous about putting himself in a position where he had a gun pointed at him and he couldn't see what was happening. Steeling himself, he walked through the doorway and into the living room.

"Everything's going to be alright, Mr Dewson," he told the dazed figure on the sofa reassuringly, imbuing his voice with as much confidence as he could muster. He hoped he sounded convincing.

Nathan turned his attention to his fellow detective then. He saw at a glance that Grey's arm had been broken, as well as his nose, and that led him to wonder what other injuries Grey had that weren't visible. Concerned that he was going to hurt his colleague, despite him being unconscious, or perhaps make his injuries worse, Nathan bent to take hold of him under the armpits.

His chest was heaving by the time he got to the front door, which he hooked open with his foot, so he could drag Grey outside.

"You can leave him there," Kurt called out once Nathan had the unconscious detective on the path. "Get back in here." He didn't want to give him an opportunity to try and escape now he had got his injured colleague out of the house.

Nathan looked up, a protest on his face. "I need to get him to the paramedics."

"Your friend can do that," Kurt said with a nod of his head.

It surprised Nathan to see Burke when he looked over his shoulder, though at the same time it didn't surprise him. He should have realised that his partner would try to stop him. Determined not to be stopped, and concerned that if he didn't do what Walker wanted he would take it out on Tim Dewson, he quickly left Grey to be collected by Burke and hurried into the house, closing the door noisily behind him.

"Good, now get in there," Kurt ordered, indicating the living room with a jerk of his head.

Nathan again felt a shiver of apprehension run up and down his spine at exposing his back to a man with a shotgun. He did his best to ignore it, but couldn't get rid of the feeling altogether. He focused on Tim Dewson in an effort to put it from his mind.

"Are you alright?" he asked, running his eyes over the man in a search for injuries - he couldn't see any, but realised that that meant nothing; even if he hadn't been hurt physically, there was no denying that he was caught in a stressful and traumatic experience, which was almost certainly going to require that he and his children undergo months, if not years, of therapy.

"No talking," Kurt snapped as he entered the room. He had no intention of letting Stone take charge of the situation, on any level, or of letting him settle Tim Dewson down and relax him to the point where he might be willing to do something stupid. "Turn out your pockets," he ordered.

"I've emptied them, like you told me to," Nathan said.

"I wanna be sure." Kurt made no effort to hide how little he trusted the detective.

BURKE STOPPED AND STARED for a moment as Nathan left Grey and hurried back into the house. The abruptness of his partner's departure, and the way the door banged shut behind him, was startling and it left Burke wondering what was going through his partner's head. There was nothing he could do about the situation, other than hope that Nathan was thinking at least semi-rationally and had some kind of a plan, so he turned his attention to Grey, whom he could help.

He wasted no time with a quick examination of his colleague - he had first-aid training, but there were paramedics on hand who were much better equipped to both assess and treat whatever injuries Grey had - instead he copied his partner, took hold of Grey by the armpits and began dragging him down the path and away from the house.

He called for help the moment he reached the street, and three officers came running to assist him. Together they lifted the unconscious Grey and carried him to where the ambulance had been moved, and where the paramedics waited.

Nathan's plan - a grand-sounding title for what was really little more than a half-formed idea - was suffering; Walker proved to be smarter than he anticipated, leaving Nathan to wonder how he was going to do anything in his present situation. He needed to get the curtains open, so Paulson and MacNamara could see into the room to use their rifles, if it was necessary for them to do so, but he didn't see how he could do that when he was on the floor, with his hands cuffed in front of him.

Kurt made a quick check of the cuffs he had had Tim Dewson put on Stone, just to be sure there had been no trickery, and then he moved over to the window, so he could peek out and see what was going on. It surprised him that the street had actually been cleared, he hadn't expected to have that request filled, at least not without him making a serious threat to the life of one of the hostages; he did wonder how far back everyone had been moved, not far, he was sure, just far enough for it to be said they had complied.

Satisfied, at least for the time being, he collected the phone from where he had left it and pressed the redial button. He knew what he wanted and needed to accomplish next, but wasn't sure how to go about it. For now, the most important thing was for him to maintain control of the situation; as long as he had control, he could manoeuvre things the way he wanted them to go - at least that was what he told himself.

Nathan kept one eye on Walker as he peeked out of the window, while with the other he looked around the room. He was after anything he could use, either to distract or disarm Walker, or simply to gain himself some kind of advantage; he could see nothing, however, at least nothing that he could use. Everything he saw that might be useful was too far away; he would be in danger before he could get to any of them.

Carefully, so as not to draw the attention of the killer by the window, he shifted position so he could look around better.

He felt something jab him in the hip as he moved about by the sofa, it wasn't painful, but it was uncomfortable, and he moved about again in an effort to find out what it was, and whether it might be useful to him. Adjusting his position was awkward to manage with his hands cuffed - at least they were cuffed in front of him, if they had been cuffed behind his back there would have been virtually nothing he could do - especially since he didn't want to draw attention to himself, but after a minute or so he managed to put himself in a position to see the shoe he had almost sat on.

It was a small thing, a kid's shoe, Sonia Dewson's he was sure, though he didn't recall seeing her minus a shoe when she left the house. It might be small, but it was the only thing he had within reach that even remotely resembled either a weapon or a distraction; it wasn't heavy enough to make a good weapon, but he figured it would suffice as a distraction.

THE PHONE RANG AND rang, and with each ring Kurt became more frustrated. There should have been someone standing by the phone, ready to answer it if he rang, and the lack of a response made him wonder what was going on, and if something was being planned. He looked out the window again, searching the street for some sign of what the police were up to; he had no intention of being caught by surprise, not if he could help it.

Because his attention was all on the street, he was unprepared when the attack came, from within the room not outside of it.

Nathan leapt to his feet as athletically as he was able and launched himself at Walker, following the shoe he had thrown at the killer's head. He had his cuffed hands stretched out in front of him, reaching for the sawn-off shotgun in Walker's hand; he was all too aware of how important it was for him to gain control of the weapon, or at the least to deny the weapon to Walker.

He was successful in his first goal, he reached the killer before Walker could recover from being hit in the face by the shoe, and was able to get his hands on the shotgun. Pushing the weapon away from both himself and Tim Dewson, Nathan twisted and wrenched at the shotgun in an effort to pull it from Walker's grasp. If he could disarm the killer he stood a chance, a slim one, but a chance nonetheless, of subduing Walker and putting an end to the hostage situation, despite being hampered by the handcuffs around his wrists.

Nathan flinched as the shotgun went off in Walker's hands. He anticipated pain, and was surprised when there was none. His grip on the barrel of the weapon loosened when it was fired but he quickly tightened it again as he looked around to see where the shot had gone; the muzzles were pointing out of the room, not into it, yet he still worried that Tim Dewson had been injured. He was relieved when he saw that the shot had plucked at the curtains and smashed the main window.

He was sure the blast from the shotgun would have panicked the officers outside; Paulson and MacNamara would be desperately trying to see through the curtains, to get some glimpse of what was going on in the house. At the same time Collins, Burke and Sergeant White would be hastily trying to decide what the shot might mean, and whether it might be necessary for the armed response team to take the risk of forcing their way into the house.

While that raced through his mind, the thought occurred to Nathan that the double-barrelled weapon now only had one shot left. If he could push Walker into firing it - without injuring anyone - and then keep him from reloading, the situation would be over.

KURT WAS ANNOYED THAT he had wasted one of his shots, and he moved his finger from the triggers to avoid doing so again. What both magnified his annoyance, and kept it in check, was the thought that the shot might push the police into storming the house; he realised he had to regain control of the situation before that could happen.

Anger flooded his system with adrenaline, giving him the strength to turn them both round and throw Stone against the wall, winding him. He then twisted the shotgun so he could bury the butt of the weapon into Stone's stomach, doubling him up. He followed that by hitting him in the face, rocking his head back and making him let go of the gun.

The moment he had full control of the shotgun, Kurt stepped away from Stone so he could get the room to use it. As he moved he bumped into the coffee table, which made him stumble, and that was when Stone struck.

Nathan had let his body sag in the hope of avoiding the hail of pellets he anticipated, and as he fell he kicked out. He wanted to catch the shotgun with his foot and knock it away, but there was no chance of that, so he settled for hitting Walker in the knee. At the same time he grabbed for the curtain behind him, using his weight and the momentum of his fall to tear it down, so the two marksmen could see into the room.

Already off-balance, Kurt nearly fell, only a quick step back kept him from doing so. His aim was thrown off as he wobbled, but he maintained enough control over the shotgun to avoid wasting his second shot. Once he recovered his balance he brought the shotgun to bear on the figure at his feet, his finger tightening on the trigger.

After the loss of his family, Nathan had felt certain he was ready for his life to end - he wasn't about to take his own life, it wasn't in his nature, but he had thought he would have no problem with accepting it when he was confronted with death - he soon learned he was wrong. His body flinched in anticipation of being struck by the shotgun's second round, and his eyes clenched tight when he heard the report of a fired weapon.

# 43

"**S**he made it through the surgery, Mr Stone, that's a good sign."
Nathan barely heard what the doctor said, his attention was all on his wife, who lay on a bed inside an oxygen tent. Very little of her was visible through the tubes and other medical attachments that were keeping her alive, but he could see the monitors that displayed her continuing efforts to live.

"If she makes it through the next twenty-four hours, there's every chance she'll make a full recovery."

'Full recovery.' Even with his limited medical expertise, Nathan knew that was a lie. His wife might recover from the burns that had nearly killed her, but she would never make a full recovery, she would never be how she used to be. He didn't care about that, though, he just wanted her to live. So long as he still had her, nothing else would matter.

He wanted to hold her, to touch her or kiss her, but he couldn't. He had been told when he was shown into the room, Melissa had to remain within the oxygen tent, and nothing that wasn't completely sterile could go inside it.

"Can...can I stay with her?" Nathan asked of the doctor. He might not be able to hold her, or even touch her, but if he could be near her, that was enough for the time being.

If he had known it was to be the last time he would see his wife alive, he would have held her, regardless of the prohibition against doing so.

IT WAS SEVERAL LONG moments before Nathan realised he was alright, that he wasn't in pain because he hadn't been hit by a single pellet. It was another second or two before his brain came up with the information that the shot he had heard had not been the coughing roar of a shotgun fired in close proximity, but rather the sharper bark of a rifle.

Cautiously, afraid of what he was going to see, Nathan opened his eyes.

HE KNEW IT WAS STUPID, and dangerous, but the moment he heard the shotgun blast Burke left the ambulance and ran towards the house.

"What's going on?" he demanded urgently of the marksmen as he sprinted along the road, his radio pressed to his ear. He was almost at the path when the rifles barked. The noise made him increase his speed until he was sprinting. As he ran he worried about what the shots might mean; neither Paulson nor MacNamara would have fired without an order, which hadn't been given, unless they were both certain of their target and convinced that someone's life was in imminent danger. He prayed, as fervently as a non-religious person could, that nothing had happened to his friend.

He could see that the window had been smashed, and the curtains were no longer concealing the living room, but he could see nothing of what was going on inside the room. The inability to see anything only increased his concerns.

"Target down," MacNamara reported after a second, during which time he scanned what he could see of the living room.

Burke reached the front door of the house ahead of anyone else, but by the time he kicked it in, which didn't take much effort,

Sergeant White and Constable Owens of the armed response team were right behind him.

He allowed himself to be nudged aside by White, acknowledging that it made sense for the armed officers to go in first, but did follow them in. He knew White would prefer it if he stayed outside until the house had been secured, but he was keen to get in there and make sure his partner was alright.

He found Nathan in the living room. His partner was handcuffed and on the floor, but otherwise appeared to be okay, at least as okay as circumstances allowed.

"Are you alright?" Burke asked, squatting alongside Nathan. From his pocket he took out his keys so he could un-cuff his friend.

Nathan didn't answer straight away, his attention was fixed on Kurt Walker, who lay unmoving on the living room floor. There were two small red stains on Walker's top, and a much larger stain on the carpet beneath him; that, plus the lack of movement, should have told him the killer was dead, but somehow it wasn't until White made the pronouncement that his brain registered what had happened and the result of it.

"What was that?" Nathan asked, dragging his attention away from the body on the other side of the coffee table so he could focus on his partner.

"I asked if you're alright," Burke said. "No broken bones, no unexpected holes?"

Nathan shook his head. "I'm fine, a bit bruised maybe." He gave his wrists a quick rub where they had been chafed by the handcuffs, and then reached up to explore the back of his head with his fingertips. He didn't think he had suffered any real damage when he hit his head on the wall, but he suspected he was going to develop a lump - a small price to pay given the alternative.

"You're damned lucky, you bloody idiot," Burke told him, his anger at the risk his partner had taken gave his voice an unintended volume. "You tried to get the shotgun away from him, didn't you."

Nathan nodded shamefacedly. Now that his insane - he could admit as much to himself - wish to seek death was gone, he felt embarrassed by it. He still felt an intense sense of despair at the loss of his family, a loss he was sure would never diminish, but he realised that getting himself killed wasn't going to change things - he didn't follow a religion, and he didn't believe in an afterlife, so his death would not enable him to see his family again.

"Come on, let's get you out of here." Burke took his partner's arm and helped him to his feet.

The two of them left the house, while White and his team checked that Tim Dewson was alright, made sure the rest of the house was secure - not that there was any reason for them to think it wasn't - and dealt with the other necessary chores that resulted from an armed response action.

"HE'S ALRIGHT," LOUISA said when she saw Nathan and Burke appear on the street. "Nathan's alright." She had to shake April by the shoulders to get her attention for she had gone into a panic following the sudden flurry of gunshots.

It was several long moments before April calmed down enough to register what Louisa had said. Hope dawned on her face and she looked around quickly, searching for her brother so she could reassure herself that he was alright.

"Thank God!" she gasped when she saw Nathan walking towards her.

Her relief quickly died away, to be replaced by anger, when she saw her brother hadn't been shot, that he showed no sign of being injured at all. Ignoring the protests of the nearest constable, she pushed through the barrier and hurried to intercept Nathan.

"What the hell were you thinking?" she demanded when she reached him. She shook him angrily before throwing her arms around him; she almost crushed him, so fierce was her embrace. "Do you have any idea how worried I was? Do you have any idea what's been going through my mind? I thought you'd been shot; I thought you'd been killed. How could you be so damned selfish? You're all the family I've got now, apart from gran, you can't leave me alone."

Thoroughly abashed, Nathan endured the tirade from his sister, aware that it was fully deserved. It hadn't occurred to him until then that his sister might be affected by the decision he had made in the depths of his despair; it wasn't just her, he realised, his gran, already struggling with her health after a cancer diagnosis, would have been affected as well, it might even have finished her off - that was a thought that sent a cold shiver of remorse racing up and down his spine, and made him mentally castigate himself for his lack of sensitivity.

"Sorry." Even to his own ears the apology sounded woefully inadequate.

April hugged him again, it held as much feeling as her first hug, but lacked the rib-crushing intensity. "Come on, let's get you out of here." She turned to Burke. "It's alright if I take him home, isn't it, Stephen?"

Burke nodded. "Sure, I'll need to get a statement from him at some point, but I think it can wait a while. There's plenty here to get sorted out. I'll pop by your place later, to see how Nate's doing and get his statement, if he's up to it. In fact," he looked around quickly, "it might be a good idea for you to get him away; the vultures - by which he meant the news crews and journalists, most of whom, thankfully, were at the other end of the street - are already starting to circle. They're bound to home in on Nate, and he's in no condition to deal with them."

Worried about his partner, but knowing that he was in the best hands he could be just then, Burke watched as Nathan was led away by his sister; Louisa Orchard trailed along, a step or two behind them, as if unsure whether she should be going with them. Only when the trio had slipped through the barrier and disappeared from view amongst the onlookers at that end of the road did he turn away to get on with his job.

There was a lot to do, he thought, but at least he could rely on Collins to handle the media for him; that was one major headache he didn't have to deal with. Looking down the road he saw that the DCI was already arranging an impromptu press-conference - Burke didn't doubt that Collins would claim that everything that had happened had been as a result of his instructions, and that the brave actions of his officers was made possible by his leadership.

Another officer might have been bothered by Collins' usurping of the credit for ending the hostage situation without loss or injury to the hostages; it didn't matter to Burke, however, and he doubted it would matter to Nathan, even if he became aware of what was happening.

By claiming credit for the successful operation, Collins made himself responsible for all the paperwork, and for the review of the situation to make sure the correct action had been taken at every step. It was unlikely, but should the review board decide that the use of deadly force could have been avoided, and the situation resolved without loss of life, he would be the one held accountable.

# 44

Alert for trouble, though he expected none, Frank Luder scanned the road ahead as they approached Salter Gaming's warehouse on the Stafford Trading Estate. When he was satisfied there was nothing to worry about, he nodded to the man next to him; Pat Drummer immediately swung the truck off the road and to a stop in front of the gates.

While Drummer remained behind the wheel, Luder got out and moved quickly to the rear of the truck, where he swung open the doors to let out the two men who had ridden there in the back.

"We're here, time for you guys to do your thing." He took up a position where he could watch the road, while the brothers got to work on the padlock and chain that secured the gate with their cutting equipment.

A whistle, following immediately after the cessation of the acetylene torch, signalled that the gates had been breached. Luder quickly moved out of the way so Drummer could drive through, and then followed as the truck headed across the yard and round the side of the building to the warehouse's loading bay. Behind him, Justin and Neville gathered up the padlock and chain they had cut away and shut the gates, so everything would look normal to a passer-by, before following in his wake.

The lock on the roller door at the loading bay took half the time to burn through that the chain at the gate had. In under a minute it been taken care of, and Luder was able to heave the door up so they could enter the building.

While Jason and Neville made for the nearest of the shelves, so they could begin loading up the truck, which Drummer had backed up to the loading bay, Luder headed for the alarm box. He was the man in charge, the one who had put the gang together, but he still had his part to play, beyond the purely physical one of helping to load the truck - his job was to disable the alarms of the places they hit.

The moment he reached the alarm box, and before he could even think about opening his tool-kit, he saw there was something wrong - the alarm wasn't on. It was possible, he supposed, that the person responsible for setting the alarm had forgotten, but he found that unlikely.

BURKE SAW THE FIGURE at the alarm box look around as he watched him on the cameras he had had set up around the warehouse. The quick way the figure's head turned this way and that told Burke he had realised there was something up.

Lifting his radio to his lips, he gave the order to move in. He had thought there would be more time for his team to get into place after the gang broke into Salter Gaming's warehouse, but he was prepared, and his officers were fully briefed on what to expect, so he felt confident things would go well.

Without waiting to receive acknowledgements, or to check that the two officers with him were following, Burke ran from the office where he had set up his surveillance post. As he hurried to the stairs he heard shouts and rapid conversation from the main floor of the warehouse, and a rumble as the engine of the truck he had observed entering the warehouse grounds was revved in preparation for a hurried departure.

He descended the stairs three and four at a time before jumping the last half dozen. He landed heavily, but recovered quickly, and spun away from the stairs so he could head for the alarm box and the nearest of the gang members.

The figure he had seen was gone, but that didn't surprise Burke, so he didn't let it bother him. He paused for a moment to listen in case the loading bay was not where he would find the gang, and then hurried to the broken open roller door when he was sure the gang were no longer in the building.

LUDER NEITHER SAW NOR heard anything that suggested a problem, other than the alarm not being set, yet his instincts screamed that there was something wrong. He had learned to listen to his instincts over the years, it was how he had managed to avoid being caught for so long, and why he had no record with the police - he only wished he had listened to the niggle he had had that morning that said he should cancel or postpone the job.

"Guys, we're leaving," he yelled, making his decision.

"What's up?" Neville asked, skidding to a halt alongside Luder.

"I don't know," Luder admitted. "But something's not right. The alarm's not been set."

"Somebody could have forgot to turn it on," Neville said, not seeing the problem.

"Maybe, but I don't think so. We're going. Back to the truck."

Had he not been wearing a balaclava, Jason's expression would have made it clear he wasn't happy with the decision. "We're already here; we're in, it'd be stupid to leave now," he protested. "We'll have wasted our time. There's no-one here, nothing to worry about; you're just getting paranoid."

Before he could react to the anger that flashed in Luder's eyes, thunderous footsteps sounded from the upper level of the warehouse. The heads of all three whipped round, searching the dim interior of the warehouse for the source of the noise.

Luder recovered the quickest of the three; he grabbed the brothers by their arms so he could turn them around and shove them towards the loading bay. "Get going," he snapped sharply when they showed every sign of staying where they were.

Together the trio hurried from the building. Jason and Neville leapt into the back of the truck when they got there, pulling the doors shut behind them, though there was no way to keep them closed from the inside. Luder in the meantime ran along the side of the truck and quickly climbed in when he reached the cab, signalling for Drummer to get going as he did.

The truck lurched away from the loading bay, picking up speed as Drummer shifted through the gears as rapidly as he could.

BURKE AND THE OFFICERS with him reached the loading bay in time to see the truck turn the corner of the building. None of them seriously thought they could catch the truck on foot but they still gave pursuit, aware that there were other officers, the bulk of the team, approaching who should be able to stop the escaping vehicle.

An ear-splitting crash came less than a quarter of a minute after the truck disappeared around the corner. It was so loud that it would have drawn the attention of everyone on the estate, had it come during the day.

Whether the noise signalled something good or something bad, Burke didn't know, and he picked up his pace so he could find out. He came to an abrupt halt almost immediately after rounding the corner as he was confronted by the sight of the truck and the police van being used for that night's operation; it was clear that the two vehicles had collided, and equally clear that the truck had come out better off.

The van was on its side, having been spun and flipped, and the officers it had been carrying remained inside, though whether they were trapped, or simply too stunned to get out, was unclear. The truck, on the other hand, appeared to be almost unscathed by the impact, yet it sat unmoving in the middle of the yard. Burke approached cautiously.

The rear doors of the truck stood open, having been thrown wide by the collision. One of the two men who had been trying to hold the doors closed was on the ground, as immobile as the vehicle he had been catapulted from. The other was on his feet, moaning in pain and holding his right arm as he stumbled away from the truck towards the gates.

A third member of the gang was on the ground a short distance from the open passenger door. Burke guessed the man had thrown himself from the truck before it collided with the van, though whether that was the best thing he could have done, Burke wasn't sure. The figure looked around wildly as he pushed himself to his feet, shook his head to clear it, and then took off towards the gate on the heels of his companion.

Burke was torn between giving chase to the fleeing robbers and checking on his colleagues in the van. He was concerned by the fact that none of them had made it out yet, and by the size of the dent made in the side of the van by the truck, which strongly suggested his team was both injured and trapped.

The decision was made for him when Constable Braun, who had been in the surveillance post with him, ran past on a beeline for the van. He reached it in a matter of seconds, and quickly climbed up so he could try and get the driver's door open. Reassured that the occupants of the van were at least being checked on, Burke set off after the two fleeing suspects, who were already being pursued by Constable Yarrow.

The nearest of the pair was soon brought down by Yarrow, who threw his arms around the man's shoulders and bore him to the ground. Burke kept half an eye on the pair as he passed them, but he saw no need to stop and help; the experienced constable appeared to be having no difficulty subduing his man, who seemed to still be dazed from the crash.

After a fifty-yard chase, his own pursuit came to an end in a way he would never have predicted. One moment his suspect was running along, slowly being overhauled but showing no sign of stopping, and the next he was sprawled on the ground in the middle of the road, having gone flying.

Burke was bewildered as to what had caused the man to fall in such a spectacular fashion, there was nothing he could have tripped over that Burke could see, but when he got close he thought he saw the cause.

"Weren't you ever told," he said breathlessly as he slowed over the final few yards and took out his handcuffs, "not to run with your laces undone because you'll trip up?"

Alert for an effort at resistance, though he didn't really expect any since the man appeared too exhausted from the chase to put up any kind of fight, Burke took the man by the arm and rolled him over. He then dropped down alongside him so he could secure his wrists, before taking hold of the balaclava.

"You're nicked, Mr Luder," he said when he saw which of the gang members it was he had caught. "For breaking and entering with intent to steal," he would have liked to have caught the gang after they began loading the van, but events had not gone in his favour on that score, "and for robbery, and I think we can probably add vehicular assault and attempted murder to that."

He felt a great deal of satisfaction at having caught the gang, even if things hadn't gone how he had planned, but he couldn't help wishing his partner was there and in charge, not because he didn't want to be in charge, but because the Jennings case had been Nathan's and his. Unfortunately, Nathan was in no fit state to be handling anything, and there was some doubt as to when he would be up to returning to work.

"Come on, on your feet." Burke hauled Frank Luder up and then, with a hand on his arm to keep him from trying to get away, guided him back down the road to join the rest of his gang in waiting for a new van to arrive and take them into custody.

## 45

The music was appropriately soft as people filed into the room, if not necessarily sombre. Distantly - as he seemed to hear everything now, a mark of his separation, mentally if not physically, from the world around him - Nathan heard the whispered comments that expressed surprise, and in some cases disapproval, at his choice of music for such an occasion.

He ignored them all, he didn't care what other people thought, he wasn't sure he would ever care again what other people thought, except for his gran and his sister, and Stephen; the three of them had been there for him during the fortnight it took to arrange the funeral for his wife and kids.

Nathan felt his grandmother squeeze his arm reassuringly, and turned to offer her a smile of thanks. The smile was a little forced for he could find no reason for smiling these days, but the gratitude behind it was genuine.

"How are you holding up?" he asked quietly.

"Don't you worry about me," Barbara Stone told him. "Just you stay strong. I know it's hard, but this will be over soon." Tears stood in her eyes as she craned her neck to see who the latest arrivals were, more strangers, she noted, strangers to her at least. There was a strong attendance from Melissa's family, who occupied the seats on the other side of the aisle, but there was only herself and April left as family for Nathan; that could have left his side of the room empty, were it not for the numerous colleagues who had shown up to pay their respects, a testament to how well-liked Nathan and his family were.

About twenty minutes after the first mourners arrived, the doors were closed and the ceremony began.

"We are gathered here today..." the clerk said, taking his position at the front of the room, alongside the table that held the three coffins, one normal-sized and two distressingly small, "to pay our final respects to Melissa, Robert and Isobel, whose lives were tragically cut short..."

His head bowed, Nathan listened to the words of the clerk, who had never met his family, and who only knew what he had been told about them a couple of days ago when the arrangements were finalised. Despite the fact that the words were the result of formula, not feeling, they caused tears to stream down Nathan's cheeks. He had cried often during the past two weeks, but just then it felt as though he had built up a lifetime's worth of tears, and they were all now coming out.

The clerk's oration did not last long, but Nathan's relief at that was short-lived, for Melissa's father rose once the clerk had moved away so he could deliver his own eulogy. That only made Nathan feel worse. He had blamed himself many times for Kurt Walker's arson attack, which had killed his family, but listening to Harold Starr, Nathan felt he hadn't been hard enough on himself.

His father-in-law had not blamed him for what had happened, but there was something about the way he spoke that gave Nathan a sense of guilt and responsibility that eclipsed what he already felt.

Melissa's brother followed her father, and if the accusation in Harold Starr's words was more in Nathan's imagination than in truth, there was no mistaking who Lee Starr blamed for his sister's death.

April bristled protectively as she wrapped an arm around her brother, whose head was bowed while his body was wracked with silent sobs. She was tempted to get to her feet and challenge her brother-in-law but resisted, knowing that a scene was the last thing Nathan needed; she focused instead on supporting her brother, whom she had never seen so broken.

Finally, after an interminable period of time, everyone who had something to say had spoken and returned to their seats. The service finished with a final few words from the clerk, and then the mourners began to slowly file out, most of them detouring to the front of the room to offer some last words, intended as comfort, though Nathan barely heard them.

He was still seated at the front of the room, no longer sobbing, though tears continued to run down his cheeks, when the coffins containing his family were taken away. His wife's family had wanted burial, so they could have graves to visit, but Nathan had held firm to the decision he and Melissa had made - cremation - and now he waited for the ashes of his wife and children, while his sister, gran, and partner waited with him, offering support without intruding on his grief, for which he was grateful.

In a surprisingly short time the three urns were delivered, all of them small enough that it didn't seem possible they could hold the remains of a person, even a child. Holding the urns as though they were the most precious items in the world - to him they were - Nathan allowed himself to be led away so he could return home; home at that time being his sister's flat.

The chapter of his life that had seen him be a husband and a father were over now, a new chapter was beginning, though what that chapter was likely to involve, he didn't know. Just then he wasn't even sure he was going to return to work as a detective.

# Don't miss out!

Visit the website below and you can sign up to receive emails whenever Alex R Carver publishes a new book. There's no charge and no obligation.

https://books2read.com/r/B-A-BNVD-CYWN

BOOKS 2 READ

Connecting independent readers to independent writers.

Did you love *An Eye For An Eye*? Then you should read *A Perfect Pose* by Alex R Carver!

**A dead model, a studio suspected of abuse, and a depressed detective.**

Three months after losing his family in a deadly blaze the discovery of a teenage girl's body on the riverbank draws Nathan Stone back to work and into a complicated case.

Ellen Powers was a popular internet model with many adoring fans, so who would want to kill her?

The investigation soon turns up many secrets, including the fact that Ellen was pregnant and planning an abortion. Was the studio she worked for covering up a dark secret of exploitation? Or was this a crime of passion?

When Ellen's stepbrother is attacked soon after her body is discovered Nathan is sure there's a connection. The guy's not talking, though; what is he so determined to keep secret, even if it puts his life at risk?

As the case deepens and they discover more about the murdered teen can Nathan Stone overcome his demons to find justice for an innocent young woman?

Read more at https://alexrcarver.wordpress.com/.

# Also by Alex R Carver

**Cas Dragunov**
An Unwanted Inheritance

**Inspector Stone Mysteries**
Where There's a Will
An Eye For An Eye
A Perfect Pose
Into The Fire
A Stone's Throw

**The Oakhurst Murders**
Written In Blood
Poetic Justice

**Standalone**
Exposed
Inspector Stone Mysteries Volume 1 (Books 1-3)
The Oakhurst Murders Duology

Watch for more at https://alexrcarver.wordpress.com/.

# About the Author

After working in the clerical, warehouse and retail industries over the years, without gaining much satisfaction, Alex quit to follow his dream and become a full-time writer. Where There's A Will is the first book in the Inspector Stone Mysteries series, with more books in the series to come, as well as titles in other genres in the pipeline. His dream is to one day earn enough to travel, with a return to Egypt to visit the parts he missed before, and Macchu Picchu, top of his wishlist of destinations. When not writing, he is either playing a game or being distracted by Molly the Yorkie, who is greedy for both attention and whatever food is to be found.

You can find out more about Alex R Carver at the following links

https://twitter.com/arcarver87
https://alexrcarver.wordpress.com/
https://medium.com/@arcarver87

https://www.facebook.com/
Alex-R-Carver-1794038897591918/
Read more at https://alexrcarver.wordpress.com/.

CPSIA information can be obtained
at www.ICGtesting.com
Printed in the USA
LVHW072055230623
750625LV00002B/271